A MAN POSSESSED

Lucien opened his eyes slowly. Bright white sunshine flooded through the uncovered window, lighting the long-neglected room. Dust motes danced in the air. The candle on the dresser had been snuffed out when it burned down to a height of less than one inch. For a moment he was surprised to realize that he was alive. Hadn't he been sure at one moment that he was going to die?

He was warm, beneath the covers. Warm, because Evie was under the covers with him, snuggled up against his body, her arms wrapped around him and her head resting against his side. She had said that if she ever needed to be there to pull him from the world of the dead into the world of the living, she would do it.

Last night, she had done just that. . . .

SHADES OF WINTER

Linda Fallon

ZEBRA BOOKS
Kensington Publishing Corp.
http://www.kensingtonbooks.com

ZEBRA BOOKS are published by

Kensington Publishing Corp.
850 Third Avenue
New York, NY 10022

All Kensington titles, imprints and distributed lines are
available at special quantity discounts for bulk purchases for
sales promotion, premiums, fund-raising, educational or
institutional use.

Special book excerpts or customized printings can also be
created to fit specific needs. For details, write or phone the
office of the Kensington Special Sales Manager: Kensington
Publishing Corp., 850 Third Avenue, New York, NY 10022.
Attn. Special Sales Department. Phone: 1-800-221-2647.

Zebra and the Z logo Reg. U.S. Pat. & TM Off.

First Printing: April 2003
10 9 8 7 6 5 4 3 2 1

Printed in the United States of America

For Beverly, a true friend.
May all your dreams come true.

One

Plummerville, Georgia
January 1886

Eve perched on the edge of the wing chair by the window and clasped her hands in her lap. On occasion she watched her fingers tapping against the skirt of her new dress as if the simple motion were fascinating. The simply cut day dress was blue, flecked with pale yellow flowers. The dressmaker, Laverne, said the color suited her. Lucien liked it well enough. Earlier in the day it had seemed a suitable choice for the occasion. Oh, she should have worn something brown! Something plain and muted that would help her to fade into the woodwork.

She had seen many frightening things, in her years as a ghost researcher, but nothing had ever terrified her this way.

Uncle Harold and Aunt Constance sat side by side on the parlor sofa. Constance Phillips was Eve's mother's younger sister. Eve didn't remember her departed mother well enough to know if she had ever been this sour. The loving way her father had spoken of the wife he'd buried too soon . . . she thought not.

Constance's daughters, Eve's cousins, stood behind the sofa with their backs straight and their eyes wide as they stared at Lucien. Both girls were dark-haired and green-eyed and well-dressed in matching shades of moss green. Penelope was eighteen, and pretty in a delicate way. Millicent was twenty, shorter and rounder in shape but still very attractive. The girls had a tendency to whisper in high-pitched voices and giggle until Eve wanted to throttle them both.

Lucien, the object of their attention at the moment, stood before the fireplace, a roaring fire behind him. If anything about this situation calmed Eve, it was watching Lucien. He had dressed nicely for the arrival of her relatives, in a new white shirt and his second best black suit. He had not cut his hair, but he had combed the longish dark strands. Six foot two, lean and handsome, he looked very dignified.

"I don't understand, Mr. Thorpe," Uncle Harold said crisply. "You make your living . . . how?"

"Lucien is a scientist," Eve said brightly. Informing her staid aunt and uncle that she was marrying a man who spoke to the dead on a regular basis would send them into a tizzy. Explaining to them that he made his living ridding houses of unwanted ghosts would not go over well. And she did want her wedding to be perfect!

"A scientist specializing in studies of . . ." Lucien began.

"It's all very boring," Eve said, standing quickly and stepping toward Lucien. "Physics and mathematics and mechanics and that sort of thing. I don't understand most of it myself." She put her arm through Lucien's, but when Constance gave her a disapproving glare Eve dropped her arm and clasped her hands once again.

Lucien fought back a smile. Eve caught the twitch at the corner of his fine lips, the twinkle in his blue eyes. "Very boring," he said.

The last time she and Lucien had planned to marry, her only family and the man she loved had not met. Her aunt and uncle and cousins had arrived the day before the wedding, not several days ahead of time as they had for this ceremony, and Lucien . . . Lucien hadn't shown up at all.

That disaster of a wedding was behind them, now. He'd explained what had happened, and while she didn't like the idea that she'd been forgotten in favor of an interesting ghost, she had forgiven Lucien. It was just as well. She loved him so much more now than she had then. Their wedding would be all the more special, since their love had grown.

Aunt Constance shook her head. Her brown hair streaked with white had been piled atop her head, and tightly restrained curls bobbed. "Eve, what were you thinking to plan a January wedding! Spring is a much better time for such an event. There are more flowers to choose from, and travel is much easier for your guests, and personally I much prefer the fashions which suit warmer weather. Early summer would have been ideal."

How to explain to a prim woman that waiting was impossible? She and Lucien were already lovers. Hiding their relationship, sneaking about so no one would suspect the nature of their relationship, had been horrid. She wanted the world to know that Lucien was hers and she was his. She wanted to wake every morning to see his face beside her, not usher him out before dawn so he could sneak into his room in the Plummerville boarding house.

While Eve searched for an explanation, Lucien took her hand and raised it to his lips. "I must admit," he said as he lowered her hand, keeping it clasped easily in his, "the rather hasty timing of the wedding was my idea."

Aunt Constance's lips pursed tightly.

"I could not take the chance that such a wonderful woman might come to her senses and decide not to become my wife, when she could have any man in the world as her husband," he said. "I don't deserve Evie, and I want her to marry me before she realizes that for herself."

Aunt Constance seemed slightly mollified, Penelope and Millicent sighed in unison, and Uncle Harold rolled his eyes.

Harold Phillips was a reserved, quiet, difficult man. He wasn't at all mollified. "You will show up this time, won't you?"

Until now, no one had dared to mention aloud that Lucien had left Eve waiting at the altar, more than two years ago.

"Of course I'll be there," Lucien said, unsmiling. "Nothing could keep me away."

"Because if you embarrass my niece again," Uncle Harold continued, "I will kill you."

"Daddy!" Millicent gasped.

Aunt Constance patted her husband on the knee. "Now, now, Harold," she said calmly. "Eve is my dearly departed sister's child. If anyone kills Mr. Thorpe, it will be me."

"Please!" Eve said, growing concerned for the safety of her groom.

"It's all right, Evie," Lucien said with a smile.

"Your aunt and uncle are being protective of you. I can understand that. And I don't fear for my life because I will be there. On time."

"You'd better be," Uncle Harold murmured.

"I really should be going," Lucien said. "My landlady gets concerned for me when I'm out too late."

His landlady was Miss Gertrude, the biggest busybody in town.

"I'll walk you to the door," Eve said. "Let me fetch your coat."

"Don't be long, Eve," Aunt Constance called after them, censure in her tight voice.

Eve collected Lucien's long, black overcoat from the entryway coat rack, and mouthed *I'm sorry* as she offered it to him. Aunt Constance had particularly sharp ears, so she didn't dare speak aloud.

Lucien grinned as he took the coat and slipped it on. Oh, she wished he were going to be here with her tonight! Instead of holding him close as she fell asleep, she'd be crowded into her bed with Penelope and Millicent. And she was quite certain they giggled in their sleep.

Lucien took her hand, opened the front door, and hauled her onto the small sheltered front porch of her cottage. "I must love you very much," he said softly, as he pulled her into his arms and the red door of her cottage closed behind them. The night was cold, but it was very warm here with Lucien's arms around her.

"You must," she whispered. "I imagine most men would have run hours ago."

"Immediately upon the arrival of your relatives."

"Yes."

He tilted her head back and kissed her quickly. "I will miss you tonight," he said, his wonderful mouth close to hers. "And tomorrow night, and the next. But on the night after that you will be my wife, and there will be no more slinking off to a rented room I don't want or need. No pretending that I don't crave you to distraction. No pretending that your bed isn't my bed."

"Soon," she said.

"Not soon enough to suit me." He lowered his head and kissed the side of her neck. That quick caress sent shivers up and down her spine. "You could sneak out tonight," he whispered. "Come to my room. I promise to have you back here well before sunrise."

"I can't," she answered softly. "If my aunt didn't catch me sneaking out, Miss Gertrude would surely catch me sneaking in."

Lucien groaned. "You're right. I know you're right. Dammit, Evie, I am a very patient man, under most circumstances. But where you're concerned I have no patience at all."

"Our wedding day will be here soon enough," she promised.

"Soon enough?" Lucien asked with raised eyebrows.

Eve smiled. *"Soon,* then. In just a few days I'll be Mrs. Lucien Thorpe, and no one will be able to run you out of this house. Not ever. I love you, Lucien," she said gently.

"And I . . ."

The door behind them flew open, and Aunt Constance appeared there, the light of the brightly lit entryway behind her. Eve and Lucien jumped apart.

"Eve Abernathy," the persimmon-mouthed woman snapped. "Get into this house this instant. You'll catch your death of cold out there."

"Good night, Lucien," Eve said as she backed toward the open door.

"Good night, Evie," he said with a soft smile. "I'll see you tomorrow."

"Not likely," Aunt Constance said as she drew Eve into the warmth of the house. "We have so much to do tomorrow, I feel quite sure Eve won't have time for visitors."

"But . . ." Eve began.

"Good night, Mr. Thorpe." Aunt Constance slammed the door in Lucien's face.

"You needn't have closed the door so violently," Eve chastised gently.

"It's cold outside," Aunt Constance explained.

"And tomorrow . . ."

"Have you allowed that man to kiss you, Eve?" Constance interrupted.

"Well . . ."

"Don't say a word," Constance said with a raised palm. "I see the way you two look at each other. You have allowed him to kiss you." She tsked loudly, and then leaned in close. "Tomorrow afternoon, when Harold and the girls are busy with wedding preparations, you and I will have a little chat. Woman to woman. Since your mother isn't here, I suppose I must stand in."

"That's really . . ." Not necessary? A frightening concept? At twenty-seven, Eve hardly needed instruction on marital relations. "Very sweet, but . . ."

"It's my duty," Constance said, patting Eve on the arm. "You musn't be afraid, dear."

"I'm not . . ."

Constance spun around. "Harold, I'm quite exhausted from the day's travel. I'm off to bed. We have so much to do tomorrow!"

Eve watched her aunt and cousins climb the stairs and head for their bedrooms. Her heart was heavy, and she missed Lucien already!

Blast him, he'd been right all along. They should've eloped two months ago.

On his walk to town, Lucien stopped in front of the Cassidy house. He didn't knock on the door, not at this late hour, but he did stand there on the roadway and study the place for a few minutes. It was a nice little one-story house, not as nice as Eve's cottage, perhaps, but cozy and well kept. Katherine took good care of the home her husband had left to her upon his death.

He'd thought ridding the house of Katherine's late husband's ghost would be simple work, but it had not been easy at all. Jerome Cassidy was hanging on with every mean-spirited bit of his measly soul.

The widow Katherine Cassidy was a member of the Plummerville Ghost Society, a secret club of six people interested in the study of the psychical world. He and Evie were among those six. The others were . . . well, they had no supernatural gifts, that he had been able to discern, but they were all accepting of his own abilities. That in itself was amazing, to him, after a lifetime of being treated as an oddity, or worse. He suspected they accepted him because of their affection for Eve. She loved him, and so they welcomed him into their midst.

He wished Hugh and Lionel, friends and fellow researchers, were arriving sooner. They would be here late in the afternoon on the day before the wedding, according to Hugh's last telegram. Friday. Almost two days from now. Perhaps if they could be persuaded to stay a while after the wedding, they could assist in Lucien's attempts to send Jerome Cassidy on.

It was too cold to stand still for long, so Lucien resumed his trek to town. He would much rather be taking Eve to bed, right now, than walking to a dreary room where he would have to pretend that they weren't already man and wife in every way except legally. But Eve's reputation was important to her, and therefore important to him. She cared about what her aunt and uncle saw and heard. She wanted this one part of their lives, their wedding, to be as normal as possible.

He wanted to give her that, since the rest of their lives would likely be anything *but* normal.

"Look!" a familiar voice called from the darkness. "It's our happy groom!"

Lucien turned as Garrick Hunt, president of the Plummerville Ghost Society, and Buster Towry, a young man who worked a nearby farm and also a member of their secret association, stepped from the shadows. Garrick was well on his way to drunk, as usual, and Buster was doing his best to keep Garrick out of trouble. Lucien didn't think the two had been friends before the formation of the Plummerville Ghost Society, but these days the son of the richest man in town and the pleasant farmer were often seen together.

"A drink!" Garrick offered his flask as he and Buster joined Lucien on the roadway. "A toast to the upcoming wedding!"

"No, thank you," Lucien said.

Garrick drew the ever-present flask in close to his chest. "You're a bit of a stick-in-the-mud, Lucien. Have I ever told you that?"

"Several times." Lucien resumed his walk, and

the two men bracketed him so that they sauntered along the roadway side by side.

"I have an idea," Garrick said. He wasn't yet drunk, but he was certainly on his way. "We haven't done much, as an organization, and as president I feel it's my duty to make sure that things move along for our little group."

"Move along in what way?" Lucien asked suspiciously.

"We really should do something besides meet for pie now and then. Old ladies could do what we've done so far."

"Well, we did try to get rid of Katherine's husband," Buster said defensively.

"A dismal failure," Garrick said darkly. "Besides, Katherine's house is right here in town, on this very street. How tediously ordinary. I think we should have ourselves a grand adventure."

"Adventure?" Buster asked suspiciously.

"We'll discuss it at the next meeting," Lucien said, in hopes that by that time Garrick would have forgotten his whiskey-induced idea.

"Yes, we'll tell the ladies all about it at that time," Garrick said with a wave of his hand. "But don't you want to know what site I've chosen for our escapade?"

"You've already chosen a place?"

Garrick nodded. "The Honeycutt Hotel," he said proudly.

"Never heard of it," Lucien said.

"Oh, I had forgotten about that place," Buster said.

It was the peculiar tone of Buster's voice that grabbed Lucien's attention. "What's so special about the Honeycutt Hotel?" he asked.

Garrick grinned widely. "It used to be some kind of resort. Rich people from Atlanta and Savannah used to come to spend a week or two soaking in the waters from a nearby underground spring that supposedly had some sort of healing power. It was an impressive business, for a while, and then six years ago the doors to the exclusive Honeycutt Hotel were closed."

Garrick tried to make his voice sound ominous, but so far, Lucien was not impressed. "Hotels, even fancy spas, do go out of business on occasion."

"Not like this one," Garrick said gleefully. "Apparently there was a ghastly murder at the Honeycutt Hotel, and in the ensuing investigation it was revealed that over the years a number of guests had checked into the hotel and never left. They simply . . ." Garrick paused for effect before whispering, *"disappeared."*

"And no one knew about these disappearances?" Lucien asked skeptically.

"Oh, the hotel owner, one Marshall Honeycutt, knew very well. He and his staff had gone to some trouble to cover up the disappearances. And then one day . . ." Garrick gave a dramatic wave of the hand that clasped his flask. "He vanished, too."

It was nice to have something to think about besides the upcoming wedding and how he'd be sleeping alone for the next three nights. "That might be interesting. Where is it, exactly?"

"North and west of here," Buster said. "Not too far off the road to Atlanta. Less than a day's trip, I reckon."

"Just a few hours away," Garrick added.

"I would want to check it out first," Lucien said thoughtfully. "I wouldn't want to drag the ladies into a house I hadn't yet explored."

"In the spring, perhaps," Garrick suggested. "You can examine the hotel and make sure it's safe for the ladies, and then we'll all go spend the weekend there."

"Send the night in a haunted hotel?" Buster asked, obviously worried about the possibilities. "I can't. Spring is a busy time for me. The rest of you will just have to go on without . . ."

"Nonsense!" Garrick said, clapping his friend on the back. "If necessary we will hire someone to take on the farm chores until we return. You are one of us, Buster. You must join us." He offered Lucien the flask again. "Are you sure you don't want a drink?"

"Positive."

Garrick pulled the flask close to his chest. "So, after the wedding, you can check out the hotel to make sure everything is acceptable, and then the six of us will have ourselves an adventure."

"How far away did you say this hotel was?"

"A few hours," Garrick said.

A few hours. He had two and a half days to kill before the wedding. Two and a half long, boring, Eve-less days. He had a feeling Aunt Constance would do her best to keep him and Evie as far apart as possible.

His ectoplasm harvester and Thorpe Specter-o-Meter were both stored in a closet in one of Eve's empty bedrooms. She hadn't wanted her family to see the devices and ask questions she didn't care to answer. Still, he didn't have to carry those devices with him for the initial visit. If the hotel was active, he could take them on the next trip. Besides, he'd travel quicker without those heavy pieces of machinery.

Just what he needed. A way to pass the next two

days and an excuse to stay far, far away from Aunt Constance and Uncle Harold.

Eve lay in the center of her big bed, Penelope on one side, Millicent on the other. They should all be asleep by now, but only Penelope was sleeping. She snored gently.

Eve stared at the ceiling and wished for sleep to come. She wished for happy dreams of Lucien. Most of all, she wished he were here.

"He's very handsome," Millicent whispered.

"Yes, he is," Eve replied.

"I don't really think Daddy would kill him."

Small comfort. "I'm sure he wouldn't." Of course, there would be no need. Lucien would be at the church this time. He would arrive promptly, not three days late.

"But Mama . . ." Millicent drawled, a touch of unexpected humor in her voice. "She's likely to do just about anything."

Millicent was fully grown and very pretty. Not only that, she had a decided femininity about her that most men found attractive. She knew what to wear, how to style her hair, what to say in any social circumstance. Those were attributes Eve had never possessed.

Eve wondered if Millicent had had that woman-to-woman chat with her mother. She thought not.

"Do you have a beau?" Eve asked, keeping her voice low so as not to disturb Penelope.

Millicent sighed. "A few. No one special, I'm afraid. There's certainly no one who would stand before my family and tell them that I'm so wonderful I could have any man in the world that I wanted. You're so lucky, Eve."

"I know I am," Eve whispered.

"Lucien is so . . . so handsome and smart, and he adores you!"

How do you tell a young woman who has never been in love that while all those things were nice, they weren't a reason to promise yourself to a man for the rest of your life?

"We belong together," Eve whispered. "I know it more strongly and certainly than I have ever known anything." She had never spoken to anyone about her feelings for Lucien. Her friend Daisy knew she loved Lucien to distraction, as did all her friends. But she had never actually told anyone out loud how she felt. "Sometimes I feel like he's inside me, all the time. Like he lives in my heart and in my bones, and without him . . . without him I would be nothing."

Millicent sighed. "I hope one day I love someone that much. But . . ." her head popped up. "Is it painful? To love someone so deeply, does it hurt?"

"Sometimes," Eve whispered.

But there would be no pain in the next few days, as she planned for her wedding. Her family and friends were either here in Plummerville or on their way. Her dress, the most beautiful wedding gown ever created, was almost finished. Laverne wanted to sew on a few more seed pearls, around the scooped neckline. Miss Gertrude, Lucien's landlady and the best cook in town, was going to bake a tasty and lavishly decorated cake to be shared with friends and family after the ceremony.

Most important, Lucien was *here*. If she needed to see him all she had to do was take the walk to town.

It didn't matter what Aunt Constance said about the days ahead being too busy for Eve to see her groom. If she needed to see Lucien, he would be there for her.

And since he was *here*, Lucien wasn't likely to get distracted by an intriguing ghost that would make him forget what day it was. He would always be close by, in the days to come, near enough to see and speak to at a moment's notice. She wouldn't have to worry about where he was. She wouldn't have to worry about his missing a train, oversleeping, forgetting where he was or where she was or when the wedding was to take place.

Millicent sighed and rolled over, very soon beginning to breathe in a deep and even way that told Eve she was asleep. It wasn't long before Eve relaxed and drifted toward sleep herself. She had nothing to worry about. All was well, in her world. Three days from now the wedding would be over and she and Lucien would be husband and wife at last.

Two

Lucien stood on Eve's front porch, eye to eye with Eve's less-than-charming Uncle Harold.

"I just need a moment," he said.

"You'll have to come back later," the portly man said, already beginning to close the red door.

"That's not possible." Lucien stopped the progress of the door with his foot. Later he'd be on the road. He only wanted to tell Eve where he was going and assure her that he would be back late tonight. By tomorrow noon, at the latest. "I must have a word with Eve."

Harold stared down at Lucien's shoe as if he wanted to stomp down on it with his own heavy foot. "The ladies are all upstairs with the dressmaker. I believe Eve is trying on her wedding gown. It would be bad luck for you to see her."

Damned superstition! "I could speak to her through a closed door. It will only take a moment."

Harold opened the door a bit wider and stepped onto the porch. "I don't like you, Thorpe," he said in a lowered voice. "There's something strange about you." He narrowed one eye. "I don't know what it is, exactly, but you're a bit peculiar. Eve's father was peculiar, so maybe that doesn't bother her none, but it bothers me."

"Mr. Phillips, I'm sorry if I offend you in some way, but the truth is I don't care if you like me or not. I want to speak to Eve."

"Last night you said you weren't good enough for her. Sounded like a bunch of bullshit meant to appease the ladies, if you ask me, but it's also the truth." His grim mouth thinned. "There are at least half a dozen solid businessmen in Savannah I know personally who would make fine, stable husbands for my niece. Instead she's marrying a . . . a scientist. What the hell does that mean? Who pays you at the end of every week?"

Lucien hated lying. Eve knew that, and still she'd gone to a great deal of trouble to see that her family did not know exactly what he did for a living. Instead of compounding the lies, he preferred to skip right over them.

"Mr. Phillips, I didn't come here to argue with you. I need a moment of Eve's time. That's all."

"Give me a message and I'll see that she gets it."

Lucien had no doubt but that the message would be distorted, if it was delivered at all. "No, thank you," he said as he turned away. A moment later he heard the front door slam.

It was cold this morning, but the sun was shining and that made the chill bearable. Lucien started his walk back to town, strides long and more than a little impatient. The weather was the least of his worries! The thought of another two days of this was more than he could stand. The preparations for the wedding had been made. All he had to do was be there on time.

He could tell Garrick or Buster where he was headed, but there were a few problems with that idea. Garrick was likely at his father's mill this morning, and Lucien would prefer to face Uncle Harold again than to come face to face with Garrick's father, Douglas Hunt. They shared too many secrets, and seeing the elder Hunt would only make things worse. Besides, if Garrick knew where Lucien was going he'd want to ride along.

Buster was most likely at his farm this morning, and it was several miles to the south of town, the opposite direction from the road he needed to take to get him north and west.

What was he worried about? Since the hotel was only a few hours away, he could be there by early afternoon at the latest, explore the place in no more than an hour, and then head for home. He'd be back by late tonight.

Worst case, the hotel might be farther away than he'd been informed, and he'd return tomorrow. He'd be here before Hugh's train arrived.

On his way to rent a horse from the blacksmith, he stopped by the boarding house and borrowed paper and ink from Miss Gertrude. He couldn't say much, since the old lady was certain to read the note before it was delivered to Eve. Uncle Harold and Aunt Constance would surely take a peek at it, as well.

My dearest Eve,
  I'm leaving town for the day and will be back late tonight. A tiny bit of unexpected business has come up.

                              All my love,
                              Lucien

Eve would understand what he was talking about, but she wouldn't have to worry about her relatives discovering the true nature of his scientific study.

He wanted Eve to have everything she wanted, grand wedding included. But deep in his heart he knew they should have eloped months ago!

Eve paced in the parlor. She had expected Lucien to call on her at least once today. It would soon be dark, and she'd had no word from him all day! Her relatives had scared him away, and she couldn't really say she was surprised.

"Sit down," Aunt Constance ordered.

"I'm just a little worried about Lucien," Eve said. "He should have stopped by." He always did. A day didn't pass that they didn't see each other!

"Oh," Uncle Harold said absently. "He did. This morning. I sent him on his way," he added with a dismissive wave of his hand.

"Uncle Harold!" Eve said, her breath catching in her throat.

"You were trying on your wedding dress."

Early in the day then. Why hadn't he come back? What had Uncle Harold said to him?

"Oh, and there's a note," Aunt Constance said, rising from the sofa and heading for the fireplace mantel. "It was delivered this afternoon by an urchin and I forgot all about it."

A note? Eve's heart climbed into her throat. Why would Lucien send a note and not come himself?

She scanned the short message quickly and then read it again. Her heart climbed into her throat, her head swam. If she were given to fainting, she would be on the floor right now.

Lucien wouldn't do this to her! He wouldn't leave town two days before the wedding on . . . on business! His *business* was the study and eradication of ghosts, and when he got caught up in a haunting nothing else mattered to him. Nothing. Not even her.

In a fit of anger she tossed the note into the fire.

"Is something wrong, Eve?" Aunt Constance asked calmly.

"No," she said in a low voice. Why was she worried? The note had been sitting here all day. Lucien was probably already back!

So why wasn't he here?

"Rather inconsiderate of him, to leave so suddenly and with such a poor excuse," Aunt Constance said.

Eve faced her aunt. "You read the note." She was too shocked to be offended, at the moment.

"I wanted to make sure there wasn't an emergency," Constance explained.

Lucien headed out for a haunted house two days before the wedding was an emergency!

"Then we got so busy with the girls' gowns and preparations for supper, I simply forgot."

Eve hated to think poorly of her aunt, but she didn't quite believe the excuse.

"I'm going to town to see if he's back," Eve said, heading for the entryway and the heavy wool cloak that hung near the door.

"You are not," Aunt Constance said primly. "It's much too late and too cold, and it's very unladylike for you to go chasing after the man. Tomorrow morning will be soon enough to track down your wayward fiancé."

Eve threw the cloak over her shoulders. "No. Tomorrow morning is not soon enough."

She left the house, slamming the door on her aunt's protest.

Eve practically ran to town, in part because it was so cold and almost dark, and also because she was afraid.

She was afraid Lucien wouldn't be back in time for the wedding. She was afraid he wouldn't come back at all. He'd get caught up in something exciting and absorbing and he'd forget all about her. It had happened before, it could happen again.

Why couldn't she have fallen in love with a farmer? Or a shopkeeper? Someone who stayed in one place without growing restless and distracted.

But she hadn't fallen in love with a farmer or a shopkeeper. She'd fallen in love with Lucien. Faults and all.

The warmth of the boarding house lobby was comforting, and Eve took a deep breath of air as she tried to calm herself. Miss Gertrude came bursting out of the dining room.

"Miss Abernathy!" the older, plump lady said with a wide grin. "Can I help you?"

"Lucien," Eve said breathlessly. "Is he here?"

Miss Gertrude shook her head. "No, dear. He hasn't returned from his excursion. Is there a problem?" she stepped forward, head cocked and eyes wide. "Goodness, you're so flushed."

"There's a cold wind," Eve explained, embarrassed to admit that she'd been running.

"He did say it might be tomorrow before he returned," the landlady said. "I'm sure he'll come rolling in here in the morning, none the worse for wear."

"I'm sure you're right," Eve said, trying to calm herself. Lucien did love her. He wouldn't ruin their carefully planned wedding for a ghost!

She tried not to worry. She did her best to stay

calm. But the truth was, he had forgotten her for a ghost once, and he hadn't changed all that much.

"Lucien," she muttered as she walked out the boarding house door and back into the wind. "How could you do this to me?"

Lucien approached the abandoned hotel from a winding road. A weather-beaten sign identified the edifice as the Honeycutt Hotel.

Bad directions from a man at the general store at a crossroads had cost Lucien several hours of travel, so he was arriving at the hotel as darkness fell. The chill in the air seemed more pronounced here, but then it was probably because the sunshine had gone, leaving him with a cold gray evening.

The Honeycutt Hotel was three stories high. It had once been white but the paint was now peeling in some places. Across the front of the hotel was a wide covered porch, and the portion of the roof that sheltered that porch was supported by four fat, white columns. Tall weeds encroached upon the porch. Other than the large porch and tall columns, the design was plain. Ordinary, but ordinary on a huge scale.

And even from here he could tell that the place was quite active. He felt it, as well as saw it in sparkling bits of light behind the panes of glass in the many windows. Bits of light those without his gift would not see. He wished he had his specter-o-meter and ectoplasm harvester with him, now that he'd seen the place. After the wedding he might even drag Hugh and Lionel here, if they had no plans elsewhere. They would be as fascinated as he was.

The hotel might be a bit too active for the Plummerville Ghost Society's first outing, though. He didn't think the ladies would like it here at all. Buster certainly wouldn't. Even though they couldn't see and hear what he did, everyone had instincts that warned them when something wasn't right.

The Honeycutt Hotel was definitely not right.

Lucien dismounted and tossed the horse's reins across the hitching post. Three creaking steps took him onto the deep front porch, and he stood there for a moment, staring at the double front doors. Since it was getting late and he would never be able to find his way back to the main road in the dark, he would be spending the night here. He had a feeling he wouldn't get much sleep, though. Even from here and without any special effort, he could tell that the old hotel was filled with unhappy residents.

He reached out, touched the doorknob, and as he turned the knob a gust of wind caught the door and caused it to swing open easily and quickly—almost as if he were being invited inside.

Lucien took a match from his coat pocket and struck it against the doorjamb. The lobby was cavernous, furnished with dust-covered chairs, a long sofa and a collection of intricate spiderwebs. And the room was inhabited by a number of ghosts. He didn't have a lantern with him, but he was in hopes that he might find one about. The lobby was still furnished. Perhaps there were supplies here as well.

And if not, it wouldn't be the first time he'd passed the night in a dark, haunted house.

The wind extinguished his match, so he closed the door behind him and struck another, holding it high. There was a candelabra on the long front desk. The candles there were burned at least halfway down, but it would certainly do.

He lit the candles, one by one, and then turned to study the room. It was nice enough, if a bit cold and neglected. Strange, that someone had left this place as it was. There were framed pictures on the walls, nice tables, neatly arranged, dusty furniture. It looked as if the last residents of this hotel had simply walked out and left everything behind.

There were spirits here, and most of them were hiding. He saw them, though, in those bits of bright light that hovered at the ceiling and in the corners. As usual, they were more afraid of him than he was of them. Soon enough they would realize that he was no threat to them, and he might be able to communicate with one or two of the braver souls. He would like to know what had happened in the Honeycutt Hotel.

Something besides those frightened ghosts lurked here as well. He felt rather than saw it. Something dark was hiding in this hotel, just as the timid spirits hid. He'd seen a lot in his lifetime, enough to know he didn't much like this hotel. A shiver of warning traveled up his spine. No, this would not be a fitting place for a Plummervile Ghost Society outing. But it was interesting, and nothing he couldn't handle.

He'd thoroughly study the hotel tonight, and then early tomorrow he'd head back to Plummerville. He never should've left, he knew that. But the plans for the wedding and Eve's relatives had pushed him to the limit. Why couldn't they simply be married by the local justice of the peace and be done with it?

Eve wanted more, and so she would have more.

Lucien lifted the candelabra high and turned to illuminate and scan the entire room. He'd have to bring her with him, next time he came here. He would speak with the ghosts and she would take notes. Together they would discover why the spirits were trapped and then they would send the unhappy shades home.

Just thinking about Eve calmed him, down deep. She was more than the woman he wanted as his wife, she was his partner. His lover. His friend. It was miraculous, to find such a woman. All his life he'd been alone. All his life he'd been peculiar, as Eve's unpleasant uncle said. With Eve . . . he was different. He was better. She had changed his sorry existence, just by loving him and letting him love her in return.

At the sound of footsteps above, Lucien lifted his head. The walls creaked, the flames of his candles flickered.

Oh, if only he had his specter-o-meter!

Morning came, and Lucien was still absent. Morning turned to afternoon, and Eve had left her family behind to speak to the people in town. It was embarrassing, to be searching for her groom the day before the wedding.

She'd run into Daisy and Garrick at the general store. The two were close friends, and Garrick had asked Daisy to marry him more than once. She always turned him down. On the outside, they made the perfect couple. Both fair-haired and both pretty, both longtime residents of Plummerville—and members of the Ghost Society—they made a striking couple. But Daisy swore she didn't love

Garrick, and in truth Eve didn't think he loved her either. He asked Daisy to marry him on occasion because marriage to her would be easy. A lifetime with a friend as your spouse could be a good thing. Daisy wanted more.

Daisy was alarmed to hear that Lucien was missing. Garrick was not surprised at all.

Eve faced Garrick with hands on hips as she shouted, "You sent him *where?*"

"I didn't actually send him," Garrick said defensively, as the three of them stepped out of the store and onto the shaded walk, the eyes of curious shoppers following their progress. "I merely mentioned that he might be interested in the old Honeycutt Hotel."

"Where is this old hotel?" Eve seethed.

"A few hours away, somewhere off the road to Atlanta."

"A few hours?" Daisy said breathlessly. She gathered her emerald green cloak close, against the wind. "Goodness, he should be back by now. Shouldn't he?"

"Somewhere off the road to Atlanta," Eve repeated slowly. "How do you expect Lucien might have found the place with those inadequate instructions!"

"I guess he stopped to ask for directions along the way," Garrick said sheepishly.

At least she knew where he was. She didn't like it, but an old haunted hotel certainly explained Lucien's absence.

"We can go after him," Garrick suggested. "Buster and I, we'll go."

"No," Eve said. She was still angry with Garrick, but in truth this was all Lucien's fault. He couldn't resist checking the place out, not even for a few days! "You'd probably just miss each other on the road, and when he got here he'd go back after you, and then . . . and then . . ." and then they would never get married. "He'll be here," she said confidently. "If the hotel is at all interesting, he won't come back until the last possible minute, but he will be here."

She had been hoping Lucien would arrive by tonight, so he could meet Hugh and Lionel at the train station. But as long as he was here tomorrow . . . that was all she asked.

The perfect wedding required a groom.

Lucien sauntered down the stairs into the lobby, his candelabra held before him to light his way. The Honeycutt Hotel was a fascinating place. It wasn't at all safe for the ladies of the Plummerville Ghost Society, but it was fascinating. After the wedding, he'd come back for a brief visit. A daytime visit. He'd bring his equipment and document what he'd found here.

After the wedding. He loved Eve with all his heart, but he dreaded the wedding itself. He hadn't told her so, of course. She had her heart set on something specific and special, and so she should have it.

Lucien didn't normally care for preachers, but the Reverend Watts was a decent sort of fellow. The widower Watts was new to Plummerville, had arrived to lead the flock of the Methodist church just two weeks before Christmas. Eve liked him, and that was all that mattered. Lucien hated the idea of getting dressed in his best suit and taking his vows in front of everyone he knew and some he didn't, but for Eve, he would happily make a fool of himself.

Eve amazed him, every day. She was beautiful, not only on the outside but down deep. In her heart. In her very soul, she was a good person. And she was his. To protect. To love. To care for forever.

He'd almost ruined everything, but all was well, now. They had forever ahead of them. One day to give Eve the wedding she wanted wasn't too much to ask.

Was it getting warm in here? Lucien placed the candelabra on the front desk, where he had found it. The flames flickered gently. His overcoat had been thrown over the sofa a while back, and now he removed his suit jacket, as well. Still, he was overly warm. It was cold outside, and he hadn't yet built a fire in the fireplace. Why was it so hot in here?

The ghosts that had been bits of light began to take shape, as they often did. He forgot the heat and watched, unalarmed, as they took form and stood before him. Men, women, even a child. They all wore the tragic expressions of those whose lives remained unfinished.

"You're all dead," he said in a calm voice. "It's time to move on. You'll be happier when you do, I promise you that." What held them all here? Most spirits willingly and easily went to the other side after death. Trauma or emotional pain held some here. Those were the spirits he helped on their way.

Moving as one, the ghosts came toward him. Such sad faces. Such deep unhappiness. A pale figure of a woman reached out to him with one hand. A child opened his mouth as if to speak. And then all at once they disappeared, fading into nothing.

Lucien sighed. Well, it wasn't usually so easy. Telling the trapped spirits to go sometimes worked, but there was something else at work here. After the wedding, he'd return and see what was necessary to send the souls on. He didn't think Eve should come here, though. Something about this place was wrong. He'd see about persuading Lionel and Hugh to stay on after the wedding. They could offer assistance, he was certain.

Eve. Heaven above, he missed her. He didn't want to be in this blasted hotel alone! He wanted to be with her. In her bed. In *their* bed. Being away from her was painful in a way he had not expected.

Since all had been quiet for a few moments, Lucien was not prepared for the restless spirit to enter his body without invitation. It was like a blow to the chest, a knife to the heart. He fell to his knees when a second spirit jumped inside him, then another, then another. He tried to push them out, but they were prepared to resist him. And he couldn't fight them all. They came at once, a flood of angry spirits that had been trapped here for too long. They all wanted to speak to him, through him. And they all wanted to talk at once.

Voices not his own came out of his mouth, his head was filled with pain and rage and horror and a deluge of tormenting memories. It was too much for one mind to manage, but he did try.

"Get out," he managed to say in his own voice.

But it was too late. He couldn't control this many spirits, and since channeling one spirit always tired him, having an endless number forcing their energy inside him very quickly drained him of all strength.

There was death here. Death and pain and fear. And something evil lurked behind it all.

All strength gone, he dropped to the floor, his hot forehead resting against cold wood. "Evie," he whispered once.

* * *

Tea would calm her, Eve thought as she puttered maniacally through the kitchen. It was a nice thought, but she didn't believe it. Nothing would calm her. Nothing but seeing Lucien walk through her door.

Garrick had promised to meet Hugh and Lionel at the train station and see them settled into the boarding house. She had wanted to be there herself, but there were so many things to be done before tomorrow! Besides, Aunt Constance had insisted that it wasn't proper for her to greet *men* at the train station. It simply wasn't done, according to the older woman.

As Eve spooned too much sugar into her tea, Aunt Constance slipped into the kitchen. "Here you are, Eve," she said softly.

Oh, no. Eve had an idea she knew what was coming. "I'm off to bed in just a few minutes."

"A few minutes is all I need." Aunt Constance grasped her hands together and lifted her chin. "Since your mother is gone, it's my duty to prepare you for marriage."

"That's very kind of you, but . . ."

"No, don't thank me," Aunt Constance said. "For the sake of my dear, dear sister, I must." The expression on her face told, too clearly, that she'd rather not.

"Yes, but . . ."

"A woman has many duties," Aunt Constance said, her eyes on the back door. Was she wishing for escape? Or merely avoiding making eye contact with her niece? "You must keep a man well fed, and keep his clothing in good repair, and keep the house nice and clean so he'll have a pleasant place to come home to at the end of a long day. You must smile when he tells you tedious stories about his work, because no matter how boring it might be, he considers it to be important."

Eve sighed and sipped at her tea. Not the talk she had prepared herself for, thank goodness.

"Men can be very selfish, and we women must endure such foolishness in the name of keeping a happy home. They are beasts, and it is our job to tame them without allowing them to know they have been domesticated."

"Thank you for that advice," Eve said, relieved.

Aunt Constance took a deep breath. Oh, dear. She wasn't finished. "A wife's duties in the bedroom are more arduous. A man cannot be completely tamed, you see, and in some ways a wife must simply surrender." She sighed. "They have . . . A man isn't like . . . A husband will expect . . . It's very private and . . . and . . ."

"Perhaps it is a husband's place to explain these particular duties," Eve said, saving her aunt from the sudden loss of words. She'd never known Constance not to complete a sentence! "Since it is private."

Aunt Constance's chin came up. "Why, I believe you're right, Eve." She smiled. "It is most certainly a husband's duty to explain such personal matters." She leaned closer and lowered her voice. "Just don't be disappointed," she whispered.

"Disappointed?" Eve swallowed a smile.

Aunt Constance nodded. "Disappointed," she whispered.

Eve sipped her tea and hid the tiny smile she could not contain. Lucien had never disappointed her when it came to intimate matters. He had taken her by surprise. He had shocked her. He had taught her more about love and pleasure than she had known was possible.

If Lucien wasn't here *on time* tomorrow, she was going to be more than disappointed. She would be crushed. Leaving her at the altar for a second time, once again forgetting her in favor of a ghost . . . that would be unforgivable.

Three

Eve sneaked a peek from the rear of the church, studying the backs of the heads of those who filled the pews. She saw elaborate hairstyles, more elaborate hats, and fresh, crisp haircuts for a few of the men in attendance. Whispers filled the resonant church, guests leaned toward one another as they spoke in low tones. Some of them probably wondered why the ceremony had not yet begun. Others knew that Lucien had not returned from his blasted excursion.

Everyone was here, on this cold, wintry day. The small church was packed. Just about everyone in Plummerville was in attendance, as well as a number of visitors from out of town.

Aunt Constance, in a horridly ornate hat decorated with oversized silk flowers, and Uncle Harold sat in the front pew on the bride's side. Millicent and Penelope, dressed in slightly different shades of rose, sat silently between them.

The members of the Plummerville Ghost Society who were not a part of the wedding party sat together. Garrick and Katherine and Buster. Garrick was finely dressed for the occasion, but then he usually was the best-dressed man in town. Buster wore what was surely his best suit. Even though he was twenty-five years old he was obviously outgrowing his suit. Katherine wore her usual widow's black, though it was a nicer gown than usual for this occasion. She was covered in black from her chin to her boots. Daisy, who waited in the anteroom where she and Eve had changed into their dresses, was the sixth member of the group and Eve's maid of honor.

Many people had traveled a long way to see her and Lucien get married. Hugh Felder was here, along with Lionel Brandon and O'Hara. O'Hara hadn't been invited to the wedding, Eve thought with a wrinkling of her nose. Apparently Hugh and Lionel had asked him to accompany them, thinking his invitation must've been lost in the mail. Or else he had invited himself. O'Hara wasn't known for his fine manners. They'd arrived on yesterday's late afternoon train, and none of them had been surprised to hear of Lucien's whereabouts.

The three men all had abilities much like Lucien's, though the gifts they shared manifested themselves in different ways. They were a striking group of men, especially when Lucien joined them. Hugh Felder was approaching his mid-forties and carried himself with quiet dignity. His black hair was marked with white at the temples, his spectacles suited his face, and his features were even and pleasant. He had been known to wear a mustache, but not today. Lionel Brandon was twenty-six years old, inordinately gifted, and was almost as tall as Lucien. He wore his hair on the longish side, as Lucien did. His long locks were pale blond and perfectly straight instead of dark with a hint of a wave, though, and his blue eyes were a much lighter shade than Lucien's. Lionel's appearance in town last night and this morning had caused quite a stir among the ladies.

Eve had once considered O'Hara handsome, also, though in a more conventional way. His brown hair was conservatively cut, and his face was pleasant in a rugged sort of way. He could be charming, when he so desired, even though he had a tendency to dress himself badly. For some reason he found stripes and checks appealing, and he owned more than one bowler hat. Still, she had once found him adorable, but that had been before he'd made an attempt to reach under her skirt and grab that which he had no right to touch.

Eve had worked with them all in the past, documenting hauntings and writing articles for books and magazines devoted to psychical research. They were friends, of a sort, or at least they had been.

Oh, Lucien was going to have a fit when he saw O'Hara! She never should have told him about the unpleasant and brazen incident. Lucien still claimed he had a score to settle with O'Hara.

Hugh was to be Lucien's best man, and he waited at the front of the church in a corner, along with the fidgeting Reverend Watts. Lionel and O'Hara were seated on the groom's side, their heads together. They whispered, like just about everyone else in the church.

In addition to the visitors from out of town and the Plummerville Ghost Society, practically everyone from town was here. Half of them believed in Lucien's abilities, the other half still thought him a scam artist. But they all wanted to see him get married.

So where the hell was he?

Half an hour late was nothing to cause alarm, not

where Lucien was concerned. Still, Eve found herself growing more and more nervous as the minutes ticked past. He'd left her at the altar once before, and the feeling in her stomach then had been much like the wrenching pain she experienced now. That instance had been explained away, and Lucien had apologized many times. Surely he wouldn't do that to her again!

Daisy crept out of the anteroom and came up behind Eve. The only sound that gave her away was the rustle of her full skirt.

"Where is Lucien?" she whispered. "He should have been here ages ago!"

"He'll be here," Eve said confidently.

Daisy was beautiful, as always, in her lavish blue gown that was adorned with bows and silk flowers. The color was perfect for her, matching her eyes and bringing out the pink in her cheeks.

Eve's wedding gown was simpler in design than Daisy's fancy dress, but elegant all the same. She had splurged this time. The gown was snow white, and decorated with seed pearls and the most delicate lace that Laverne, the Plummerville dressmaker, had been able to find. The skirt was full, the train not too long, the headpiece simple—a circlet of silk flowers with fine netting attached. Lucien would love it; he would love her in it.

If he ever got here!

It was her aunt and uncle who had sent him packing, she supposed. They were hard to take, she knew that. But by tomorrow they'd be on their way back to Savannah! It wasn't as if they were going to live together as one big, unhappy family.

In her mind and in Lucien's they were already man and wife. Her family couldn't know that, of

course. The wedding was a formality, a celebration
. . . a convention.

But it wouldn't be much of a wedding without a
groom.

Eve's stomach roiled. Lucien obviously thought
investigating an old hotel would be better than
passing a couple of days with her aunt and uncle
and those two twittering cousins who thought he
was handsome and worthy of their most annoying
giggles. He hadn't given a moment's consideration
to her feelings. He should have known that she
needed him here, even if they did have those annoying relatives between them. Even if he did have
to stay in his own room for a few days. He should
have known . . .

"What are you going to do if he doesn't show
up?" Daisy whispered.

Eve stared at her best friend. Her heart thudded
too hard. "He'll be here."

"But if . . ."

"He'll be here!"

Daisy laid a hand on Eve's shoulder, cocked her
head and smiled pleasantly. Daisy Willard was everything Eve was not. Fair and beautiful, delicately
feminine. She always knew what to say.

"Of course he will be here. I don't know what I
was thinking to suggest that he might not. He
adores you, Eve. You're right. He will be here at any
moment."

It was a blatant and very sweet attempt to soothe
Eve's rattled nerves.

Daisy straightened a bit of lace on Eve's sleeve.
"That nice Lionel Brandon," she said too casually.
"Did he mention me this morning when you saw
him?"

"Um, no," Eve said.

"I met him briefly, last night, as he and his friends checked into the boarding house. He's very dashing, don't you think? He looks rather like a nicely dressed Viking."

Eve turned her attention to the waiting crowd in the church proper. She didn't have time to ponder Daisy's interest in Lionel. *A Viking? Good Lord.*

"He is attractive, I suppose," she said in a casual voice. "But I do doubt that you two have anything in common."

"We have you and Lucien in common," Daisy said brightly.

Eve ignored her friend. The wedding guests were getting restless. People fidgeted, the whispers grew louder.

When the door behind her opened, Eve breathed a sigh of relief, then turned around quickly. A gust of cold wind pushed her skirt and her veil back, before the church door closed again.

It wasn't Lucien who'd come bursting in out of the cold. It was a boy, surely no more than twelve years old with a sheet of crumpled paper in his hand.

"Are you Evie?" the boy asked breathlessly.

"Yes." Her heart leapt. Now she knew something was wrong. Lucien had sent this boy. No one else called her Evie.

She hesitated before taking the note. Yes, something was certainly wrong. If not, Lucien would be here himself. He wouldn't do this to her again. He wouldn't leave her waiting in the church in her wedding gown, not if he could help it.

"I came as fast as I could," the boy said. "He said I had to hurry. I ran home and told Ma what was going on, and then I got here as quick as I could."

"I'm sure you did," Eve said as she unwadded and unfolded the note the boy had pressed into her hand.

Her blood ran cold as she read the note. One sentence was repeated over and over again. *I didn't forget. I didn't forget. I didn't forget.* The page was filled from top to bottom with that sentence. The writing was not consistent. It often changed in midsentence from crude, childlike penmanship to an elegant script to small, perfectly formed letters. There were at least six different styles of handwriting here, that she could discern at first glance.

"Where is he?" she asked the boy.

"I found him at the old Honeycutt Hotel."

Right where Garrick had said he would be.

"I hunt over that way just about every day," the boy continued, "and his horse was out front of the hotel and had been for more than a day. I was worried that something might have happened. After I looked in on him and he asked me to deliver this note, I took his horse home, told Ma what was going on, and took my Ma's horse for the trip, since I'm more comfortable with Buttercup than with a strange animal. You don't have to worry about his horse, though. My Ma's taking care of it."

"Very good," Eve said crisply. She wanted to cry, and she wanted to scream that she didn't care about the horse or how the boy had gotten here. Her chest was tight and her stomach was in knots, the scream caught in her throat. But there was no time for hysterics. "What's wrong with Lucien? Is he injured? Is he sick?"

"I don't rightly know, ma'am," the boy said in a lowered voice. "He was just sitting on the floor, rocking back and forth sorta slow and easy, and he kept talking."

"Talking about what?"

"I don't know. Most of the time it was just gibberish." The boy leaned in close. "Ma'am, I don't think he's quite right in the head, but he insisted that I deliver this to Evie at the Plummerville Methodist Church, and here I am."

"Thank you . . ." Eve said, glancing down at the note again. "What is your name?"

"Elijah, ma'am." He looked past her to the waiting wedding guests. "My Ma woulda gone to check on your friend herself, but she hurt her hip a few weeks back and she doesn't walk too well."

"That's quite all right," Eve said absently.

Elijah craned his neck to see into the church. "Are you getting hitched today?"

Eve sighed. "Apparently not," she said under her breath. She folded the note and grasped it tight. "Elijah, I want you to wait right here for a moment, and then I would like you to take me to this hotel."

"Yes, ma'am," he said dutifully. "You'd better hurry, though, if you want to get there before dark."

She nodded and turned around with a dramatic swish of her full skirt, and finally began her walk down the aisle, skirt lifted off the ground so as not to impede her quick step. Daisy was right behind her. "Eve," Daisy whispered as she hurried to keep up. "What are you doing?"

"You heard what the boy said. Lucien's in trouble. I'm going to get him and bring him home."

As Eve approached the altar, the Reverend Watts stepped from his station to the side of the front pew. Hugh moved forward, too, and Eve waved them both off as she turned to face her guests.

"I'm afraid there's not going to be a wedding today," she said emotionlessly, while her heart pounded and that stifled scream crawled into her throat once more.

Aunt Constance stood quickly. "Not again!" she snapped. "Eve, this is simply unacceptable behavior."

Eve looked at her aunt. "I've just received word that Lucien is ill, and I'm going to fetch him."

"Ill?" Hugh stepped around the preacher. "Where? What happened?"

"There's no time to explain," Eve said. "I must hurry if I'm going to get there before dark."

Aunt Constance moved toward Eve with dainty steps, lowering her voice as she said, "You are not going to chase after a man who has left you waiting at the altar twice. It simply isn't done."

There had been a time when Eve would have agreed with her aunt. The last time Lucien had done this to her she had been devastated. She would not have gone after him, no matter what kind of note he'd sent.

But now she knew without doubt that he loved her, and she would not let him stay all alone in a deserted old hotel where he had obviously been trapped or weakened or made ill by the possession of unhappy spirits. The note, with its variation in handwriting styles, told her that much. He should have known better than to go to such a place alone!

"I have to go," Eve said softly.

"What will I tell my friends?" Aunt Constance asked haughtily.

Eve sighed. "I really don't care what you tell your friends. At the moment, I only care about Lucien."

Aunt Constance pursed her lips in disapproval.

"I'll go with you," Hugh said, stepping into the aisle to meet her.

Lionel and O'Hara stood and nodded their heads. "We'll ride along," Lionel said in his deep, soft voice. "Perhaps we can be of help."

"Me, too," Daisy insisted.

"And us." Garrick, president of the Plummerville Ghost Society, stood, and so did Katherine and Buster.

"It's really not necessary for all of you to come with me," Eve protested. "I'm sure I can handle . . . whatever I find."

"You'd rather go alone?" Garrick asked. "You don't know what you might find there. Besides," he said sheepishly, "this is at least partially my fault."

"It's just that I have to hurry," Eve explained.

"I'm going too," Aunt Constance said with a nod of her well-coiffed head.

"No!" Eve protested. If they were going to find what Eve thought they might find at this hotel, she definitely didn't want her staid aunt and uncle along for the trip. "If you would see to closing up the house for me, I would appreciate it. You can stay if you'd like, or . . . go on home. I have no idea when I'll be back."

Aunt Constance pursed her lips. "I still say it's not at all proper to go chasing after a man who has left you at the altar not once but twice!"

She couldn't explain, not in the little bit of time she had. It would certainly be best if they reached the Honeycutt Hotel before dark, as Elijah had suggested.

"I have to go," Eve said, turning and practically running down the aisle. Her friends and Lucien's were right behind her.

* * *

It would be night soon. Dark again. The sky outside the windows was growing gray. The spirits loved the night.

The first night in this place had not been so bad, in the beginning. He'd walked about the place with the candelabra in his hand, explored empty rooms, and then come downstairs to rest for a few hours before heading home. He hadn't been paying enough attention to his work. His mind had wandered, it had opened, and the spirits had grabbed him from the inside out. He'd been overpowered so quickly defense was impossible.

Yesterday had passed in a misty daze. But the day hadn't been nearly as bad as the night that followed it. Last night this room had grown so dark, and the hours of blackness had been so very, very long. He'd lost all track of time. Was it just past midnight or almost dawn? Had he been lying here hours or minutes? The spirits had descended upon him in the dark, they'd danced around and inside him. Lucien wasn't sure he'd live through another night like that one.

He lay on his back on the lobby floor, feeling oddly boneless, staring up at the ceiling. This old hotel that had been unoccupied for six years was a lively place. It was filled with ghosts who didn't know they were dead, empty spirits, and mischievous phantoms who delighted in being seen.

They all wanted to talk to him, to talk through him. Usually he had a high degree of control when it came to channeling, but the spirits in this house had seized him. Possessed him. All day yesterday, all night last night, they had used his body until he had nothing left. He had no physical strength, and his mind . . . his mind was in shreds.

Something else was here, too. Watching. Waiting. Taking pleasure in Lucien's pain. He couldn't quite grasp what that evil was . . . but he felt it, and it made him cold to his bones.

In his occasional lucid moments he thought of Eve, and those thoughts kept him sane.

He was so cold, lying on the floor. Cold and then hot. And he was utterly alone. He had been alone most of his life. Until Eve had come into that life he hadn't much cared, or even noticed. But now—he didn't want to be alone anymore. He wanted her with him, badly.

The sky outside the windows grew darker. Something pattered sharply against the panes of glass, like a shower of tiny pebbles.

Sleet. Sleet and a wind so strong it blew the bits of ice beneath the porch overhang. He tried to laugh, and inside he did. He did. No sound came out of his mouth, though, and he didn't move at all. The sleet would be followed by snow. The winding road to this place, which was filled with potholes and even a low ditch at one point, would be impassable. No one would find him, and he would not survive the night.

A voice that was not his own drifted from his mouth. "You'll like it here."

He had asked, a hundred times, that the spirits that held him here let him go. Yesterday, in a lucid moment before he had grown so weak, he had tried to leave by way of the front door. It had refused to open. He'd then tried a window. It had also been stuck. The door at the back of the house, off the kitchen, would not open.

But this morning, when the boy had come in and found him, the front door had opened quite easily, for him.

The house and the spirits in it didn't want Lucien to leave.

"With your spirit here," the strange voice coming from his mouth continued, "we'll be more powerful than ever."

"I won't stay," Lucien insisted in a gruff, low voice. "You will."

He closed his eyes and thought of Eve. She was the only good thing in his life, the only good thing he had ever had. And he had left her waiting for him, once again. He had humiliated her, broken her heart. That's why she wasn't here. She wasn't coming, because she had been unable to forgive him a second time. She wasn't coming. No one was coming. And if the spirit who was currently inside him was right, he would never leave this place.

Sleet! It was bad enough that the gulley across the road had forced them to abandon the wagon that she, Daisy, and Katherine had been riding in, now sleet whipped across her face.

Eve and the other women each rode with a man on horseback. None of the ladies were accustomed to such methods of travel and they all held on tight. Eve rode behind Hugh, Katherine rode with Buster, and Daisy was currently holding onto Garrick for dear life. O'Hara and Lionel and Elijah rode alone, with Elijah leading the horse that had been pulling the wagon.

"There it is!" Elijah cried.

Eve peeked around Hugh to catch her first

glimpse of their destination. The Honeycutt Hotel was a huge monster of a building, square and solid and standing three stories high in the last light of day. The sight made her shudder. There was nothing for miles around, except for Elijah's home, and it was not close enough to be in sight. The boy had said it was well beyond the hotel where he'd found Lucien.

Why would anyone build a hotel out here in the middle of nowhere?

Freezing rain pelted against her face. It was almost dark. She wanted to urge Hugh to move faster, but she knew he was going as fast as the weather and the condition of the animal they rode would allow. Lucien was in there. Hurt? Alone?

"Hurry, Hugh," she said softly.

"We'll be there in a few minutes," he assured her.

It was a long few minutes. The cold air whipped through the black wool cloak she wore over her wedding gown; sleet stung her cheeks. Now that the hotel was in sight, she didn't dare hide her face behind Hugh's back. She wanted to keep the place in sight.

As they drew closer, Hugh spurred his horse past Elijah. They reached the steps that led to the wide front porch before the others, and Hugh helped her down.

"Wait!" he called as Eve ran to the front door. "It might not be safe."

She heard Hugh, but nothing could stop her. No warning. No concern for her own safety. She threw the front door open, and even though it was dark in the cavernous lobby she saw the outline of a body lying on the floor. He didn't move.

"Lucien," she whispered as she ran toward him

and dropped to her knees. "Dear God, what happened?"

Her heart stopped. The man she loved, the man she was supposed to spend a lifetime with, was dead. He didn't move. She laid her hands on his face, finding him still warm. Too warm, in fact. She lowered her head so she could be close to him. She held her breath as she listened closely. Yes, he breathed.

"Wake up," she said softly. "Look at me, Lucien."

His eyelids fluttered, and then his eyes opened.

"Am I dead?" he whispered.

"No." She leaned down and kissed his cheek. Did he have a fever? Perhaps.

"But you're here, and you're so beautiful. I didn't think I'd ever see you again. I'm dead, and you won't tell me . . ."

"You're not dead," she insisted.

Lucien's eyes rolled back in his head, his body twitched, and then he looked at her again and smiled. In a voice slightly higher and more clipped than his own, he said, "Not yet."

Four

Eve used all her strength to pull Lucien into a sitting position. He leaned into her, limp and lifeless, as the others began to parade through the door. A brave Elijah led the way. "There are candles in the kitchen, I believe," he said, pointing out the way. Katherine and Buster hurried in that direction together. "And there should be plenty of blankets upstairs. Y'all should be comfortable enough for the night."

"No," Eve said. "We're not staying here. We have to get Lucien out of this place. Now."

Hugh knelt down beside her and lifted Lucien's arm, laying his fingers over the pulse at his wrist. "We can't leave here tonight, Eve. I'm sorry. It's almost dark, the sleet is coming down hard, and Lucien is in no condition to travel."

All she could think of was that he should be cold. His overcoat was thrown over the back of the sofa, his suit jacket was on the floor several feet away. All he had to protect him from the cold was a white shirt, his trousers, his socks and shoes.

"They want him dead," Eve whispered, as if the spirits couldn't hear her if she kept her voice low. "He can't stay here."

"Lucien is no longer alone," Hugh said in a soothing voice. "We'll protect him."

"How?"

Hugh smiled softly. "Don't worry. He'll be fine, now that we're here."

Since Bernard Abernathy's death four years ago, Hugh Felder had been like a father to Eve. Kind and supportive, quiet and reserved, he was more family to her than Aunt Constance would ever be. And he was Lucien's family in that same way. Hugh had guided them both, as he had guided Lionel and O'Hara. At one time they had all been lost, and Hugh had shown them the way.

O'Hara walked around the room, searching dark corners and talking to himself, laying his hand against the wall, here and there, pausing to absorb the information he gathered in that way. When he passed Daisy, he brushed up against her, much too closely. Daisy jumped and leapt out of his way with a muted screech, and O'Hara responded with a gentle smile. Every family, whether by birth or by choice, had a black sheep. He was theirs.

Katherine and Buster returned from the kitchen with candles and matches, and began to light them one by one until the lobby of the Honeycutt Hotel was bathed in a soft, warm glow. Katherine righted a candelabra that had fallen onto its side and lit the short candles there.

Lucien opened his eyes. "They won't let me leave," he said weakly. "I tried. I would not have left you waiting there for the world."

"I know that," Eve whispered.

"The doors wouldn't open, the windows wouldn't open, when I tried to break a window they

. . . they took over and pulled me back. I've never lost control that way before, Evie. Never."

"Don't talk." She didn't want to stay here, but Hugh was right. It was too dangerous to try to move Lucien in these circumstances. Tomorrow would have to be soon enough, whether she liked it or not. "Tonight you're going to rest, and tomorrow morning we'll get you out of this place. If I have to knock down a wall to get you out of here, I will."

Lionel, his long blond hair tangled by the wind and wet with melted sleet, stood over them. "This hotel is extremely active."

"Yes it is," Hugh said.

"I have a very bad feeling about this place. I believe Eve's initial instincts were correct. Perhaps we should try to get out tonight."

Hugh glanced around the room. "I don't know. Moving Lucien in his current physical state won't be easy. Where's the boy?"

At that moment, Garrick came bursting through the front door. He slammed it behind him. "The sleet's turning to snow," he said as he shook off the white flakes.

"Snow?" Daisy said, rushing to the nearest window. "We almost never get snow!"

"We did have that one big snowstorm a few years ago," Katherine said.

"Yeah," Buster said. "Don't worry. It never lasts very long. We'll get a few flakes and by tomorrow afternoon the sun will be out and everything will melt."

Hugh asked again, "Where's the boy?"

It was Garrick who answered. "Elijah took the horses to his place. He and his mother have facilities to care for and shelter the animals, there. He also said he would bring us some food in the morning."

Lionel sighed. "I guess we really are stuck here for the night."

Eve brushed a long strand of dark hair away from Lucien's cheek. He was so pale, and that oddly bloodless color of his skin was accentuated by dark stubble on his face. When had he last eaten? Had he even bothered to eat before he left Plummerville? Sometimes he forgot to take care of himself, when he got involved in a haunting. It was only one of the reasons he needed her. She was supposed to take care of him, the way he took care of her. At the moment, she didn't know how to help him.

They were trapped here, by the darkness, by the sleet and snow, by the simple fact that their horses had been led away. "I don't like this," she said. "I don't like it at all."

Lucien locked his blue eyes on her face. "Neither do I."

Daisy stood against one wall and clasped her hands together. She should have volunteered to stay in Plummerville and see to entertaining Eve's family during her absence. There was nothing she could do here. She didn't fight ghosts. She didn't see things in dark corners the way Lucien's friends obviously did.

But when Eve had said she was going after Lucien, Daisy had felt compelled to join her. Any good friend might offer support in such a trying time. The fact that the handsome Lionel Brandon had volunteered first meant nothing to Daisy. Well, almost nothing.

Now that she was in the Honeycutt Hotel it occurred to her that feeding and entertaining Eve's family would have been a better use of her time. Of course, she came to that conclusion because she absolutely, positively, did not like it here.

She might not be able to see the things Lucien and his associates saw, but she had instincts. This hotel was a bad place. A very bad place.

O'Hara walked past Daisy again, and once again his hand brushed against her. He came very close to her hip, even though she was standing against the wall and he had plenty of room to maneuver without touching her. She moved out of his way and gave him a warning glare he ignored. At least she didn't squeal, this time.

Feeling the need to do something productive, Daisy stepped to the center of the room. O'Hara wouldn't dare to grab her here where the others might see. "I suppose we should settle in for the night, then. Is there any food, do you think? We could wait for morning and Elijah, but if there's anything in the kitchen . . ."

"I didn't see any food," Katherine said.

"Oh." So much for spending the evening cooking. She wasn't a very good cook, but she did like puttering about in the kitchen better than standing around and allowing some annoying scoundrel to grab her improperly whenever he passed by.

Hugh Felder stood, leaving Eve sitting on the floor and holding on to Lucien tightly. "We might not have food, but you're right, Miss Willard. We should settle in for the night. We'll need a fire, and if there are suitable beds above stairs they will certainly come in handy."

Daisy stared past Mr. Felder, wide-eyed, to study the perfectly even and almost pretty features of Lionel

Brandon's face. She had seen handsome men before. Most of the men she knew had some sort of
pleasant features that made them handsome in their
own way. But she had never before met a man who
was so beautiful!

"Would you mind checking into those details,
Miss Willard?" Hugh Felder asked. Daisy pulled her
eyes away from Lionel Brandon and nodded at Mr.
Felder. Eve always talked about the man as if he
were ancient, a grandfatherly type, so Hugh Felder
had definitely taken her by surprise. He wasn't all
that old, though he was significantly older than the
other men in his group of colleagues. His spectacles and the white at his temples made him look
very distinguished, but not at all like a grandfather.

"Of course. We need to hang our coats and
cloaks up to dry, once we get a fire going," she suggested. "We'll need them dry and warm for the trip
home tomorrow."

Mr. Felder smiled at her. "Excellent idea." He set
Garrick and Buster to the task of fetching wood
and building a fire, and Daisy shook off her own
heavy cloak. She had no desire to ensconce herself
in a bedroom all alone, not in this place. But they
were apparently in for the night. She shivered.

Eve spoke softly to Lucien, stroking his hair, touching his face. Bless her heart, she was so scared for
him, and Daisy couldn't blame her. Lucien didn't
look well, not at all. He was pale, his fingers shook.
And it was all Eve could do to keep him sitting up.

Lucien and Eve loved each other so much, sometimes Daisy envied them. She'd had proposals of
marriage, but the kind of love her friends had
found eluded her. Deep in her heart she wanted
that kind of love. She wanted nothing less than

what Eve and Lucien had found. At the same time, love scared her. It required something she wasn't certain she had to give, anymore. It was like she was being torn in two, craving love and being afraid of it at the same time.

"Eve," Daisy said gently as she stepped toward her friend. "Let me take your cloak. It's wet."

"I can't let Lucien go," Eve insisted with a shake of her head. "I don't want him to lie on the floor like he was when I found him. The floor is cold. He wasn't . . . he wasn't himself," she added in a whisper. "This is better. As long as I'm holding him, maybe they'll leave him be."

Mr. Felder dropped to his knees on Lucien's other side. "I'll support him while you get that cloak off," he said sensibly. "We can't have you catching cold."

Eve shrugged off the cloak quickly and handed it to Daisy, muttering, "Everyone's so concerned about me catching cold." She was so beautiful in her wedding gown, Daisy thought as she took the cloak. Eve always insisted that she was plain, but she wasn't. Not really. Especially not today. Eve's honey-brown hair had once been elaborately styled, but the jolting trip had loosened many of the once-restrained strands. Her gown was wrinkled, her green eyes bright with fear for the man she loved. And still, she was lovely.

When Eve wrapped her arms around Lucien again, Hugh released his hold and stood. "Lionel," he said crisply. "See if you can find a quiet room above stairs. Take O'Hara with you."

"A quiet room?" Daisy asked as the two men cautiously climbed the stairs.

"In a house like this one, where there's an unusual amount of activity, there are usually a few quiet spots.

Places in the building, small rooms usually, where the activity is much less than in the rest of the structure." He appeared to be suddenly serious. "We must find a quiet spot for Lucien so he can regain his strength."

She nodded. "Of course."

Mr. Felder returned his attention to Lucien, and Daisy stepped back. Since Lucien's three friends had come to Plummerville just last night, they'd had the entire town atwitter. Lionel was striking, of course, and had a winning smile and a slight limp that made him seem rather mysterious, even though Eve had revealed the limp was temporary, the result of a fairly recent broken leg.

The younger girls in town were fascinated with O'Hara and his flirtatious manner. He was not at all like the farmers and shopkeepers who populated Plummerville, and so they were intrigued. He did have a certain appeal, Daisy conceded. But then, didn't all rogues possess some kind of charm?

Even Hugh Felder, well into his forties, managed to turn a few heads. There was something very dignified about the man, and he did have his own quiet charm.

Her mind quickly returned to Lionel again. She didn't know him well enough to recognize if there was any possibility of a romance. At the moment she was simply intrigued by his smile and his face and, she blushingly admitted to herself, his long, lean body.

There was only one problem. She would never know if she and Lionel suited one another or not unless they spent time together. Most men usually gave her lots of attention, and finding a few moments for a telling conversation was not difficult.

There was a specific expression that came over the face of a man who was interested in her in a romantic way. She knew that look. She'd ignored it many times.

Lionel Brandon might be the perfect man for her, but since his arrival in Plummerville twenty-four hours ago he had not so much as glanced her way, much less given her that all-telling infatuated look.

Daisy wrinkled her nose as she continued to stare at the man who ignored her. Once Lucien was all better, she'd have to make sure Lionel noticed her.

O'Hara and Lionel assisted Lucien up the stairs. Eve stayed close behind them, the candle in her hand casting strange shadows across the walls. Hugh led the way, his own candle throwing light onto the stairs and up into the hallway of the second floor.

The quiet room Lionel and O'Hara had chosen for Lucien was at the end of the long hallway. She was grateful the safest place wasn't on the third floor. The hotel was huge, rambling and cavernous. Their footsteps echoed in the long-empty building. Moving Lucien at this point was no easy task. The sooner they got him into a bed, the better off they'd all be.

Hugh placed his candle on a dusty dresser and then assisted the other men as they carefully lowered Lucien onto the prepared bed. The place had been neglected for years, but Daisy and Katherine had given the linens a quick shake and had fluffed up the old pillows. This place had obviously once been elegant, extravagant even, but the years of neglect had dulled the luster. For now, it would have to do. It was certainly preferable to the lobby floor.

A single candle didn't provide much light, but they were conserving what they had found. Eve handed her candle to Hugh as she sat on the side of Lucien's bed and straightened his covers.

"I'll stay with you," Hugh said, passing the candle to Lionel.

"No," Eve said softly. "Go ahead and get the others settled for the night."

"Are you sure?"

She tilted her head back and smiled weakly at the older man. "My friends from Plummerville are shaken, I'm sure. They're not accustomed to this sort of thing. Tell them I'll be fine, and help them settle in."

"If anything happens . . ." Hugh began.

"I'll scream so loud they'll hear me in Plummerville," she said.

He nodded, and the three men left the room. Lionel was the last to leave, and he very gently closed the door behind him.

Lucien's eyes were closed, but his breathing was deep and even, and it seemed his color was already better. Eve reached out and brushed a strand of dark hair away from his face. If anything happened to him . . . What would she do? Losing her father had been difficult, but she'd managed to continue on with her life. If she lost Lucien, she would never recover. Never.

His eyes fluttered and opened, and he looked at her. Eve's heart skipped a beat. Oh, she loved him so much. She knew this face in a way she had never known another. She knew his laughter, his quirks, his faults and his most precious attributes. He was strange, to many, getting lost in his work and seeing things others did not. But he was capable of the deepest of loves, and that love was hers. She would care for it and him in whatever way was necessary.

At the moment, the light in those eyes she knew so well was dimmed.

"Is everything all right?" Eve asked. "Should I call Hugh?"

Lucien shook his head, the simple movement leaving him weak. "No. It's quiet, now. They're gone."

"If they come back, you must tell me right away," she insisted. "I'll call Hugh and the others, and they'll take care of everything."

He nodded once and closed his eyes.

The events of the day came crashing down around her, and Eve started to shake. She leaned down and placed her head on the pillow beside Lucien's. A shudder worked through her body, a single tear ran down her cheek. "You scared me," she whispered.

"I'm sorry," he replied, his voice just as soft as her own. "I'm not sure how it happened," he added, sounding truly puzzled. "They blindsided me, Evie. I was walking through the house, picking up hints of spirits here and there, and then I started thinking about the wedding. Out of nowhere they were just . . . with me. Pushing, shoving. I tried to close those doors, the way Hugh taught me to, but it was too late. They were already inside and they didn't want to leave."

"You can tell me all about it tomorrow, when we get home," she said, snuggling close. "Right now you need to sleep. Lionel said this is a quiet room."

"It is," Lucien whispered.

"Nothing will bother you here."

"That's good." Already he was drifting toward much needed sleep.

"I won't allow it," she insisted, and another tear slipped down her cheek.

Daisy's eyes shifted to the stairway once again. Mr. Felder and the others seemed sure that Lucien and Eve would be safe up there, but she wasn't so sure.

No one was anxious to retire for the night. Buster and Garrick had gathered wood and built a fire in the fireplace, and the lobby was much warmer than it had been when they'd arrived. There were many rooms and beds above stairs, and Daisy didn't mind too terribly that they were dusty and long-neglected. She did mind that there were restless spirits here. It didn't matter if she could see them or not. They were here and she didn't like it.

Katherine, who sat on the sofa beside Daisy, yawned. She tried to hide that telling sign with her hand, but that yawn was catching. Soon Daisy was yawning, too. Garrick and Buster talked, their heads together and their voices low. Were they having second thoughts about coming along on this excursion? Probably so, not that second thoughts at this late date did them any good. Buster was rightfully scared of ghosts and didn't mind letting everyone know about his fears. He was a simple farmer, and he didn't like confronting things he couldn't see and touch. Garrick was definitely out of his element. He was most comfortable with a bottle of whiskey in one hand and a wad of cash in the other. All his troubles were either drowned in whiskey or paid off with his father's money. They were both involved with the Plummerville Ghost Society because it was fun and interesting, not because they wanted to spend the night in a haunted hotel.

Of course, the same could be said of Daisy. The social aspect of their club was the highlight. She loved being a part of a secret society, and she adored all her friends. Daisy had been so excited at the outset that she had even embroidered each of the members matching hankies. She still couldn't understand why Lucien and Garrick had found that contribution so amusing.

Katherine's motives went beyond the social, Daisy suspected. For one thing, she wasn't an overly friendly person. Until she'd joined the Plummerville Ghost Society she'd kept to herself, most of the time. Katherine wanted to be rid of the ghost of her late husband. So far Lucien had attempted to send him on twice, but had been unsuccessful. They had planned to try again, after the wedding.

None of them were prepared for such an excursion. Ghosts! Abandoned, creepy hotels!

Daisy shuddered. She didn't like the way Lucien's three friends looked around the large, dusty lobby, as if they saw something she herself did not. Of course they did! They were all extraordinary men who had gifts she would never understand. Gifts like the one Lucien possessed.

Lucien talked to the dead. Did the others do the same? Or were their powers different? She wanted to know . . . but at heart she was not a brave woman. She didn't want to see those powers manifest themselves in this particular situation.

A scholarly and distant education was more her style.

Katherine stood slowly. "Gentlemen, I would like to retire for the evening. Which room would be most suitable? Does it matter?"

Daisy's heart lurched. "Katherine!" she said. "Surely you don't intend to . . . to sleep upstairs."

Katherine glanced down with a smile. "Well, I'm not going to sleep here."

"But . . . but there are *ghosts!*" Daisy whispered.

Katherine shrugged. "According to Lucien, there are ghosts everywhere. Since I don't have his gift, I don't see how I can be in physical danger."

"Is that true?" Daisy asked, her eyes turning to Hugh Felder.

It was that annoying O'Hara who answered, stepping away from the corner and into the light. Daisy tried to concentrate on his faults. Where Lionel was very pretty, O'Hara had sharper, more masculine features. Some women might find those features handsome, she supposed, but she most certainly did not. O'Hara was shorter than Lionel and Lucien, probably standing no more than five foot ten. Since she was barely five feet tall herself, that was hardly short, but still . . .

O'Hara dressed differently from the others, too. Lionel was given to simple, plain, black, and Mr. Felder wore conservative suits. O'Hara had chosen the most outlandish suit for the wedding. The pants were *checkered,* and the jacket was a muddy brown.

And he stared at her in what could only be called an insolent manner. "Most likely. There are doors within Lucien that are standing wide open, inviting the spirits in. He was born with those doors, and has spent a lifetime opening them wider and wider. If you have such doors at all, they are firmly shut and locked."

"But . . ." Daisy began.

O'Hara stepped closer, his hand outstretched. He seemed to be coiled like a snake, ready to strike. "Take my hand, Miss Willard, and I will assure you that those doors within you are inaccessible, and that you are safe."

Daisy clasped her hands in her lap. She had no intention of touching the rogue. "I think not."

O'Hara smiled. "Afraid?"

Terrified. "Of course not."

"Here," Katherine said, offering her own hand to the scoundrel. "Reassure me so I can go upstairs and find myself a comfortable place to sleep."

O'Hara took Katherine's hand and clasped it tight. They stood face to face, and for a long moment neither of them moved. Did they even breathe? O'Hara's smile faded. His jaw clenched. The firelight danced over them both, almost as if it were drawn to them. Katherine was tall . . . almost as tall as O'Hara. But at the moment she looked much smaller than he, in her fine black gown.

"You have a ghost of your own," O'Hara said, his voice low.

"My departed husband," Katherine said without emotion. "We've tried to get rid of him but he refuses to go." She attempted to appear nonchalant, but something on her face changed, as it always did whenever she spoke about her late husband.

"He won't go because you have not released him," O'Hara whispered.

"That's ridiculous." Katherine tried to retrieve her hand, but O'Hara held on tight.

An intense O'Hara continued. "Lucien's efforts at releasing Jerome's spirit have failed because you won't let him go."

"That's not true. I despise him. I want him out of my house!" Katherine insisted as she continued to tug at her trapped hand.

O'Hara leaned in close and lowered his voice, his fingers tightening around Katherine's hand. No one but Katherine and Daisy could hear him as he whispered. "Let him go. He can't hurt you anymore."

Katherine tugged once again and O'Hara released her. She almost fell back, but caught herself quickly and regained her composure. After taking a deep breath, she backed away from the man who had touched her hand and told her more than she wanted to hear. "I'm going upstairs to sleep. Is there a particular room I should stay in or one I should avoid?"

Hugh Felder glanced at O'Hara and raised his eyebrows.

"She's fine," O'Hara said.

"Second floor, either the second or third door on the left," Lionel instructed. "Actually, most of the rooms on the second floor are relatively quiet. I would suggest that anyone who wants to rest tonight stay away from the first and second door on the right, and avoid the third floor entirely."

"We really should get some rest," Mr. Felder suggested wisely.

"I'll go with you, Katherine," Daisy said as she quickly stood. "If you don't mind." She had no desire to spend the night in a room of her own!

"Miss Willard," O'Hara said as she stepped past him. "Don't you want to take my hand?"

Daisy hurried away from him, "I think not," she said primly as she chased after Katherine.

He laughed softly as she all but ran to the stairway.

Five

Eve slipped beneath the covers and reclined along the length of Lucien's long body. Her wedding dress was draped over the chair by the bed, her corset had been removed and tossed aside. She would sleep right here, wearing only her chemise. Convention be damned, this was her place in the world. Sick or well, Lucien was hers to keep.

She'd left the candle burning as long as she dared, but there wasn't much left. Snuffing out the flame had left this room in darkness. Snow continued to fall, so there wasn't even the light of the moon to illuminate the room.

As long as she had Lucien to hold on to, she didn't care.

"I didn't think you would come for me," he whispered.

Eve shifted her body along his. She couldn't get close enough, not tonight. "I didn't mean to wake you."

"You didn't." Lucien ran his hand down her back. "I'm exhausted, but I keep waking up." His hand found her hair and he threaded his fingers through the loosened strands. "I can't seem to stay awake for long, and when I sleep it's a deep and dreamless sleep."

"You need the rest." She laid her hand against his chest. Heavens, it was a relief just to feel his heartbeat! Had she really thought for one moment that she couldn't forgive him? She lifted her head. "Why on earth did you think I wouldn't come?"

She had missed this, lying with Lucien, touching him as she pleased, having him touch her. He was long and strong, rough and hard. He was the perfect contrast to the curves she pressed against him, to the softness that seemed more pronounced when they were side by side.

"I left you waiting again," he answered. "I didn't mean to, and I certainly didn't want to. But that doesn't change the fact . . ."

She silenced him with a soft kiss. "You would come to me, if I needed you."

"Yes."

"So why did you doubt that I would come for you?"

He hesitated. Maybe he was already drifting back toward the sleep he needed so badly. "Your uncle is right, Evie. You deserve better," he whispered.

"Better than you?" she teased. "Impossible. You are the best."

He wouldn't allow her to make light of this moment. "I can't give you everything you should have. This disaster proves that beyond a doubt."

"You can give me everything I need and want, Lucien Thorpe," she assured him as she cuddled against him. "Do I deserve a lifetime with the man I love?"

"Yes."

"Then sleep, and get better, and when we get out of this place we'll see what we can do about that."

She pushed aside the nagging doubt that her life

would always be this way. Uncertain. Filled with dangers she would never fully understand. Lucien Thorpe would never be a shopkeeper or a lawyer or a businessman of any kind. He would always be drawn to things she could not see or hear, to things she tried to understand but never fully experienced.

Still, living with uncertainty was much better than living without Lucien.

"Do you know how much I want to make love to you right now?" he asked in a weak voice.

This should be their wedding night. Lucien, who was a very detail-oriented and thorough lover, should be making love to her right now. Lying beside him, she couldn't help but remember all the nights they'd spent exploring, laughing and screaming until they were completely spent and then sleeping entangled, as if to let go would mean death. He wanted her. She wanted him. Since he could barely move, that would have to wait.

"Soon," she whispered. "When you're better."

"I hate this," he said. "I hate being weak and trapped in this place, and most of all I hate that I disappointed you again."

"You'll be yourself soon," she assured him. "And we'll have our wedding, and then we'll have our wedding night." Right now that wedding seemed like a distant dream, a castle in the clouds.

"Kiss me again," he requested in that thin voice that scared her more than anything else.

She did just that, rising up to lay her mouth over his and give him a sweet kiss. When she took her lips from his he immediately fell asleep.

"I love you," she said as she settled in close at his side. "But for goodness sake, Lucien. You left me at the altar twice!"

Once again she had been utterly humiliated. The people in Plummerville would talk. Aunt Constance would never recover.

And still, Lucien was the only man for her. Was it her curse, to never have him completely? She would never love anyone else, she knew that. She didn't doubt that he loved her. She only wondered if love would be enough for them to build the life they wanted.

Katherine tried to keep her eyes closed, tried to will sleep to come, but she stayed wide awake. If she let Daisy know she was awake, the girl would probably want to talk the night away. Katherine didn't want to talk.

Daisy dozed fitfully beside Katherine, tossing and turning in the bed they shared. After a restless bout of turning this way and that, Daisy woke with a start. "Oh, I hate this awful hotel!" she said as she sat up. She shook off the dream that had scared her with a shake of her head, sending blond curls this way and that. "We haven't seen anything out of the ordinary, except for Lucien's dreadful state, and still I know with every ounce of my soul that I would prefer to be anywhere else tonight. Anywhere but here."

Katherine had seen something to keep her awake, hadn't she? She hadn't seen any ghosts, she hadn't seen any monsters of any kind. But she had felt something odd when O'Hara had taken her hand. What if that disturbing man was right, and she was actually holding Jerome here, somehow? She shuddered at the thought.

Daisy leaned over Katherine awkwardly, as if making certain she was awake and listening to the tirade. Katherine groaned. "Can't you be still?"

"I had a bad dream," Daisy said quickly.

"I'm not surprised."

"Is that why you're awake? Did you have a bad dream, too?"

"No."

"I don't think I can sleep," Daisy whispered. "That dream . . . I don't even remember what it was about, and still my blood is running cold. I need something to take my mind off that dream, before I can even think about going back to sleep."

Katherine just sighed.

"We can talk for a while." Daisy rolled onto her side and moved closer to Katherine.

It was dark in this room, but Katherine's eyes had adjusted. She could see well enough. There was nothing frightening here. Nothing but Daisy Willard and her need to chatter. "Talk about what?" Katherine snapped.

"Well, we could talk about your . . . umm . . . ghost."

"Absolutely not," Katherine said sharply.

"But you have to get rid of him, don't you, before you can move on? When you get married again you certainly don't want . . ."

"No!" Katherine took a long, shaky breath. The idea of another man in her house, in her bed, in her *life*, terrified her. "I won't get married again. Not ever. Not ever," she said again, more softly.

"But you might find a really good man, this time," Daisy said optimistically. "The way Eve found Lucien."

Katherine scoffed. "If you ask me, Lucien Thorpe is no prize."

"Eve loves him."

"For now," Katherine whispered.

She'd once loved Jerome, hadn't she? It had been so long ago, but she still remembered. She had once loved her husband, before he'd shown his ugly side. In the end she'd discovered that everything about him, everything but his face, had been horribly, deeply ugly.

"But . . ."

"I don't want to talk," Katherine said. "I want to sleep. I suggest you try to do the same."

Daisy settled back down and pulled the covers to her chin. She stared at the ceiling, eyes wide open.

Katherine sighed, feeling a little guilty. It was only for one night, after all. She could humor the girl. "What about you," she asked. "Why aren't you married?"

Beneath the covers, Daisy shrugged her shoulders. "I don't know. The right man just never asked, I guess."

That was such a lie! Katherine, who had learned to live with lies, knew it too well.

"Do you hear that?" Daisy whispered.

"Hear what?" Katherine snapped.

"*That.*"

They were both very quiet for a long moment, and sure enough, there it was once again. It sounded very much like there were soft footsteps above their heads. Faint, quick, footsteps.

"Someone decided to spend the night on the third floor," Katherine suggested.

"But that nice Mr. Brandon said not to go up there," Daisy whispered.

"Perhaps someone in our party is more brave than wise."

Daisy took a deep breath. "I'm sure that's it." She didn't sound at all sure.

At that moment, a woman's laughter drifted down to them. Daisy turned to glare, wide-eyed, at Katherine. "That's not Eve, and we're the only other women here."

"A trick of the wind," Katherine said sensibly.

As if to prove her wrong, the trill of laughter came again.

Daisy pulled the covers over her head and started to pray.

O'Hara paced in the lobby. He wouldn't be able to sleep, not tonight. Luckily for him, he didn't require much sleep. His body sometimes functioned on an energy he had never understood.

Lionel sat on the lobby couch, now that the others had gone to bed, and Hugh dozed off and on in a wide, fat chair near the stone fireplace. The fire had died down, but it continued to burn so the room wasn't lost in darkness.

Some of the furniture that had once adorned this lobby had been taken, either moved when the hotel closed or stolen in the years since then. But a sofa, three chairs, and a writing desk remained. Drapes covered one of the long windows, but the others were uncovered. A long front desk was situated against one wall, where happy, unsuspecting guests had once checked into this damned hotel.

Touching the walls proved to O'Hara that this hotel was wrong. They needed to get out of this place, and the sooner the better. Many of the guests who had checked in had never left. Not every trapped spirit was evil—in fact, most were not—but there was evil here, and most of all there was pain. The place was definitely *wrong*.

He felt the wrongness when he touched the walls, when he laid his hand on a doorknob, even when he ran his fingers along the back of the sofa. There was darkness in this hotel.

There had been a time when he'd thought his ability to see into and beyond things and people when he touched them would make him a raving lunatic. Nothing in his life was simple. Shaking a man's hand might reveal secrets he had no right to know. Touching a woman always uncovered fears and hopes he didn't want to know. Even picking up an item of clothing or jewelry gave him an abrupt glimpse into the life of its owner. Years ago he'd reached the point where he didn't touch anything or anyone, unless he had no choice. He told no one of his ability. In the end, he became the one with the fears and the secrets.

And then he'd found Hugh, who had introduced him to the others. To know he was not alone was such a relief O'Hara had cried—once he was alone, of course. Lucien was able to channel spirits, Lionel was incredibly psychic, and Hugh had a weaker but still impressive combination of psychic skills.

O'Hara had the power of touch. He accepted that, now. He could take a person's hand or hold an object and know things about them. He never knew what kind of message he would receive, and Hugh had taught him to turn the power down when he so desired. He was still trying to perfect the art of turning it off completely, but learning how to mute the power had saved his sanity, perhaps even his life.

The widow Cassidy had been an interesting study.

She was tough on the outside, but inside . . . inside she was teeming with fears and insecurities. She'd had a bastard of a husband, and in an instant O'Hara had known all the terrible things he'd done to her. The hitting. The way he had forced himself upon her. And still, Mrs. Cassidy felt guilty because she was so relieved that her husband was dead.

O'Hara was relieved for her.

The day had been draining. First the failed wedding, then the hotel, and then Katherine Cassidy. It was not at all what he'd expected when he'd traveled to Plummerville to watch Lucien and Eve get married. Hugh had proposed that his invitation to the wedding had been mishandled in the mail. O'Hara knew better. Eve wanted nothing to do with him these days. He'd hitched a ride to the wedding anyway, thinking it might be fun.

So far, nothing about this trip had been fun. Of course, it could be. What he really wanted was to lay his hands on Daisy Willard. Could she possibly be as sweet and innocent as she appeared to be? Brushing up against her didn't give him enough of a reading to be sure, but he suspected there was more to her than met the eye.

He would prefer to learn all about Miss Willard someplace other than the Honeycutt Hotel.

The entire house creaked, and Hugh opened his eyes. Lionel stood.

"It's the wind," Hugh said uncertainly.

"Not entirely," Lionel added. He closed his eyes and became very still, the way he often did when he worked.

O'Hara laid his palm against the wall. "The place is angry," he said.

"Because we arrived before Lucien died," Lionel

said, eyes remaining closed. "Something in this hotel wanted him, very badly."

"Someone," O'Hara said.

"No," Lionel said, "Some *thing*. Once a man but no longer. It was trapped here long ago."

"Older than the house," O'Hara said.

"Much older."

Hugh grabbed a pencil and paper and began to write down what they said. So often they forgot.

"It's frustrated," O'Hara said. "It trapped all these souls here, feeding itself, but it's not enough."

"Yes," Lionel said. "But not enough for what?"

"I don't know." The knowledge was just out of reach. If he could reach into the wall, into the house, into the heart of the spirit that had almost killed Lucien, maybe he could see.

The flame in the fireplace flared high, and O'Hara felt the heat in his hand, as if the fire itself sparked through the walls of the house, and then shot inside him. He drew his hand away, in pain, and Lionel's eyes popped open.

"Stop," Hugh commanded.

When Hugh made such a request, they obeyed. Immediately.

The flame in the fireplace subsided, the heat in O'Hara's hand disappeared.

The dark force that had once been a man had grown very strong, over the years, and was now a part of the house itself. O'Hara suspected they had never faced anything so dark and powerful.

"Do you hear it?" Lionel asked, his eyes closing again.

"Hear what?" O'Hara asked.

"Laughter."

* * *

Scrydan's eyes opened, and he looked around the room. He could see well in the dark, and he could feel the woman beside him. She was warm, delicate and soft, and she liked to stay close to him. A hand here, the brush of her body against his. It was an unremembered human comfort, this touch.

He inhaled and caught the scent on her skin. Lavender. Closing his eyes for a moment, he breathed deep again and held the air inside his lungs. Lavender and the fragrance of a woman. It was unexpectedly tantalizing. Unexpectedly *human*. Sweet and almost intoxicating. When he rolled to the side and fixed his mouth on her shoulder, he tasted her. She tasted good.

His fingers probed, and Scrydan felt the intriguing swell of the woman's breasts through thin linen. She sighed in her sleep, undulating slightly, pressing that softness more deeply into the palm of his hand.

He was stronger than he had been in years.

But not as strong as he would be when he got out of this room.

The witch who had cursed this room, many years ago, had thought a few whispered spells and a sprinkling of herbs would protect her. It had, for a while, and this room had never been the same. But in the end, he had won. He had killed her, just as he'd killed the others. Why did a hint of her damned spell linger? It weakened him, here. It held his power in check.

It didn't matter. He wouldn't be here forever. He wouldn't be trapped in this room for long.

The sleeping woman beside him was tempting,

but he had other things on his mind. Freedom, most of all.

He slipped out from beneath the covers, being careful not to disturb the sleeping woman. Strong as he was, his limbs were weak, his hands shook.

Scrydan looked down at his new body, a tall, lean body clad in nothing but a pair of wrinkled trousers. It was weak at the moment, yes, but it was healthy enough. All the senses functioned well, as the woman had proved to him. He placed the palm of his hand against his own bare chest, felt the rhythm of the heart beating there and the warmth of his own skin. Yes, it was weak, but soon the body would be as strong as the spirit.

For years he had been stuck in this place, without a body, without a way to communicate clearly with those who walked and rode past. There had always been a few who answered his call, but too many did not. They rode on, oblivious, just out of his reach. And then they'd built the hotel, and he'd found a home at last. Lonely, after so many years of solitude, he had trapped the spirits of those who had died here. When he became hungry for another, he slipped into the body of an unsuspecting person and took over, long enough to take a life, to add to the collection of souls that kept him strong.

This place had fed him well, until the people stopped coming. None of them had ever been as welcoming as this one. He hadn't known there was even the possibility of finding a body that not only allowed him to stay within, but to grow and flourish. Usually his time within a human body drained him. It was an effort to stay in control for even a few minutes. But this one . . . this one was different. He was opened to possession in a way Scrydan hadn't known was possible.

The woman on the bed rolled over, and he sat down beside her. She was pretty enough, he supposed, and she liked this new body he lived within. She craved it, she knew it well. And he hadn't had a woman in so long.

He reached out and laid his hand on her throat, and with the fingers of the other hand he touched the place on her shoulder where he had tasted her. He had forgotten softness. He had forgotten the feel of skin like silk. The woman had such a delicate throat, and this hand was so large. He squeezed, very gently.

Something in him wanted her. It was the function of the body, male to female, and perfectly understandable. Animal instinct. A human need for pleasure. But more than he wanted this woman, he hated her. She was the one who had pushed him away, who had pulled the other one back from the brink of death. The other one, the soul of Lucien, still lived deep inside this body, but it was weak. Much weaker than anyone knew. Memories of the man Lucien Thorpe had been were still here, and Scrydan knew things about the man's life and heart. He remembered almost everything the man who had once used this body had known. The soul that had been Lucien Thorpe held on too tight. It lived still, in part because of this woman who lived so deep in his heart.

He shouldn't hate the woman. He should thank her. If not for her the body would be dead, and Scrydan never would have discovered the miraculous power that allowed him to remain within.

When Lucien Thorpe had stumbled into this

house, Scrydan had planned to add him to his collection of souls, and what a powerful soul it was! He had known all along that Lucien was special, but he had not known this was a body he could stay inside for such long periods of time. He had not known he would ever find a man who had a power he could use, a body he could inhabit and eventually own.

Scrydan was here, now, he was inside, and once he was strong enough and Lucien was no more, he could walk out of this house and start a new life.

He'd be walking out alone.

Eve woke to find Lucien sitting beside her, one hand on her throat, his bare chest surely too cold. The snow must've stopped. Moonlight shone through the window, at last.

"What are you doing?" she asked. "You should be asleep."

He blinked once. Twice. And then looked around as if he'd just awakened from a long sleep. "I don't know."

She drew back the cover and scooted over. "Get in this bed, right now."

He complied, slipping under the covers and drawing her close. Holding on tight. Was he stronger than he had been earlier when she'd found him? Yes, she was certain of it.

"You're not going to start sleepwalking, are you?" she asked.

"I certainly hope not."

"That could be dangerous. You can't wander around this awful place in your sleep."

"Then maybe you'd better hold me close."

She smiled as she did just that. Lucien's body against hers was familiar, a comfort and a joy. Yes, she still worried about whether or not they could make this work, she wondered if they would ever get married . . . But she didn't want to think about that right now. She wanted to savor the joy of holding the man she loved close.

"Lucien," she whispered, feeling incredibly warm and safe in his arms. "I don't like this place."

"Neither do I."

"But as long as we stay together, we'll be all right, won't we?"

"Of course," he assured her.

"That . . . that thing that attacked you, he can't hurt you while I hold you, can he?"

Lucien hesitated before answering. "No. No he can't."

Eve smiled and sighed in relief. "Together we can face anything."

Lucien stroked her hair, as if he were comforting her. "Sleep, love. Sleep."

She did.

Six

Lucien opened his eyes slowly. Bright white sunshine flooded through the uncovered window, lighting the long-neglected room. Dust motes danced in the air. The candle on the dresser had been snuffed out when it burned down to a height of less than one inch. For a moment he was surprised to realize that he was alive. Hadn't he been sure at one moment that he was going to die?

He was warm, beneath the covers. Warm, because Evie was under the covers with him, snuggled up against his body, her arms wrapped around him and her head resting against his side. She had said that if she ever needed to be there to pull him from the world of the dead into the world of the living, she would do it.

Last night, she had done just that.

He was amazingly alive, but still so weak that he could not lift his head. The spirits had been doing their best to suck the life out of him. Hadn't he felt it, draining away? Thoughts of Evie had kept him going, and still . . . he'd been very aware of the effects of the spirits invading his body.

Vague memories of the night before danced through his tired mind. Evie, coming to him when he thought he was dead. Holding him, sitting beside him, telling him everything would be all right, while she cried just a little. Late last night she'd finally taken off her wedding dress, snuffed out the candle, and crawled into the bed with him.

He didn't remember much else about last night. And in truth, nothing else mattered except that Evie was here.

It was amazing that she had come to him, after he'd managed to ruin yet another wedding. The woman he loved wanted an elaborate ceremony, and it didn't seem too much of an imposition to let her be a bride in white, with her friends and family gathered around. He wanted Evie to be happy, to have what she wanted. That didn't mean he had to enjoy the tumult that came with the wedding.

In the far corner of the room a few twinkling lights appeared. They danced there, not coming any closer, not attacking him as they had when he'd been alone. And they wouldn't. Not here. Not now.

"Go away," he whispered hoarsely, and they did.

Evie slept on, and that was good. She was exhausted; he could tell by the way she breathed so even and deep. He drifted toward sleep himself, still drained by his encounter with the residents of the Honeycutt Hotel.

Something dark he did not grasp held the spirits here. Some force he did not understand had ensnared those spirits the way they wanted to ensnare him. This place, this abandoned hotel—it was more than haunted. It was a trap. One in which he had almost been inextricably caught.

He ran a weary hand through Evie's hair, pulled her close, and let his eyes close. And he wondered, as he quickly fell toward sleep again, if she had thought to bring his specter-o-meter or the ecto-plasm harvester.

"No," she whispered. Daisy stood on the front porch, her green wool cloak over her bridesmaid dress not nearly warm enough for the bone-chilling weather. The sun was shining, and day was unbearably bright. The day was bright because the sun shone down on at least a foot of snow. "No! This just isn't fair," she added.

O'Hara came up behind her. "Life isn't usually fair, Miss Willard."

Daisy snapped her head around and her chin came up. How had he sneaked up on her like that! Surely this porch had a number of loose boards that would creak when unwanted intruders came about.

"We never get this kind of snow," she said sharply. "Never."

"Can't say *never* anymore, now can we," O'Hara said, apparently not at all disturbed by their predicament. He was relaxed as he studied the admittedly beautiful scenery that surrounded the hotel. He rocked very gently back and forth on his heels, his hands in his pockets, his eyes focused on the evergreen trees touched with snow. A half-smile made him look somewhat handsome, and as if he knew a secret. But then, O'Hara knew many secrets, she imagined, thanks to his gift.

Daisy had slept much later than she'd expected she might. When she'd awakened, Katherine was already gone from the room. Daisy had dressed hurriedly, not wishing to be alone any longer than necessary. All the while, as she dressed in her blue gown once again and gathered her hair into a bun with her hands and a few pins, she'd been certain that she'd be headed home soon. Very, very soon. And when she got home she would stay there! Daring escapades might be just fine for some people, but she preferred her nice, quiet, mediocre life.

And then she'd come downstairs, opened the front door, and walked onto the porch to discover that she'd slept through the snowstorm of a lifetime.

"Can we travel through this?" she asked.

"Not easily," O'Hara answered, turning his gaze to her and maintaining that all-knowing half-smile. "It would be hard on the horses. As you said, they are unaccustomed to this kind of weather. In an emergency we could attempt to leave, but it would be risky."

"This is an emergency, is it not?" she asked.

She didn't like the way he looked at her! His eyes were a greenish blue, intelligent and full of humor and somehow piercing. Perhaps he didn't really need to touch a person to know what they were thinking. The thought gave her a chill unrelated to the cold.

O'Hara grinned. "What's the matter, Miss Willard? Not having a good time?"

"Of course not!"

"No sense of adventure?"

"Absolutely none," she replied frostily.

The annoying O'Hara seemed amused by her answer. "That really is too bad."

She gave him her haughtiest glare, an expression he seemed to find amusing.

Fortunately, Lionel Brandon stepped onto the porch before O'Hara could say more. Daisy managed a smile for the handsome man. "Good

morning, Mr. Brandon. How is Lucien this morning? Have you spoken to him?"

"Lucien is sleeping soundly," Lionel said. He
gave her a reassuring smile. "He'll be fine."

"Will we be able to travel today?" She held her
breath as she awaited an answer, hoping that his answer would be different from Mr. O'Hara's.

"I'm afraid not," Lionel said.

"Oh," Daisy turned to look at the wintry landscape. "Well, if you say so. I'm sure you and Mr.
Felder know what's best."

Lionel laid a comforting hand on her shoulder.
That hand was large, warm, and very friendly. Did
he, perhaps, feel something of what she felt?
"There's nothing to be afraid of, Miss Willard. All
will be well."

"Thank you, Mr. Brandon. And you must call me
Daisy."

O'Hara snorted, and she glanced at him quickly
to see that he wore a wicked grin.

"Daisy," Lionel said. "Elijah delivered some supplies early this morning. Mrs. Cassidy has prepared
a delicious breakfast. You really should eat."

In truth, she was starving, and when Lionel offered his arm she gratefully took it.

From everything she'd heard, Lionel's own powers
of seeing beyond what he should be able to see were
not limited to the things and people he touched. He
could see anything he chose to see; he had the power
to peek inside a person's mind. And yet, she didn't
worry about him the way she worried about O'Hara.
Lionel was much too much a gentleman to pry.

"Miss Willard," O'Hara said with a touch of glee
in his irritating voice, as he followed them into the
hotel. "May I call you Daisy?"

She tossed a glance over her shoulder. She almost said, "Absolutely not!" but held her tongue. It would be rude to say no at this point, she supposed. She didn't want Lionel to think her rude. Still, she certainly didn't want O'Hara to believe that they were friends or ever would be. "I suppose," she said with a lack of enthusiasm.

"Given the circumstances, it would be foolish for us to remain so formal," Lionel said. "We should all be on a first-name basis, at least for the duration of our adventure."

As Lionel led Daisy into the dining room, she cast a quick glance to the man who followed. "And what about you, O'Hara? What is your given name?"

"Everyone calls me O'Hara."

She was overcome with unexpected curiosity. "Your given name must be dreadful, to make you blush that way."

"I am not blushing," he insisted.

Daisy smiled up at Lionel, dismissing the man behind them. Why did she care what O'Hara's name was? She would talk to him as little as possible, while they were stuck in this horrid place. With any luck, she didn't have to call him anything at all!

Eve muttered a word that was not fit for a lady. Then she said it aloud and quite distinctly.

"Snow!" She spun around to face the bed where Lucien reclined, awake but obviously still shaken.

"So?"

"It doesn't snow here very often," she explained more calmly. "How will we get out of this place now?"

"It will melt," he said calmly.

"Not today." Eve grabbed her wedding dress

from the chair where she'd tossed it last night. She'd slept in her chemise, but if she wanted to go downstairs she'd have to don her wedding gown once again. She wouldn't bother with the corset that was tossed over the dresser. Most of the time she enjoyed wearing fancy, colored corsets, but for her wedding she had chosen something white and simple, with just a touch of lace. There was no need to squeeze herself into it now.

Maybe she was cursed, she thought as she stepped into the white satin gown. Two failed weddings were surely a sign of some kind. And not a good sign, either. If she believed in fate, signs from above, bad luck, then she would have to consider that maybe she and Lucien weren't meant to be, no matter how much they cared for each other.

She struggled with her gown. Without the corset it was a snug fit, and the last of the buttons down the front were difficult to fasten. Maybe she should've taken the time to change before riding to Lucien's rescue, but at the time she'd been unwilling to delay for any reason.

"I smell food," she said, not letting on to Lucien that she was having doubts. Not about the fact that she loved him and he loved her; she knew that without question. But maybe they simply weren't meant to be together. Not forever. Not the way she wanted. "I'll go down and get you something to eat. Will you be all right here? I'll send Hugh up to sit with you . . ."

"I don't need a sitter," Lucien said. If he'd had the energy, that might have been a biting retort.

Gown in place, Eve stood by the side of the bed. "We need to be careful, until you have your strength back."

"I'll be fine here," he said.

Eve nodded and walked toward the door.

"Evie." Lucien's soft voice stopped her, and she turned to face him. He was so pale, and there were circles under his eyes. Dark, ominous circles. But his attempted smile had a bit of the old Lucien in it, something she had not seen so much as a hint of last night. "You are so beautiful, in your wedding dress."

She glanced down. The gown was wrinkled and misshapen, and her hair was a tangled mess. "It really did look much better before I spent several hours in a wagon and then on horseback." Her elegant, expensive dress was ruined. "I wanted you to be overcome when you saw me in this dress. I wanted to be the perfect bride for you. And look at me now. I look like a . . . a well dressed beggar."

"You do not," Lucien said. "And it doesn't matter what condition your wedding clothes are in. It's the woman in the gown who makes it beautiful."

She smiled at him. "I see you have not lost your ability to try to sweet talk yourself out of any predicament."

"Only the truth for us, Evie," he said, closing his eyes again. "Only the truth."

She ran down the stairs, not wanting to leave Lucien alone for more than a few minutes. He needed to eat, and she was starving. She'd make a large plate of whatever that was she smelled, and she and Lucien would share it.

The dining room was full. Daisy and Katherine, Buster and Garrick, Lionel, O'Hara, and Hugh. They all ate from a massive spread of eggs, biscuits, and ham.

When she walked into the room, everyone started

speaking to her at once. Lionel and Garrick both stood, and after a moment Daisy jumped to her feet.

"He's much better," she said, answering all their questions about Lucien. "Still weak, but more himself than he was last night."

Hugh breathed a sigh of relief.

"I told him I wouldn't be gone but a few minutes," she said, grabbing a plate and piling it high. "If someone would fix us a couple of cups of that coffee and bring them up, I would appreciate it. I don't suppose there's tea?" she asked. Katherine shook her head. "It isn't important." Coffee would do.

"I'll get the coffee," Daisy said, hurrying toward the kitchen. Daisy was always happiest if she had something to do. And besides, Daisy knew how she and Lucien liked their coffee. Was there sugar and cream? It would be nice, but in truth it didn't matter much.

"Can he tell us what happened?" Hugh asked.

"Let him eat first and then we'll see," Eve replied.

She rushed from the room with a full plate in her hands. O'Hara was right behind her.

"Let me help with that," he said, trying to work his way around her.

"No, that's really not necessary." Lucien didn't need to be confronted with O'Hara. Not yet!

"It's heavy," he said.

"It's only one plate!" Eve protested as she came to a halt at the foot of the stairs.

O'Hara leaned in close. "Actually," he said in a low voice. "I wanted to speak to you about Miss Willard, privately."

"Daisy?" Eve sighed. "Really, O'Hara, she's not your type at all."

"I know. I seem to irritate her, and she's much

too prim and proper for me, and she's obviously frightened of the things I face every day." His eyebrows rose and fell in a rakish manner, and she was subjected to the boyish grin he apparently thought was charming. "I just want you to tell me how to get on her good side."

Not now! She didn't have time to humor O'Hara. Besides, it would never work! "Daisy isn't accustomed to men who are so . . . bold. She likes men who are polite, and well-spoken and . . ."

"Boring," he finished for her.

Eve glanced up. Lucien was waiting in his room, weak and ill and needing her. "Can we finish this conversation later?"

"I don't have that much time," he said in a lowered voice. "Once we get out of here, I might never get Daisy cornered again."

"Cornered?" Eve asked, outraged.

"You know what I mean."

"I'm afraid I do."

She turned toward the stairs, and O'Hara grabbed her arm. "Wait. I said that wrong. You know how horribly inept I am with women."

Eve rolled her eyes. "O'Hara," she said, exasperated.

He leaned in close and whispered. "I like her."

O'Hara and Daisy. Eve closed her eyes and took a deep breath. The very idea was as impossible as the concept of Daisy and Lionel together! Perhaps she could explain to O'Hara that Daisy was smitten with Lionel, and then handle the concept of that improbable coupling at another time, if necessary. "Later," she said. "After I get Lucien fed and back to sleep."

"Later," a deep, familiar voice whispered from the top of the stairs.

Eve's head snapped around. Lucien stood there at the top of the stairs wearing nothing but his wrinkled trousers, one hand on the banister as he teetered unsteadily. Pale, weak, and angry, he glared down at her.

O'Hara smiled. "Lucien! You look so much better than you did last night."

"Get away from my wife," Lucien said.

"Your wife?"

Eve handed the plate of food to O'Hara and rushed up the stairs, catching the annoyingly full skirt of her wedding gown in both hands, when it threatened to impede her progress. She had to reach the top of the stairs! Lucien looked like he might fall at any moment.

"That's right," Lucien said hoarsely. "She's not my wife, is she? She's just . . . just . . ."

Eve took his arm and held on tight. He'd been too warm, since she'd found him here, but right now his skin was cool. Almost cold. This damn drafty hotel was filled with icy drafts and cold spots, and a man half-dressed had no business wandering the halls. "Back to bed."

Lucien looked her dead in the eye. "Why is O'Hara here?" he asked.

"Calm down . . ."

"Why?!"

Eve led Lucien down the long hallway. "He came to the wedding," she said in a whisper.

"You invited him to our wedding?" he asked, incredulous.

"No, of course not," Eve whispered. "He showed

up with Lionel and Hugh. What was I supposed to do? Send him away?"

"Yes," Lucien said weakly.

"What's going on?" O'Hara came up behind them with the plate in his hands.

Lucien stopped and tried to spin around. Eve wouldn't allow him to turn to O'Hara. He was in no shape to face the man down, physically or emotionally.

"You're protecting him again," Lucien accused.

"I am not."

"Protecting who?" O'Hara asked. "Me?"

"Wait here," Eve ordered as she steered Lucien toward the door to their room.

Amazingly, O'Hara obeyed.

Inside the room, Lucien headed for the bed. He was already fatigued.

"Why on earth did you leave the room?" she asked.

"I don't remember," Lucien said as he lay back and closed his eyes. "I dozed off, I think. Suddenly I was just there, looking down the stairs, and you were whispering sweet nothings to O'Hara . . ."

"I was not!"

"Making plans to meet him later."

"That's not . . ."

"Last night while I slept, did you go to him?" Lucien glared at her, accusation in his dark blue eyes. She usually loved his eyes. They were full of life and intelligence, and love. He didn't hide his emotions. They were right there for her to see.

"You know I didn't," she whispered.

"How do I know?"

She should be furious with Lucien, and in any other instance she would. But he was not thinking clearly, she understood that. "You know I love you."

"Do you?"

"Yes."

The anger and accusation in his eyes faded. It didn't disappear, but the rage was gone. "Is it enough, Evie?" he asked weakly.

She didn't answer, and it didn't matter. Lucien closed his eyes and almost immediately fell into a deep sleep.

Katherine sat on the top step of the Honeycutt Hotel front porch and stared out at the snow that covered the ground and rested in the limbs of the evergreen trees. Snow even sat on the branches of trees that wouldn't see their leaves until spring. It made a pretty prison, but then she was accustomed to pretty prisons. Her own home was one, and had been since the day she'd married.

With a shiver, Katherine hugged her cloak close. The outerwear was warm, but not warm enough. Cold air whipped inside the cloak, ruffling her black skirt and slipping beneath to chill her legs.

She knew the moment she heard the furtive footstep that it was Garrick behind her, and she didn't bother to look back or rise. After a moment when neither of them moved, he sat beside her.

"What a dilemma," he said casually.

She didn't turn to look at him. All her life, she'd known Garrick Hunt, though they had certainly not been friends. He was rich and spoiled, above common folk like her. And he drank, like Jerome. The only difference was, when Garrick got drunk it was likely to be maids and a butler who tucked him in and spoon-fed him tea until he was recovered.

But lately, they had become friends. It was the

ridiculous ghost society they had formed that threw them together. Otherwise, he never would have looked at her twice.

"We shouldn't be here," she said softly.

Garrick shrugged his shoulders. "Probably not."

She turned her head sharply to look at his relaxed profile. "Probably? Garrick, there are ghosts here. Lucien is . . . is . . ."

"He's not well at the moment," Garrick said as she faltered.

"Not well. That's an understatement."

With a sigh, Katherine returned her gaze to the snow-covered land before her. Did Garrick not understand the danger in this situation? She did. She felt it to her bones. They shouldn't be here.

"I had to come," he said. "It's my fault he's here."

"How could it possibly be your fault?"

"I told him about this place, suggested that we bring the Plummerville Ghost Society here for an outing."

Katherine shook her head in wonder. "How foolish."

"I know."

"Well, you got your outing. Happy?"

Garrick shrugged his shoulders as if it made no difference that they were trapped in a haunted hotel. "It's beautiful, isn't it?"

"The snow?" she asked sharply.

"Yes." He smiled. "I've never seen more than a light dusting. I had no idea it could be so . . . so pure and bright and white."

"It is beautiful," she conceded. "But it also traps us here." A gust of wind kicked up and she shuddered.

Garrick immediately removed his coat and

draped it over her shoulders, letting his hands rest on her shoulders too long.

"What are you doing?" she asked sharply.

"You're cold."

"You'll freeze without your coat," she said sensibly, shrugging off the garment.

Garrick placed one hand on her shoulder and held the coat in place. "Allow me to be a gentleman, just this once," he said in a low voice. "I have so little opportunity to impress the fine ladies of Plummerville."

Katherine rolled her eyes. "Please. You haven't cared about impressing anyone since you turned fifteen and realized that a smile and enough money made it unnecessary for you to bother."

His smile faded. "When I was fifteen, you were . . ."

"Ten," she said.

"And you remember me from that time?"

It wouldn't do for her to allow him to think that she had ever been attracted to him, even in the most fleeting, impossible way. "Of course. You were the most obnoxious child in Plummerville, even then."

"Even then?" He laughed out loud. "Are you suggesting that I'm still an obnoxious child?"

She couldn't help but smile back. "You have your moments."

"You should do that more often," Garrick said.

"Do what?"

"Smile."

Immediately, her smile faded. She hadn't had anything to smile about for a long time. And no matter how beautiful it was here, no matter how engaging Garrick Hunt could be when he set his mind to it, nothing had changed.

Seven

Eve wrestled with her skirt as she tried to get comfortable in the ladderback chair beside the bed where Lucien slept. The skirt and petticoat rustled loudly, but Lucien was sleeping so deeply he was not disturbed. Eve was, though. She was terribly disturbed.

Laverne had been determined that the wedding gown be elaborate and elegant and special. Eve Abernathy didn't bother with special clothing to make herself beautiful, she didn't attempt to make more of herself by dressing up in elegant gowns. But she hadn't argued with Laverne, not once. Deep in her heart, she'd wanted the wedding and everything about it to be special and memorable.

Well, it had certainly been memorable.

What she wouldn't give right now for a simple blouse and skirt! Her wedding dress had been constructed for beauty, not comfort and practicality.

Giving up on comfort and silence, she reached out and rested her hand on Lucien's forehead, finding him too warm but not as frighteningly hot as before. Again, he didn't respond. He slept so deeply he wasn't even aware of her presence. No sound or touch would invade and disturb his sleep. Usually if she touched him while he slept, he woke with a smile. He wrapped his long arms around her, sighed in her ear and told her she was beautiful, and then he made love to her. Lucien Thorpe was her man, her friend and lover, the only one for her. Was she in for a lifetime of days like this one?

A fire blazed in the fireplace, warming the room on this cold afternoon. Eve pushed back a strand of dark hair that had fallen over Lucien's forehead. In preparation for their marriage she had endured numerous fittings for the now-ruined wedding gown and had allowed Daisy to pull and twist her hair every afternoon for a month, searching for the most perfect hairstyle. She had begun secretly converting one of the bedrooms in her cottage into an office for Lucien as a wedding surprise. She had entertained her family, arranged for a very nice reception, and seen to the invitations.

Lucien hadn't even bothered to cut his hair.

Was she fooling herself to believe that they could be happy? She didn't doubt that he loved her, and she certainly loved him. But was that enough?

"How is he?"

Eve withdrew her hand and twisted around to see Hugh standing in the open doorway. "Better, I think," she said softly, even though she suspected she could shout out her answer and Lucien wouldn't be disturbed. "How is everyone else faring?"

Hugh stepped into the room, his eyes on Lucien. "As well as can be expected. Lionel and O'Hara are exploring the house from top to bottom, searching for answers. There's quite enough here to keep us all busy until we're able to leave."

"And the others?"

"They're adapting to the difficult situation quite

well." He gave her a gentle smile. "The two gentlemen from Plummerville are out hunting, in order
to supplement what Elijah has provided in the way
of food, and the ladies are keeping themselves busy
in the kitchen."

"Very good," Eve said softly. She had a feeling this
was not exactly what any of them had bargained for
when they'd formed the Plummerville Ghost Society. "Keep a close eye on them for me," she added.
"They're good friends, and they truly have no idea
what they've stumbled into." She should have
forced them to stay behind in Plummerville! They
had no business here. This was not a lark. It was a
dangerous rescue mission that had gone terribly
wrong, thanks to the snow that had trapped them
here.

Hugh moved soundlessly to the foot of the bed,
and stood there looking down at Lucien. A fatherly
concern touched his features. "It's not entirely his
fault, you know," he said in a lowered voice.

She could argue with him, but Hugh saw too
much. "He never should've come here."

"I don't think he had a choice," Hugh said. "Lucien is eaten up inside, wondering why he has this
gift he never wanted. He's learned to control it, he
has made a productive life for himself, and still . . . he
is determined to discover a scientific reason for his
abilities. He wants answers he will never find. That's
why he's always fiddling with those contraptions of
his. That's why he can't resist an opportunity to
investigate a place like this one. He's driven by something even he doesn't understand."

"He could've waited two days," she said, only
slightly agitated. "Two days, Hugh! But no, he
comes here all alone, not knowing what he might

find. He is willing to risk everything, even me, to find his answers."

"He loves you," Hugh said simply.

"I know that." Her anger died as quickly as it had flared to life. "And I love him, I truly do. But does that mean I will have to watch him go through this again and again? That I will have to abide always coming second to his ghosts?"

"I can't answer those questions."

Neither could she, and that was the problem. "I love him, Hugh, with all my heart." Every fear she had been swallowing for the past two days swam to the surface. "I'm just not sure I can do this forever."

Darkness was encroaching once again, and Daisy was quite sure she did not want to spend another night in this hotel! Still, what choice did she have? Eve had spent the day with Lucien, and from what she'd heard from Hugh they had both slept away much of the day. Daisy didn't want to disturb her friend, so she was doubly glad Katherine had joined the party. They might not have much in common, but it was nice to have a woman to talk to. Even when they didn't talk, just knowing someone familiar was close by was a comfort.

The kitchen was warm, in spite of the winter's chill that cut through the drafty hotel. She and Katherine had been in this warm room most of the afternoon, cooking and cleaning, digging through the pantry for usable utensils and linens. So much had been left behind when the hotel had been abandoned. It was decidedly odd.

The day had passed quickly enough. They might not be here more than one more night, but they both wanted to stay busy! Daisy daydreamed as she wiped down a long, polished counter in the kitchen—for the sixth time. If only she had brought her latest piece of needlework with her. Now, that was an activity that made the time pass quickly.

But for today, sweeping, washing, and beating a rug or two had been her only distraction.

Buster and Garrick had spent much of the day hunting. Thankfully, Garrick possessed a small six-shooter he was rather proud of. She supposed they needed a way to pass the time, too. They had come home with several rabbits and, since Elijah had dropped off some winter vegetables this afternoon, Katherine had put together a big pot of rabbit stew for dinner. The simmering pot of stew looked and smelled delicious.

Luckily for her, O'Hara had spent much of the day exploring the house and was unable to harass her. Unfortunately, Lionel had been with O'Hara, so she hadn't had a chance to speak with him, either. The two men had knocked about the house, exploring every room. Including everything on the third floor.

She had caught glimpses of them, now and then. Completely by accident, of course. Lionel would stand in the middle of a room, close his eyes, and go stone-still. She didn't know where he went when he did that, but he certainly went *somewhere*. O'Hara worked differently, touching everything. Walls, furniture, the floor—he moved constantly. He laid his palms here and there, brushed his fingers across surfaces slick and rough. He was never still, and he talked to himself as he worked. Well, either he talked to himself or else he spoke to things she couldn't see.

She preferred to believe that he carried on a conversation with himself.

Lionel was oblivious to the presence of others as he worked, but O'Hara was not. His eyes had found Daisy more than once, when she'd been bold enough to check on the two men, and he'd smiled widely, like the rogue that he was. She had not smiled back.

Katherine steered well clear of O'Hara. Was she shaken by what he'd said last night, when he'd taken her hands in his? Was it truly possible that she was somehow holding her departed husband in the home they'd shared?

Daisy herself certainly had no intention of allowing O'Hara to touch *her*. Not simply because he might be able to find a hidden secret inside her, but because he was such an annoying man, and she did not allow such rogues to touch her in any way. Even though Lionel didn't have to touch her to see secrets, she continued to tell herself that he was too much a gentlemen to use his powers to pry into the minds of the others in this house. He directed his abilities elsewhere, in a productive and strictly professional manner.

O'Hara was not a gentleman, she felt quite sure.

During the long day Hugh Felder had taken notes, talked to himself much as O'Hara did, and often ensconced himself in a room all alone. To Daisy's way of thinking, that was unwise. Who wanted to be alone in this haunted hotel?

Not her.

"Do you think we'll ever get out of here?" Katherine asked as she stirred the stew.

Daisy jumped, startled and dismayed by the question. "Of course."

"I'm not so sure," the widow said pessimistically.

Daisy tried to be cheerful. "The snow can't last much longer. Surely by tomorrow . . ."

"I'm not worried about the snow," Katherine interrupted.

It was the hotel itself that scared Katherine, just as it scared Daisy. Neither of them wanted to talk about it. "Lucien's colleagues are quite talented," Daisy said. "I'm sure they'll be able to . . . to fix the place."

Katherine laughed darkly. "Lucien's colleagues are a large part of the problem. If what they say is correct and something in this hotel wanted to keep Lucien here to feed off of him, then doesn't it make sense that the same something is delighted to have a house full of strange men who see and hear things normal people don't?"

"Maybe," Daisy whispered.

"Maybe," Katherine snorted. "I never should have joined this ridiculous ghost society. When you invited me to that dinner party right before Halloween, I should have declined and run for my little house and stayed there."

"Just because Lucien hasn't been able to get rid of your ghost yet . . ."

Katherine spun around. The high-necked black she always wore made her face seem starkly pale. Her black hair was pulled back in a severe bun. Her dark eyes looked too large, too frightened. Katherine was not a woman to be easily frightened.

"That charlatan O'Hara says I'm holding Jerome here. Is that possible?"

"I don't know," Daisy whispered.

"What if it is my fault?" The widow took in a deep breath and let it out slowly. "What if I'm never rid of him?"

Daisy had never seen Katherine so scared. She was frightened not of the hotel and whatever resided here, but of the husband who had mistreated her when he'd been alive. "You will be rid of him," she said, in her most reassuring voice.

"You're so damned optimistic!" Katherine blurted. "You think the world is a neat, orderly place where everything makes sense and good always wins and every question gets answered."

"It doesn't hurt to expect the best."

"Yes, it does," Katherine whispered. "It hurts like hell."

Before Daisy could respond Lionel stepped into the room, that limp and his long blond hair making him look rather like a pirate. A smiling, handsome, well-dressed pirate. "That smells wonderful," he said.

"Dinner will be ready soon," Daisy said, smiling so that her dimples were shown to their very best advantage. She was glad to see the abrupt end of her conversation with the widow Cassidy. It had been leading in a very difficult direction. Katherine had turned to face the stove, so Daisy took over the role of hostess.

"Katherine is a wonderful cook," she said brightly.

"I have discovered that already," Lionel said appreciatively. "I'm sure you're a fine cook, as well."

Katherine scoffed aloud at that statement.

"Did you learn anything of importance as you explored the hotel today?" Daisy asked to change the subject.

Lionel's wicked, pirate-like grin faded. "Perhaps," he said.

Just her luck, O'Hara stepped into the room to stand beside the taller, more handsome Lionel

Brandon. "Eve's going to bring Lucien down for dinner," he said without a smile.

"That's lovely," Daisy said, very much looking forward to seeing her friends.

"No, it isn't," O'Hara snapped. "Lucien should stay right where he is until he has his strength back. The hotel is crippling him, and he has no business exposing himself to the most active areas until he's recovered."

"I'm sure he wouldn't risk coming downstairs if he thought it was dangerous."

The two men looked at each other. "I thought you said you knew Lucien," O'Hara said sarcastically.

"I do."

"Not very well," he said sharply. "The man is impossible!"

Daisy was quick to defend her friend's beloved. "Lucien has always seemed quite sensible to me."

This time even Lionel snorted.

She was anxious to change the subject. Again. "You never did tell me what you discovered today." She planted her eyes on Lionel and ignored O'Hara.

"No one should be alone in this hotel," O'Hara answered. "And I don't care what the weather looks like tomorrow, I think we should leave in the morning. Even if we have to walk out of here."

Daisy's mouth went dry. "Is it really that bad?"

Both men nodded.

"This is not a good idea," Eve protested as she took hold of Lucien's arm.

"I'm fine," he insisted for the tenth time. "I'll be just as safe downstairs with the others as I am cooped up here."

"Hugh doesn't think so," Eve said softly.

"Hugh is much too cautious for his own good. He always has been."

He did look much better, and that eased her mind. But this was a quiet room. Not completely quiet, but much safer for Lucien than most of the rooms in this dreadful hotel. If she had her way she'd keep him here until it was time to leave. Unfortunately, he didn't seem to care what she thought.

They left the room arm in arm. Eve wore her wedding gown, which was quite wrinkled but still lovely and elaborate, and Lucien had dressed for dinner in his only available suit of clothes. He did look much better tonight, she decided as they descended the stairway, even though he needed a shave and lots more sleep. There was color in his face tonight, more strength in his step and his hand, and he held himself straight and tall.

Still, he was not himself.

Everyone else was already in the dining room, seated and waiting, and their eyes turned expectantly to Lucien. At once, they all seemed relieved.

It was odd, to have these wedding guests trapped here in the old Honeycutt Hotel. Dressed in their best, a bit the worse for wear but in fine spirits given the circumstances, these were the people most important to Eve. If no one else had been at their wedding but these seven friends, she would have been happy. Of course, Lucien would have had to show up!

Eve and Lucien took the two vacant chairs that had been left for them, those nearest the dining room entrance. Fortunately, O'Hara was seated at the far end of the table. Maybe, just maybe, Lucien was too tired to start a fight over dinner.

She relaxed when Lucien reached for his coffee and didn't even so much as look O'Hara's way.

Bowls of stew and tender biscuits made a tasty, filling dinner and were a nice surprise, given the situation. Everyone at the table ate heartily, but there were suspicious glances cast Lucien's way, as if they all expected him to pass out at any moment.

Lucien must be starving. She had never seen him eat like this! He obviously loved the stew and the biscuits. When they got back to Plummerville, she'd have to get the recipe from Katherine. She needed to learn to feed this man who often got so wrapped up in his work that he forgot to eat.

Eve remained silent while polite conversations went on around her. Daisy spoke about the weather, and so did Buster. Garrick expressed an interest in the design of the Honeycutt Hotel, from a strictly business point of view. Numerous comments on the tastiness of the meal were made, compliments Katherine neatly dismissed.

Lucien said nothing at all. For someone who usually cared little for food, he enjoyed the stew. He savored it, even. His reaction made Eve wonder if there wasn't something wrong with her own cooking! When he had cleaned the bowl, Lucien leaned back in his chair and studied the people around them, one by one. Their conversations continued, in soft voices. It was a very civilized gathering of old and new friends. After a moment of silent and still reflection, Lucien smiled.

"All these heroes here to rescue me," he said sardonically. "How curious."

"Lucien!" Eve said beneath her breath. He might have meant that comment as a thanks of some kind, but it certainly didn't sound that way!

"These are our friends, Eve," he said as he glanced down at her with a touch of annoyance in his eyes. "Surely we can speak honestly with our *friends.*"

"Of course," she said. A tickle of warning crawled up her spine. She knew how important honesty was to Lucien. Still, hadn't she convinced him that some things were best left unsaid?

Lucien lifted his coffee cup in mock salute. "And what a motley group of friends these are."

"I think you should get back to bed," Eve said, setting her napkin on the table and beginning to stand. Lucien grabbed her wrist and pulled her back down so that she thumped into her seat.

"Not yet," he said softly. The grip on her wrist was tight. Where had he found the strength? Just a few hours ago he had been so weak.

He looked pointedly at Daisy, who sat at Eve's side. "Daisy, my dear, you look positively terrified."

"Well, I . . ." Daisy began.

"You're always afraid of something, poor thing. What you really need is a man in your bed," Lucien interrupted. "Someone who will spread those pale thighs and make you scream and . . ."

"Lucien!" Eve said, yanking her hand out of his grasp.

"Well, it's true," he said defensively. "The woman is tied up in knots. A bit of excitement in her bedroom, a man to make her . . ."

"Don't continue," Eve said icily. "Don't you dare." What was wrong with him? Again, she tried to rise and Lucien pulled her into her seat.

"And Buster!" Lucien continued. "A simple man. An ordinary man. A dull, countrified hick who could certainly benefit from the same cure Miss

Daisy is in such desperate need of. Perhaps the two of you . . ."

"That's enough," Eve whispered. "Lucien, what's gotten into you?"

He ignored her. "My good friend Hugh Felder," Lucien said with a widening smile. "I have never known such a martyr in all my long, weary days. Your wife is dead, Felder, and has been for fifteen years. Yes, it was your fault, but that doesn't mean you have to live your life like a monk . . ."

Eve stood quickly. "I'm sorry," she said. "Obviously Lucien is not well . . ."

"Lucien is just fine," he said. He did not try to yank her down into her chair this time. "But coming close to death made me realize how precious our lives are. We shouldn't waste a moment pretending or suffering when with a few words the truth can be out in the open. Left hidden, lies and secrets fester. You know that, darling. Haven't I always told you that honesty is best in all circumstances?"

She sat back down of her own free will. "I think you've said enough."

He ignored her as he continued his perusal of the people at the table. "O'Hara, you lecherous scoundrel. Putting your hand up Eve's skirt was a blunder you will live to regret. Or not. I believe not. I believe I will kill you for touching her."

Eve closed her eyes and then covered them with her hands. Daisy gasped. At this point, no one else at the table was terribly surprised.

"I didn't exactly . . ." O'Hara began.

"You did," Lucien interrupted.

"It was a mistake," O'Hara said defensively. "I'd had too much to drink, and I saw this piece of lint on the back of her dress, and . . ."

"Shut up," Lucien said, relaxing in his chair and moving his gaze on to Lionel.

Those two men stared at each other for a long moment. Lucien's smile died. Lionel said nothing as he stared at Lucien with a stony expression on his face. A silent and invisible power passed between them. It was an energy of some kind, like lightning. The air was charged. The hair on the back of Eve's neck stood. What passed between Lionel and Lucien was a fleeting and potent phenomenon Eve did not understand. All was silent. She wasn't the only one who felt lost at this moment. Finally Lucien moved his gaze to Katherine.

"My dear, dear Katherine," he said. "I have been trying not to alarm you, but I suppose you should know the truth. Your dearly departed husband isn't tied to Plummerville or the house in which you live. He is attached to you like the leech he was in life. He's here now."

Katherine went white. Her lips parted.

"He's standing behind you," Lucien whispered. "With his hands on your shoulders. No," he added quickly. "Around your pretty neck. He hates you, so much."

Katherine bolted to her feet and ran, and Garrick stood and glared down at Lucien.

"I don't care how ill you are, you have no right to be so callous. How dare you speak to Katherine that way?" Garrick shook his head and left the table, presumably to follow the distraught Katherine.

"Don't leave just yet," Lucien called. "I saved the best for last." He grinned wickedly.

Garrick muttered something obscene as he stepped to the wide doorway between the lobby and the dining room.

"Don't you want to know who your mother really is?" Lucien asked loudly.

"Lucien, no," Eve whispered.

Garrick stopped in the arched entrance and turned to face Lucien. "You don't know what you're talking about. Good Lord, Lucien, you really are sick."

"If you don't believe me, ask your father. Or better yet, ask the woman you have called Mother all your life. She hates you, you know. The very sight of you makes her ill. She looks at you and sees your wayward father plowing into another woman. So much hate in little Plummerville." Lucien licked his lips. "Every time she looks at you she sees your father's mistress with her legs spread wide. I can't tell you how many times she wished you dead."

Garrick went almost as pale as Katherine had. "Eve, what's he talking about?"

She'd known that someday Garrick might find out the truth about his mother, but this was such a hard way. To have the news tossed at him as if it were a joke was so very, very wrong. "Garrick," she began.

He shook his head. "I see the truth on your face, Eve. How do you know? Why didn't you tell me?"

Daisy stood and practically ran behind Eve and Lucien's chairs, making her escape. "I'm going to see about Katherine."

"No," Garrick said. "Let me speak to her. This other matter can wait."

Daisy stopped in the entrance as Garrick turned and ran. They listened to his quick booted footsteps on the stairs.

"Yes," Lucien said softly. "Plummerville is filled with nasty little secrets."

Eve took Lucien's arm and tried to urge him to stand as she did. "Come on. You're not well, Lucien. You need to get back to your room."

As one, Lionel and O'Hara stood. "We'll help you to bed, Lucien."

That offer got Lucien's attention, and he stood quickly. "Not necessary, gentlemen. I'm quite capable of taking my bride to bed without assistance."

He took her arm and together they left the dining room.

"How could you do that?" she asked when they were alone in the hotel lobby.

"Do what? Tell the truth?"

"I know you think honesty is always best, but Lucien, the things you said . . . they were rude and unkind and unnecessary."

"And all true."

They climbed the stairs together. "And I am not your bride," she said softly. "In order for me to be your bride, you have to be there for the wedding."

He dropped his arm as they reached the top of the stairs. From a door on the left, they heard muted sobs. Katherine. And a soft, comforting voice. Garrick. Eve's heart broke for them both.

"But you are my bride," he insisted. "Look at you, in that beautiful white wedding dress. All you need is a veil and a bouquet of flowers, and you become the perfect bride. More than that, you are my bride on the inside, aren't you? In the heart, in the very soul. You love me like a bride. You're my wife, my woman."

"Yes, but . . ."

Lucien stopped outside the door to the room they shared. "I'm not ready to go to bed." He glanced toward the stairway at the back of the wing, the stair that led to the third floor. "Let's do a little exploring, shall we?"

"I don't think that's a good idea," Eve said, as he pulled her along, grasping her hand tightly and smiling as he guided her to the stairway.

"I slept all day, and I'm feeling so much stronger tonight." He took a deep breath. "I haven't felt this strong in years."

An odd thing to say, given the circumstances.

He hurried up the stairs, all but dragging Eve with him. His eyes scanned the walls, and when they reached the third floor he grinned widely and dropped her hand to stride down the center of the wide hallway. He took a long, deep breath and lifted his arms, opening them wide.

"There's so much energy here," he said. "Power. Can you feel it?"

Eve shook her head. "No." At the moment she didn't care about the energy in this haunted hotel. "Don't change the subject! You owe each and every one of our friends an apology," she said.

"For being honest?"

"For being heartless!"

He turned on his heel and walked toward her, treading down the long hallway with a half smile on his face and his eyes locked to hers. Every stride was long and slow, as he walked toward her with purpose and vitality in every step.

"I didn't know you could be purposely cruel," she whispered as he reached her.

Lucien grabbed Eve close, spun her around, and pressed her back against the wall. "I don't want to talk about them right now," he said, placing his body close to hers. "I would much rather talk about us."

"Do you have something rude and insulting to

say to me?" she asked, trying to remain detached as he laid a possessive hand on one hip.

"You make such a beautiful bride," he whispered.

"I am not your bride," she said again, as he laid his other hand over the swell of her breast.

"Of course you are. You are my bride, in your lovely white gown, and I want you so badly." He laid his mouth on her throat, moved his lips subtly, and caressed her breast through the thick satin. His hands were gentle and demanding, his mouth was warm and arousing.

"Lucien, you're not well," she protested, even as her body began to respond to his. They were lovers, and had been for months. He had taught her the art of pleasure, the joy of truly being with the man she loved. She was angry, she was confused, but as his hands caressed she could not help but be affected.

"Make me well, Eve," he whispered as he stroked his hand down her side and then back up again. He cupped her breast, then flicked his thumb over the sensitive nipple. Her eyes drifted closed and she felt her own desire begin to grow. At her center, she melted. She'd thought she'd lost him, and yet here he was. Here they were. Lucien lowered his head and kissed her throat again, sucking gently until she moaned low in her throat. Then he moved his mouth to the flesh below, to the expanse of chest revealed by the low cut of her wedding gown.

"You're right," he whispered against the swell of her breasts. "I was needlessly blunt and crude tonight. I don't know what came over me. It's the possession, I suspect. A lingering weakness I have not yet conquered. I can conquer it, with your help. I need you, so much."

It was what she had always wanted from Lucien.

She wanted his love, she had his love. But she wanted him to need her. To depend on her in a way he had never depended on anyone else.

"I do love you," she whispered, taking his face in her hands and looking deep into his blue eyes. "But Lucien, you're truly not well. Something happened to you, in this hotel. Something made you . . . different."

"If I'm sick, you can cure me," he said as he lifted her skirt and petticoat with both hands. "You can make me stronger . . ." his smile faded. "Or you can kill me. Which will it be, Eve?"

"I want to make you stronger," she whispered.

"Of course you do." He pushed the full, white satin skirt high and shoved his hand between her legs, caressing her beneath the linen drawers she wore. "You're already wet," he whispered.

"All you have to do is touch me," she confessed, telling Lucien something he already knew.

His gentle fingers teased her, and once again he lowered his mouth to her throat. Oh, he knew what this did to her! He knew how to touch her, where to kiss. She began to relax in his arms, and all her doubts vanished. For now, at least. There would be time for doubts later. Much later.

She threaded her fingers through his hair. "Let's go downstairs and back to bed."

"No," he said huskily. "I want you here. Now. It's been so long."

Her body wanted him, and reacted as it always did when he was near. Her heart wanted him. She loved him so much. But her mind . . . her mind was not sure. "Lucien, darling, I think you have a fever. You're so hot."

"I'm fine, I promise you."

"You're not strong enough."

"I am," he insisted, and then he showed her he had strength by pulling her body up against his. His fingers dipped beneath the bodice of her wedding gown, caressing soft skin, brushing against one bare, hardened nipple, sparking her passion for him to a new level.

"Love me, Eve," he whispered as he held her close.

The last of her doubts dissolved. She reached between their bodies to unfasten the buttons that held Lucien's arousal trapped. She freed him, caressed his length, and when he kissed her deep she tasted a passion that matched her own.

Lucien groaned as he ripped at the opening in her drawers. With a heave, he lifted her high. Eve wrapped her legs around his waist, her arms around his neck, and she kissed him again. Deeper than before, hungrier. He took his mouth from hers almost roughly and pushed inside her in one long stroke. With her back against the hallway wall, her legs wrapped around him, and the skirt of her wedding dress bunched between them, he buried himself inside her with one long, hard thrust . . . and then became very still. For a moment he didn't move at all.

"Evie," he whispered, as he began to rock into her more tenderly. "Is this a dream?"

"No. It's very real." She held on tight and moved against him. The hands that held her gentled.

Lucien placed his mouth over hers and kissed her ardently as he made love to her. Thick and long, he filled her. He stroked her. She moaned and he caught that moan between parted lips. As they came together, rocking and swaying in their own time, Eve was able to forget how she had found

Lucien on the lobby floor, how he had changed, how he had suffered and made the others suffer. No matter what happened, when they became one the world was a better place.

He pounded against and into her, and she held on tight and moved her hips into and against his. Nothing else mattered, but that she wanted him faster, harder. He gave her everything she wanted.

She climaxed while he was buried deep inside her, and so did he. Her body shuddered; his did, too. They held on to each other as the waves of passion unleashed washed over them.

Joined with him, holding him, she knew in that moment that everything was going to be all right. Her doubts and her fears were senseless. Everything was going to be fine. They would return to Plummerville, get married, have children, and live together happily for the rest of their lives.

"That was . . . different," she said as Lucien lowered her to her feet.

"Yes, it was. Very different." He held her close and looked up and down the long, silent hallway. "Evie?"

"Yes, darling?"

"Where are we?"

Eight

Lucien sat on the top step of the stairway that led down into the lobby, his head in his hands. "I didn't say that. Please tell me I didn't say that!"

He'd gone to sleep with Eve sitting at his side, and awakened inside her, not in the bed they'd shared last night and most of today, but standing in the third floor hallway with Eve's back against the wall and her body wrapped around his.

He lifted his head and stared at the friends who surrounded him. They didn't look like friends, at the moment. Katherine was red-eyed and pale, and Garrick, who stood beside her possessively, was openly furious. Hugh hung back in a way he never had before, and Buster was blushing and embarrassed.

And Eve . . . she stood at the foot of the stairs with Daisy at her side and glared at him as if he were a stranger. Her face was still flushed, her gown more mussed than it had been when he'd last seen her, her hair fell down around her shoulders in tangled waves . . . and she was afraid. Of him, he supposed. And who could blame her?

Of all of them, she should be the one to understand. "Didn't you know?" he whispered. "Couldn't you tell that it wasn't me?"

"No."

"It was you," Lionel said, stepping forward. Apparently he had said nothing hurtful to Lionel over the dinner table . . . perhaps because whatever had possessed him had known that Lionel saw too much too easily. "You spoke with your own voice, and there was none of the weakness that usually comes when you channel. I tried to see more over the dinner table. I knew something was wrong, but I couldn't see into you. I thought you had learned to block me, but apparently you were sleeping and a dark entity had taken over. It was that entity that was able to obstruct my ability to see into your mind."

"Is he gone?"

"No," Lionel said succinctly. "He's hiding, for the moment, waiting until he's strong enough to kill what's left of you."

What's left of you. Lucien shuddered. Was he already fading? Already less than he'd been when he'd walked through the front door of the Honeycutt Hotel?

"I'm so sorry," he said. "I didn't know. I never would have said those things."

"You might not have said them if you'd had the choice," Katherine said as she took one angry step forward. "But you meant them. Every word." In her prim black dress and with her hair pulled severely back, she was the picture of propriety. And she was furious. With him. With her dead husband. "All this time you've been telling me that you could send Jerome away, and you never bothered to tell me that I was the one keeping him here. That he's somehow *attached* to me."

"I didn't think it would serve any purpose to upset you," he said, reaching for a composed tone of voice even though inside he felt like he was falling apart. Eve had been trying to teach him discretion . . . and this is where it got him. He should have told Katherine the truth weeks ago!

O'Hara advanced, tugging on his muddy brown jacket as if to straighten the garment, and bravely sauntering onto the stairway that led to the second floor. Lucien sat on the top step, tired and confused. He was not confused about this man, though. Where O'Hara was concerned, his feelings were crystal clear.

"You . . ." Lucien said hoarsely. "You I really don't like."

"Fine," O'Hara said, unconcerned. "When we get out of here in one piece, you can take all your irrational, unfounded jealous rage out on me. Until then, we need to stick together and fight this . . . thing."

"How do we do that?" Lucien asked.

"This is not your normal nasty spirit, Lucien. He's old, and irate, and dangerous, and he's actually in the hotel."

"We're all in the hotel," Lucien snapped.

O'Hara shook his head. "No, he's *in* the hotel. He's a part of the structure. This spirit, this thing, it's in the walls, in the floors, in every grain of wood and chip of stone that make up this hotel."

"Oh," Daisy squealed.

"How can that be?" Lucien asked.

O'Hara stopped when he was halfway up the stairway. "He died here, a very long time ago. Before the hotel was built, he bled into the ground beneath. He was . . ." O'Hara's brow wrinkled, his eyes narrowed. "I don't know what or who he was, but he had tampered with dark magic best left unexplored, and when he died his soul remained in the land."

Lionel leaned against the banister at the foot of the stairs. "A lot of people died here, on this ground, long before the hotel was built. People passing by, travelers, would be overcome with rage. Hate. Jealousy. There were bloody battles over the very spot where he died. And all the while he collected souls. Scrydan," Lionel said quickly, as if the name had just come to him. "His name was Scrydan, and he didn't want to be alone."

"I think this Scrydan must've somehow influenced the man who built this place," O'Hara said. "Why else would a man build a cathouse out in the middle of nowhere?"

"A *what?*" Daisy squealed.

O'Hara turned to look down at her. "Pardon me, miss. An entertainment house, a jolly place for lonely men, a . . ."

"Do you mind?" Daisy snapped. "How *rude.*"

"In any case," O'Hara said when he turned to face Lucien again, "it didn't remain a . . . house of ill repute for very long. Men did come. The place had a reputation for pretty, willing, adventurous women. But too many of the customers who came here never left. People talked, business suffered, and years before the war began the place was shut down."

"Soldiers!" Lionel said brightly, again as if the thought had just hit him. "Soldiers hid here, and they died here. They even fought here. Not just the enemy, but one another. The soldiers fought over food and imagined insults." His brow furrowed. "They killed comrades with their bare hands." He literally shook off the unpleasant thoughts. "Then after the war, the original owner's grandson decided to turn the place into a spa. There are mineral springs not far from here, and he hawked the hotel as a resort, to those who could afford to pay the exorbitant sum he asked."

"And again," O'Hara said, "too many guests died violently. That's bad for business, no matter what kind of business it might be." He turned to stare pointedly at Daisy, who ignored him.

"So this hotel is just a big trap," Lucien snapped, "and I walked right into it."

"More or less," Hugh said in a lowered voice. "I believe this . . . man, spirit, ghost . . . whatever you want to call Scrydan . . . gathers his strength from the fear and death of others. But you, Lucien, you're different. After we arrived and his plan for your death was thwarted, he discovered that he could stay within you for extended periods of time, something he had not found possible with other living beings. For years he's watched his imprisoned spirits do his dirty work for him, and on occasion he has entered living beings for short periods of time to compel a victim to kill. But he was not able to remain long inside a living being without exhausting himself, until you came along, Lucien. He is able to tap into your mind, he can live inside you. And I'm afraid he likes it."

"Why are you seeing all this *now?*" Eve asked sharply. "Why didn't you know about this Scrydan last night or this morning?"

"He was able to block us completely, for a while," Lionel answered calmly. "But what happened this evening was challenging for him. He stumbled, just enough for us to get a glimpse of what he's done and what he's capable of."

"We have to get out of here," Garrick said. "Tonight."

"We wouldn't get far," Lionel said. "It's already dark, the snow is deep, and we have no horses."

"Tomorrow morning, then," Buster said.

"Tomorrow morning. We should stay together tonight. No one goes off on their own," Hugh commanded.

Daisy nodded enthusiastically.

"One word of caution," Hugh added calmly.

"One word?" Katherine shouted, balling her fists and turning on the older man. "Given the circumstances, I think we deserve more than *one word!*"

Hugh remained serene. "This spirit, it feeds off of pain and fear. That's why it drew bits and pieces from Lucien's memories and said those upsetting things at dinner. It meant to disturb us all. Scrydan wants you to be afraid. The best thing any of you can do, to help us all get out of this place, is to remain calm."

Daisy laughed. "Calm? I can't possibly . . ."

"Try," O'Hara interrupted. When Daisy looked like she was about to argue with him, he continued. "Please, you must try."

Daisy nodded, but she remained obviously skeptical.

"Where is he now?" Lucien asked. Lionel closed his eyes, while O'Hara grasped the banister and then ran his hands along the polished wood. "Where is Scrydan?"

"He's resting," Lionel said. "Since he's not yet in complete control of your body, his time with you saps his energy, just as it saps yours."

"But at the same time he's still here," O'Hara said, "still in the walls and the ceiling and the floor, still powerful."

"And Lucien," Lionel said as he opened his eyes. "He's still inside you."

Eve sat on the lobby sofa, Daisy at her right, Katherine on her left. Eve Abernathy was not a high-strung woman. She did not sob, screech, or lose control of her emotions. There had been times when she could have lost control, but she hadn't. She was a sensible woman who knew there was no benefit in giving in to hysteria.

But at the moment something inside her wanted to scream and cry.

Why hadn't she seen that Lucien wasn't Lucien? Why hadn't she known that no matter how he valued honesty he would never insult his friends the way he had at dinner? Why hadn't she known that the man who'd seduced her was not the man she loved, but a stranger? An evil stranger who wanted them all dead.

Lucien was upstairs resting, hopefully sleeping, with Hugh and Buster close at hand. She should be there, she should be watching over him . . . but she couldn't bear to face him, not now.

Her hands trembled, and Daisy, seeing the reaction, placed a comforting hand over hers.

"It will be all right," Daisy said, trying to sound reassuring but falling far short. "Lucien will be fine, and we'll all get out of here, and you'll have a wonderful wedding."

"What if we don't? What if nothing is ever *fine* again?" Eve asked, dangerously close to hysteria. "What if we never leave this place, what if Scrydan wins and Lucien dies, and we're trapped here forever and . . ."

"Hush," Katherine insisted softly. "If you let yourself become agitated this bastard Scrydan wins."

"She's right." Unexpectedly, O'Hara knelt before Eve and laid a hand on her knee. Eve looked at that hand sharply, and it was withdrawn. "You are the key, Eve," he said calmly. "You are the reason Lucien is still with us, and if he is able to beat Scrydan it will be thanks in no small part to you." He smiled gently. "Lucien is hanging on against incredible odds because he loves you."

Tears welled up in Eve's eyes. Oh, she did not want to cry!

"I have to ask you for a favor," O'Hara said in a soothing, soft voice. "Lucien is blocking Lionel and Hugh, somehow. Not entirely, but to a certain extent. He won't let me near him, so I'm not sure if he can block me or not. Scrydan doesn't want me to touch Lucien and see too much, and Lucien is angry over a silly little accident."

"Accident?" Eve snapped.

O'Hara waved a dismissive hand. "We'll discuss it later, if you like. The most important thing is, we need to know what's happening inside Lucien's mind, and I can't get close enough to get a reading." His blue-green eyes softened. "But he has recently touched you, Eve. Scrydan and Lucien both touched you."

It was a delicate way of reminding her that she had just made love to a demon.

"If I can take your hand, maybe I can see. A little." Still kneeling before her, O'Hara offered his hand. "It's a long shot, but it might be all we have."

"Leave her alone," Daisy said protectively. "She doesn't want you pawing her."

O'Hara cast a weary glance at Daisy. "I don't wish

to *paw* anyone," he said in a less serene voice than he had used to this point. Firelight danced over his face, as he glared at Daisy. This morning he had expressed an interest in Daisy; now he seemed irked with her. Apparently things were not going as he had hoped. Just as well. There was no time for romance in a situation like this one.

In spite of the fact that he knew they all had to remain calm, O'Hara's jaw was tense and his lips were thinned. He needed a shave, as all the men did.

Eve noted with a sinking heart that O'Hara had gotten a haircut for the wedding. Even this scoundrel had put more time and thought into the preparations than Lucien had!

Daisy snorted, letting O'Hara and everyone else in the room know she did not believe his assertion that he had no intention of pawing anyone.

"It's all right," Eve said. After a moment's hesitation, she laid her palm on O'Hara's. He closed his fingers over her hand and looked into her eyes. She knew he now saw everything. Her memories, good and bad; her doubts and her love. He continued to hold her hand, even closing his eyes once and swaying slightly.

"Lucien should be gone by now," he said, "but he's hanging on because he doesn't want Scrydan to hurt you. He's fighting, deep inside, and it's a constant battle. He's doing his best to protect you."

Eve's hand began to tremble, but O'Hara held on tight. There was something else, something he didn't say aloud. "Tonight," he finally whispered, "Scrydan thought he had won. He thought Lucien was so weak he didn't dare reappear. But he did. Lucien fought his way back because . . . because . . ."

She knew why, though even the rogue was too

embarrassed to say so aloud. Lucien had come because Scrydan was inside her. He had fought his way to the surface in order to protect her.

"What can I do?" she whispered.

"Fear will feed Scrydan as it has for centuries," O'Hara said. "You can show him no fear, Eve. You can *feel* no fear."

"How is that possible?"

"I don't know," he whispered. Before he released her hand, he kissed the knuckles briefly. "I only know that in order to completely defeat Lucien, Scrydan must first defeat you."

Everyone was talking about sleep. How could they? Daisy paced in the parlor. She might never sleep again.

Eve had gone upstairs to sit with Lucien. Hugh and Buster were with her. Katherine, still understandably upset, had headed for the kitchen more than an hour ago. When Daisy had offered to help, Katherine had told her not to bother. Garrick had gone with her, though, so she wouldn't be alone.

That left Daisy here in the parlor with Lionel and O'Hara.

She continued to think that Lionel was a magnificent specimen of manliness. A Viking, a pirate, a strikingly beautiful figure of a man.

O'Hara would never be beautiful. He certainly wasn't ugly, but next to Lionel he was almost ordinary. Except for his eyes, she amended silently. He had perfectly marvelous eyes that were intelligent and expressive.

Perhaps she had been hasty in dismissing O'Hara as a rogue. He had been very sweet to Eve, earlier in the evening, and he had certainly kept his calm during this crisis. She was almost positive that he must have a reasonable explanation for that mishap in which he'd behaved improperly with Eve.

Was there a proper explanation for putting one's hand under a woman's skirt?

She tried to turn her attention to Lionel. He was, by far, the superior of the two. There was something almost regal about his bearing. She could add "princely" to the list of descriptions that fit him.

O'Hara was just a man. A nice-looking, average height, man. No one would ever mistake him for a prince, or a Viking, or a pirate. A charlatan, perhaps. A salesman. A scoundrel. Definitely a scoundrel.

Right now, both men were solemn and thoughtful. Lionel stared into the fire. O'Hara paced. She didn't have to be a mind reader to know that they were worried. Worried for everyone in the hotel, she imagined, but most especially they worried for Lucien. He was their friend, and one did not easily dismiss the sufferings of a friend.

"You never did tell me your given name, O'Hara," she said, ceasing her own nervous pacing to sit on the sofa.

"What?" he turned to her, obviously surprised that she had spoken. Perhaps he was surprised that she had spoken to *him*.

"Your given name," she repeated. "You never did share it with me."

He waved her off. "The name my mother gave me isn't important."

"Surely your mother didn't call you O'Hara."

"Of course not."

"What did she call you?"

"She called me her little sweetums," he teased. "Why this sudden obsession with my name?"

"I'm merely curious," she said. "And since I very well might die here in this awful haunted hotel, I think I should have my every curiosity resolved."

O'Hara opened his mouth, started to say something, and then stopped with a shake of his head. "I can't. It's just too easy."

"What's too easy?" she asked.

"Nothing."

"Really, O'Hara . . ."

He took a step closer to her. "Let's just say that when a beautiful woman speaks to a man about her piqued curiosity, his mind might take a decidedly forbidden turn."

"Oh," she said softly. So, he *did* think she was beautiful.

"What are you doing, Daisy?" O'Hara asked.

"I'm just trying to keep my mind occupied," she explained, "so I won't be thinking about everything that's happened and get scared all over again. You did say that we should not be afraid."

"I did," he said softly.

"So, instead of sitting here deathly terrified that I'm going to die tonight and feeding this spirit's fear, I decided to think upon your given name instead."

"What if I warn you that my given name is just as frightening as anything that lives in this hotel."

She looked him in the eye. "Then I am all the more determined to know what it is."

Lionel turned and said, "Yes, what is your given name? You've been nothing but O'Hara since the day I met you."

Daisy almost jumped out of her seat. She had forgotten, for a moment, that Lionel was in the room!

"I'll never tell," O'Hara said, quite seriously.

Daisy frowned as she stared at Lionel. "You don't know his given name either?"

"No," he said simply.

"But you can know . . . everything, can't you? You could look into his mind and see, if you wanted to know. Right?"

It was O'Hara who answered. "We have an agreement, among us. We don't pry into one another's lives or minds unless invited."

This was an interesting turn of events. "Do you mean that you can turn off your abilities?"

O'Hara nodded. "Somewhat. It's easier for Lionel than for me, but I'm learning. For the most part I simply don't touch anyone without warning. Usually," he added in a lowered voice.

So, she couldn't cajole Lionel into telling her O'Hara's given name.

Men were usually anxious to give Daisy Willard whatever she asked for, thinking that would impress her in some way. She was accustomed to asking for something and having it handed to her almost immediately.

"Your name can't be that bad," she said, growing annoyed. "And I do so want to know."

"Why?" O'Hara grinned widely.

"I told you, I'm curious."

He was not impressed.

"And besides, it's silly for everyone to call you by your surname."

"Silly?"

"Yes, silly." She nodded her head once for emphasis.

O'Hara was enjoying this much too much. He could see very well that she wanted to know what his name was, and yet he withheld that tiny bit of insignificant information. "I'll make you a deal," he said smugly.

"A deal?"

"You give me your hand, and then I'll tell you my name."

Daisy clasped her hands tightly in her lap. She had seen how O'Hara looked into a person, first with Katherine and then with Eve. She didn't want anyone to be able to look into her soul and her mind that way! What kinds of secrets would he see? Most people probably thought Daisy Willard had no secrets, but that wasn't the case. She just hid those secrets very well.

If O'Hara took her hand, there would be no more secrets.

"I suppose O'Hara will have to do," she said primly.

He dropped his hand, and his smile dimmed. "Just as I suspected."

Daisy cast a quick glance at Lionel, who had returned his attention to the fire in the fireplace. He was incredibly psychic, according to Eve. Could he turn his gift toward her and uncover her secrets? She had thought that not to be a danger, since he was obviously a gentleman. Looking at him, she suspected he simply didn't care enough to be interested in what she hid deep inside. Besides, he could turn the power off, when he wanted, he could control what and where he saw.

The way O'Hara stared at her, he most definitely cared. But she knew he would not force her to take his hand. He wanted her to lay her hand in his of her own free will.

She could never do that. Never.

The mood changed subtly when Katherine and Garrick returned from the kitchen. Garrick, who had jokingly asked Daisy to marry him several times, had been very nice to Katherine of late. Very nice. Still, Daisy couldn't see them as a couple. Garrick was carefree and never seemed to take anything seriously, and Katherine had a tendency to be aloof and sometimes downright bitter.

Garrick was probably taking a special interest in Katherine since he was, after all, president of the Plummerville Ghost Society.

Katherine sat beside Daisy, and Garrick went to stand beside Lionel. He asked a whispered question, and Lionel shook his head quickly.

"Why not?" Garrick snapped. "For God's sake, it's what you do!"

All eyes turned to Lionel.

"Garrick," Katherine said sharply. "I told you not to ask!"

"If that bastard is here, I don't see why we can't get rid of him now. Why do we need to wait until we get back to Plummerville?" Again Garrick turned to Lionel. "Isn't that what you do for a living? You can do this."

Lionel remained calm. "There are two very good reasons. The first one is Scrydan's curse of this house. Spirits are trapped here. Imagine that the house is encased in a bubble, only this is not a bubble that will burst on its own. It's sturdy, an effective prison."

"So, when we leave the hotel Jerome will be trapped here?" Katherine asked, a touch of hope in her voice.

"I can't be sure," Lionel answered. "In order to free the trapped spirits in this house and defeat

Scrydan, we're going to have to find a way to burst that bubble, freeing all the spirits."

Katherine settled back on the couch, looking almost defeated.

"But you could try," Garrick said sharply.

"No," Lionel said succinctly. "There's also the issue of keeping our energy level low in order not to feed Scrydan. The process of ridding Katherine of her late husband's ghost will be emotional and it will take a lot of energy. We don't need to expend that energy only to have Scrydan suck it in and grow stronger."

"Katherine," Garrick said, turning to face the couch. "I'm sorry. I just want to help."

She nodded her head. "That's very sweet."

Garrick had problems of his own, but he was apparently holding them inside. Since dinner and Lucien's outrageous accusations and revelations, no one had mentioned the bit of news about Garrick's mother not really being his mother. News like that had to hurt, especially when it was delivered in such a crude manner.

Daisy herself had never cared for Mrs. Hunt, a reclusive woman who always acted as if she were better than everyone else. Still, Garrick had spent his entire life believing her to be the woman who had brought him into this world. Was he relieved, just a little, to discover that the bitter woman was not his real mother? Or did he love her in spite of her faults, the way Daisy had loved her own mama? No matter, the news was a shock to him and everyone, but no one wanted to discuss the revelation. Not now.

Of course, no one had dared to mention that Lucien had suggested that a man in her bed was the cure for all Daisy's own problems, either.

Not Lucien, she reminded herself. Scrydan. She shuddered at the very thought.

"Are you cold?" O'Hara asked. "I can fetch you a blanket, if you'd like."

"No, that's not necessary." This chill had nothing to do with the winter weather. It was an icy cold that came from the bones outward. "Perhaps later, though. Would anyone mind terribly if I just stayed right here all night?" Her heart leapt. "I don't want to go upstairs, and I don't think I can sleep, anyway. I'd like to stay right here. I think we should all stay here. Together."

"Good idea," O'Hara said with a smile.

Nice eyes *and* a nice smile, Daisy conceded. A rather brilliant smile, in fact. Charming and roguish, perhaps, but definitely real and true, the way a smile should be. With a smile like that, O'Hara did seem to be beautiful, in his own coarse and rather masculine way.

Daisy was nothing if not practical. Yes, O'Hara was rather handsome, and charming, and when he spoke to her she always found herself feeling something. Anger, disquiet, a light laughter that crawled into her throat and her heart and stayed there. And yet, nothing could come of these unexpected feelings for O'Hara. She couldn't possibly entertain a relationship of any kind with a man who had the ability to see into her very soul.

"I don't think anyone wants to be alone tonight," O'Hara said sensibly.

Daisy shuddered. Alone. In this haunted hotel. Oh, not even for a moment! In fact, she needed to make a trip to the privy soon. Perhaps Katherine would like to go with her.

Nine

Lucien slept as if nothing were wrong. Eve watched over him. She would think it a peaceful sleep, if she didn't know better. He didn't toss and turn, he didn't mumble in his sleep. There was no tension on his brow or in the way he breathed.

Two candles burned softly, one on the dresser and another on a bedside table. A low fire burned in the fireplace. Hugh had sent Buster on an errand, since Lucien was sleeping so deeply, but he had stayed. He didn't want to leave her alone with Lucien. She didn't *want* to be alone with Lucien! Not until he was himself again.

The man on the bed, wearing only his wrinkled trousers, didn't move at all. There was only the rise and fall of his chest to indicate that he lived. The effects of the past few days showed on his pale face, in the dark stubble on his jaw. He looked thinner, somehow, too. Maybe even older.

Was it Lucien she watched? Deep down, where it mattered, was this the man she loved?

"How do we fix this?" she whispered.

Hugh laid a comforting hand on her shoulder. "We'll find a way."

But what if they didn't find a way? As she watched Lucien sleep her heart beat too hard, and a raging anger began to grow. Why had he come here in the first place? All he'd had to do was stay in town for a couple of days, instead of running off to explore a haunted hotel. He should've stayed in Plummerville. He never should have come to this place alone. If he had stayed in town they would be married now, sleeping together in their own home, making plans for the future. Now they were here, and she didn't know if they had a future or not.

"It's not Lucien's fault," Hugh said in a low voice. Again, he was defending Lucien!

Eve closed her eyes. With his hand on her shoulder, of course Hugh knew exactly how she felt! He was not as talented as O'Hara or Lionel, but he wasn't without gifts of his own.

"Why couldn't I fall in love with an ordinary man?"

"An ordinary man would bore you."

"You make me sound callous."

"No," Hugh said apologetically. "It's just that you're not exactly an ordinary woman."

"I am," she whispered. "I am very, very ordinary."

"I don't think so. Neither does Lucien."

She swallowed hard. "Is this man still Lucien?" He looked like Lucien, spoke with Lucien's voice . . . but inside, where it counted the most, someone or something else was taking hold.

"Let's see." Hugh stepped around her and reached out, moving cautiously so as not to wake Lucien. He had tried to lay his hand on Lucien earlier, but could not get close enough without alarming his subject. Scrydan didn't want Hugh or O'Hara to touch Lucien and perhaps see too much. Before Hugh's hand reached Lucien's bare shoulder, the sleeping man's eyes snapped open.

"Don't touch me, old man," Lucien said in a husky voice. Newly awakened eyes that were much too bright turned to Eve. The lips smiled, the eyes did not. "What's he doing here? And why aren't you in bed?" He scooted over, making room for her beside him.

Eve shook her head slowly. Her greatest fear was coming true, and there was nothing she could do. "You're not Lucien."

"Of course I am, lover." His smile widened into a wide grin. "You know that well." He looked her up and down. "You know me very well," he said suggestively. "Every inch of the body, every desire buried in the heart."

She knew without doubt that this man was not Lucien. He was a monster inside the shell of the man she loved. Lucien would never say anything to embarrass her in front of Hugh or anyone else.

And he called it *the* body, *the* heart. Not *my* body, not *my* heart.

Not only had this creature taken over Lucien's body, he was a very real danger to everyone in this hotel. As soon as he was strong enough, would he kill them all?

Buster came into the room, a length of twisted rope in his hands. Lucien's smile died, as he eyed the rope.

"You wouldn't dare," he said softly.

"I'm sorry, Lucien, it's for the best and you know it," Hugh said calmly.

Lucien jumped out of the bed and grabbed Eve, pulling her back against his bare chest with one arm around her waist and the other at her throat. His body continued to be warm, much warmer than it should have been. His touch almost burned her. "Come one step closer, and I'll kill her." The hand at her throat tightened.

For a moment, Hugh hesitated. Then he took that one step. "I don't think you will. You're not strong enough physically, not yet, and enough of Lucien still lives inside you to protect Eve. He loves her. He will protect her with his very life."

Buster came up on the other side. "Why don't you just lie down on the bed, nice and easy, and let us do what we have to do. I can tie a knot that won't hurt you none, and you can just go on back to sleep until Mr. Felder here decides what to do about this."

"You expect me to lie down and allow you to bind me?" Lucien asked. "No. Not ever." He tried to tighten the grip at Eve's throat. The fingers flexed and then loosened. She felt his frustration in the way he pressed his body to hers, in the way his muscles twitched. His fingers tightened and then, with a jerk, went slack. The arm at her waist held her firmly against his too-warm body.

In a fit of rage Lucien tossed her aside and went after Hugh. He pushed her so vigorously she fell to the floor, getting tangled in her full skirt and petticoat.

"Stop it!" Eve shouted as she scrambled to her feet. He hadn't been able to hurt her, but he seemed to have no qualms about taking Hugh's throat in his hands and squeezing tight. "Lucien!"

Buster dropped the rope and tried to force himself between Hugh and Lucien, hoping to break the hold Lucien had on Hugh's throat. The three of them struggled, and Buster was partially successful. Lucien stopped attacking Hugh just long enough to push Buster to the floor.

Those downstairs in the lobby surely heard the commotion. Eve heard footsteps running up the stairs, excited exclamations and questions. They were going to come in here and see what was happening, and something bad would happen, she knew it. Garrick had a gun, didn't he? He usually did, and he and Buster had gone hunting. What if he had that gun in his hands and he shot Lucien? There would be no saving him, then.

Eve grabbed the candle from the dresser. She moved so quickly the flame was extinguished as she swung it up and around, and hit Lucien on the back of the head with the heavy pewter candle holder.

Lucien went very still, just as O'Hara and Lionel reached the open doorway. He dropped his hands, turned to look at Eve and the candlestick in her hand, and muttered a weak "Why?" as he dropped to the floor.

In that instant, it had been Lucien in control. Lucien wondering why she had hit him on the back of the head. She'd seen the truth in his eyes. He didn't remember threatening her, trying to kill Hugh, pushing Buster aside. Eve watched the misty scene before her through tears. "I didn't kill him, did I?"

"No," Hugh said softly. He turned to O'Hara and Lionel as they rushed into the room. "Let's get Lucien onto the bed and tie him up before he comes to."

"You're sure he's going to be all right?" Eve asked as the four men lifted an unconscious Lucien and laid him on the bed.

"I'm sure," Hugh assured her, though he didn't sound confident. "He'll have a lump on the back of his head, and a nasty headache, but he'll be fine."

Buster worked quickly, taking the sections of rope he had tossed aside when he'd rushed to Hugh's defense and using them to tie Lucien to the bed. Hands first, the left and then the right. A section of rope was knotted at the wrist, then tied tightly to the post at the headboard. Buster left a little slack in the rope, so that Lucien had a small range of motion. Still, his arms were opened wide; he was horribly exposed and vulnerable. The feet were next, ankles to posts at the footboard. Again, Buster left a little slack in the rope, so that Lucien would not be motionless. He should be able to sit or lie flat, but would have little range of motion in either position.

As Buster tied the last knot, Lucien opened his eyes. When he laid those pained eyes on Eve, thick tears dribbled down her cheeks. She expected an angry outburst, an accusation, a faintly whispered "Why?" but Lucien just stared at her.

"What did I do, Evie?" he asked, and she knew it wasn't Scrydan she was talking to, but her own beloved Lucien.

"You tried to kill Hugh," she said softly.

Lucien closed his eyes. "It wasn't me, you have to believe that."

"I know," she whispered.

Hugh glanced down skeptically. After a moment, he laid his hand on Lucien's bare shoulder. He sighed in relief. "There's more Lucien than Scrydan, at the moment. I wish I could untie you . . ."

"No!" Lucien said. "Don't. Not until you find a way to get him out of me. Permanently."

No one liked seeing Lucien bound this way, least of all her. But as Lucien said, until they found a way to safely get Scrydan out, they had no choice. Still,

Eve looked down at him and sniffled. She wanted to cry out loud, to set him free and drag him out of this hotel, but she couldn't. She was horribly powerless. She reached out and touched his hand.

"Evie," he said, looking directly at her and attempting a small smile that didn't quite work. "Would you go downstairs and get me something to drink? I don't care what it is. Water, cider, cold coffee. My throat is dry."

"Of course," Eve dropped her hand and rushed into the hallway, not only anxious to do as Lucien asked, but eager to get out of the room. Just for a few minutes.

She stopped long before she reached the stairway, closing her eyes and swaying on her feet. How incredibly stupid she was! Lucien had gotten rid of her for a reason. Why would he be so eager to get her out of the room? She turned and retraced her steps, slow and soft so no one would hear. She heard Lucien's voice as she neared his room, a low whisper she could not decipher.

"No," Hugh said insistently. "You can't ask me to do that."

"You might have no choice," Lucien said calmly. "No matter what, we can't allow Scrydan to walk out of this hotel. If things continue to spiral downward, you may have to kill me in order to kill him. All I ask is that you make it quick, and that you don't let Eve watch."

Eve's knees went weak, and she leaned against the wall to keep from sinking to the floor.

Daisy shot to her feet when she heard footsteps on the stairs. When the commotion had started above stairs, O'Hara had ordered Garrick to stay with her and Katherine, and then he and Lionel had run up the stairs to see what had happened.

It wasn't O'Hara on the stairs, though, it was Eve. A pale-faced, trembling Eve who held onto the banister as if she might fall without that support.

"What's wrong?" Daisy asked as she rushed to the foot of the stairs to meet Eve.

"They tied him up," she said in a low, croaking voice. "They tied Lucien up there on the bed. I hit him," she said. "I hit him on the head with a candlestick and knocked him out. I had no choice, truly I didn't, but what if he never forgives me?"

Daisy took Eve's arm and led her to the sofa. The poor woman needed to sit before she fell! "You're not making any sense," she said calmly. "Take a deep breath, relax, and tell me what happened."

Eve plopped down on the couch by Katherine, leaving room for Daisy on the other side. The full skirt of her ruined wedding gown twisted and crinkled around her. "He wasn't Lucien when I hit him," she said weakly. "But he was going to kill Hugh! What else could I have done?"

Daisy sat beside Eve and laid a hand on her arm. "I'm sure you only did what you had to do."

"I need to get him something to drink." Eve stood too quickly, swayed, and then plopped down again. "He's thirsty."

"He can wait a few minutes, while you rest."

Garrick stood before the couch and looked down at the three ladies. "Lucien really tried to kill Hugh?"

"It wasn't Lucien!" Eve insisted. "It was that . . . that damned Scrydan." Her fear faded and her face flushed with anger. "What if we can never get him out? What if Lucien is never Lucien again?"

"That won't happen," Daisy said in a serene voice. "And Eve, remember what O'Hara said. This thing feeds on fear. Don't let him draw strength from yours. When this is all over, Lucien will be himself again. Everything will be fine. We'll go back to Plummerville and you two will get married, and everyone will live happily ever after."

Eve took a deep breath. "You're right. I can't be afraid. I can't be angry." She laid her red eyes on Daisy. "I'll try, but it won't be easy." Her lower lip trembled. "It's the worst possible fear," she whispered, "losing Lucien."

Daisy took Eve's hand. "I know."

"I love him so much. I love him so much that he's a part of me. If anything happens . . ."

Katherine and Garrick watched, saying nothing. Did they too believe this excursion would end in disaster? By the expressions on their faces . . . Daisy thought yes.

"Don't think of the worst," Daisy said. "Think of how wonderful the wedding will be, when we get back to Plummerville. If this Scrydan feeds off of fear, maybe happy thoughts and love will make him weak."

"I suppose," Eve said with a sniffle.

"You're the strongest woman I have ever known," Daisy said. "Be strong now." She was trying to be strong herself, but it was not an attribute that came naturally to her. She hid from confrontation. When the going got rough, she ran away. She didn't take chances, she was never courageous. Courage and bravery only led to disaster, for her.

"When we get back to Plummerville, I think we should change the Plummerville Ghost Society to something more ordinary," she suggested. "A garden club, perhaps, or a historical society."

"There's already a garden club and a historical society," Eve answered.

"A pie club, then," Daisy suggested. "After this, I don't think I want to speak of ghosts ever again!"

"A pie club?" Katherine asked, incredulous.

"We do all like pie," Garrick said. "I wouldn't mind being the president of a pie society. Daisy, you'll have to embroider us all new hankies. The Plummerville Pie Society. PPS." He grinned, in an attempt at levity, but it wasn't his usual devil-may-care smile.

They had tried to lighten the mood, but tension still hung in the air. There were no easy answers, not tonight. Daisy was relieved when she heard O'Hara's footsteps on the stairs.

"Come on, Garrick," Katherine said as she came to her feet. "Let's go make some good, strong coffee. I have a feeling it's going to be a long night." She headed for the kitchen, and Garrick followed her.

Eve lifted her chin to look at O'Hara. "Is he okay?"

O'Hara nodded. "He didn't much like me laying my hands on him, but physically, he'll be fine."

"What did you see?"

O'Hara waited. "Not much more than I saw when I touched you. Scrydan's hiding, but he's still there."

"And Lucien?" Eve asked. "Is he still there? Will he ever be the same again?"

"He's there," O'Hara said softly. "And he needs you. I know it's hard, but if you're able you really should be in the room with him."

Eve nodded and stood. The skirt of her wedding gown rustled, and as she ran a hand through her hair a pin came loose and dropped to the sofa, and a thick strand of honey-brown hair fell to her shoulder. With a sigh she removed the last of the pins and tossed them onto an end table, shaking her hair loose.

"I'm going to gather some extra candles," O'Hara said, following Eve to the stairway. "We don't have many left, not enough to get through the night. There must be some around here somewhere."

Daisy leapt to her feet. "Wait! I don't want to stay here all by myself." She tried not to be afraid, but at this point her greatest fear was being alone in this hotel.

"Come with me, then," O'Hara said with a half smile.

This time yesterday, she would have heartily refused to go anywhere with O'Hara. But things had changed, as they so often do. She was safer with O'Hara than without him, and heaven help her, she was actually beginning to like him. A little.

Lucien tried to make himself comfortable on the bed, sitting up with his back to the headboard and his arms and legs spread wide. Lionel, Hugh, and Buster stood silent guard, and no one came close to the bed. They were all naturally uncomfortable, especially since he had ordered them to kill him if it came down to it. Scrydan could not be allowed to leave this place.

Eve came through the door, much too pale and trying to hide the fact that she trembled when she looked at him.

She'd let her hair down. He loved her hair when it was loose, waving over her shoulders and down her back, thick and silky. She usually only let her hair down late at night, when they went to bed. That's when she was his completely. And he might never be able to touch her again.

"Katherine and Garrick are making coffee," she said softly.

"Good," he said, trying his best to sound as if this situation was anything near normal. "I could use a cup."

"I think we all could," Hugh said.

Lucien tried to smile at Eve. "You'll have to hold mine for me," he teased, wiggling his useless fingers.

Eve was not comforted. Her lower lip trembled, and so did her hands. "I don't like this," she whispered. "Can't we let him go?" she looked pleadingly at Hugh. "We'll keep a close eye on him. Scrydan usually comes while he's asleep, right? We can let Lucien go for a while and then tie him up when he falls asleep."

"No," Lucien said. Hugh and Lionel echoed the refusal.

"It's too risky," Hugh added.

Eve nodded her head and walked to the single chair in the room. She sat as if she needed to get off her feet. Perhaps she did.

"I'm sorry," Lucien said. "You know I wouldn't hurt you for the world."

"I know."

"This is for the best, until we find a way to eradicate Scrydan." He didn't tell her that the only way to eradicate Scrydan might be to allow him to take over Lucien completely, and then kill him before he grew too strong.

He didn't tell her that, but he suspected she already knew.

"It's going to be a long night," Hugh said practi-

cally. "I suggest we get prepared. You two," he said,
turning to Lionel and Buster. "Make sure there's
plenty of firewood in the lobby. I think we should
all stay there tonight."

"Are we going to try to move Lucien down the
stairs?" Buster asked.

"I don't know," Hugh said, turning to Lucien
once again. "This is still the quietest room in the
hotel, when it comes to supernatural energy. It
would be best if he stays here until we decide how
to proceed. We'll build up the fire," he added, nod-
ding to the low burning flames in the fireplace.
"Lucien, Eve, and I will stay here."

"You don't seem to have any kind of weapon on
you," Buster said in his soft, kind voice.

"No," Hugh answered. "Of course not."

Buster drew a long, narrow-bladed knife from a
sheath that hung from his belt. "This isn't much, but
if you need to cut the ropes or something," his face
turned beet red. They all knew what that *something*
might be. When Hugh refused to take the knife,
Buster laid it on the dresser. The thud of the heavy
metal on wood reverberated through the room.

That awkward moment past, Lionel and Buster
left the room. Hugh turned to Eve and tried to
smile. They were all trying to comfort her, but
nothing seemed to be working. She was too smart
to be comforted at a time like this.

Lucien heard the front door close, as Lionel and
Buster left the hotel to do as Hugh had asked. They
had gathered and cut wood that afternoon, but
they'd need to bring in plenty to get through the
night.

Doors up and down the second floor hallway
opened and then closed softly, the sounds of

movement coming steadily closer. Chattering voices, one male and one female, drifted into the room. A moment later Daisy and O'Hara passed by, barely peeking in as they walked on. Lucien heard them whispering conspiratorially, and a moment later there were a pair of footsteps on the stairway that led to the third floor.

Lucien's heart skipped a beat. A chill rushed through his too warm body. "Should they go up there?" he asked. "I don't think it's safe."

"I'm sure O'Hara will be cautious," Hugh said.

Deep inside, Lucien knew the third floor wasn't safe. He didn't know how, or why, but something that remained of Scrydan in his conscious mind knew no one should go to the third floor. What was up there? The knowledge was in his head, locked away, waiting like the name of an old acquaintance that sits on the tip of your tongue.

"Stop them," Lucien said in a low voice.

Hugh took one look at Lucien, saw that he was serious, and then turned to run into the hallway. "O'Hara," he called. And then he ran for the stairway that led to the third floor.

Lucien turned his eyes to Eve. "I love you," he said softly. The vow only brought more tears to her eyes. "No matter what happens here, remember that."

"Is he . . . still inside you? Can you tell?"

Lucien nodded. "He's still here, but he's hindered at the moment, somehow, and he's weak. Weaker than he has been. It's as if he's not all here."

"There is a part of him in the house, right?" Eve asked. "Do you think that since you're restrained he's directing his energies elsewhere?"

It was a frightening thought. They still had no idea what Scrydan could do. They didn't really know how powerful he was. "Perhaps," Lucien admitted.

The door to the chamber where he was imprisoned swung violently shut. One by one other doors in the house slammed closed. All along the corridor, above their heads, below, the house shuddered with the din and vibration of doors slamming.

On the heels of that vibration there was the startling sound of something, someone, falling. Tumbling. There was a low, muffled grunt, and then a final thud.

On the third floor, someone screamed.

Eve jumped to her feet and ran to the door, reaching out to tug on the doorknob. The door didn't budge.

"Save your energy," Lucien said. He knew just how Eve felt, as she continued to tug and finally kick at the door. He had tried for a very long time to open the front door to this damned hotel, when it had first imprisoned him here. "Scrydan is holding the door closed."

From the sound of it, Scrydan was holding all the doors in the hotel closed. And someone, probably Hugh, considering the timing and the direction the noise had come from, had taken a nasty spill down the stairs.

"Whatever you do," he said as Eve stopped pounding on the door. "Stay calm."

"Stay *calm?*" Eve stalked to the bed to glare down at him. Her beautiful eyes sparked to life with a green flame. "You're possessed, you left me at the altar for a *second* time, and I'm trapped here. Trapped! By snow and an evil spirit and . . . and by the fact that I love you so much I can't possibly leave you here."

Lucien knew without a doubt that love would either save them or kill them both.

Ten

The swinging of the door had snuffed out the candle O'Hara had been carrying, and left the room they'd just entered completely dark. All Daisy could see was the outline of the uncovered window. Hysteria bubbled up in her throat and she let it loose. Again.

"Stop screaming," O'Hara said in a low voice as he tugged at the closed door.

"I don't think I can," she admitted.

Her eyes quickly adjusted to the darkness. She still couldn't see much, but the little bit of moonlight that broke through the window allowed her to make out O'Hara's outline as he continued to pull on the door.

"It's him, isn't it?" Daisy whispered. "It's Scrydan, holding the door closed."

"Yes," O'Hara answered. "And I think I heard someone fall down the stairs. It was difficult to tell, with all the screaming going on."

Daisy lifted her chin bravely. "There's no need to be testy."

He quit fighting the door and turned to her. She saw his form, but not his face. "There is every need to be testy," he said softly. "We should have settled for the few candles we have left and firelight, to pass the night. That would have been sufficient."

"I know, but the lobby is so dark, without those extra candles . . ." She'd much rather be in the dark lobby than here. Hadn't Lionel warned everyone to avoid the third floor? And yet here she was, imprisoned in a small hotel room with no one to protect her but O'Hara.

Someone . . . something . . . in the corner of the room giggled. Daisy held her breath. The soft giggle came again, and Daisy was frozen to the spot.

O'Hara walked past Daisy, toward the corner. "Stay here," he whispered as he walked past.

It was an unnecessary instruction. Where did he think she was going to go?

No moonlight shone in the corners of the room, but O'Hara walked forward without hesitation. When he was close enough, he laid his hand on the wall. The soft, indistinct giggle turned into words so low Daisy had no hope of deciphering them. But they were words. They were words that crept under her skin and grabbed hold of her bones and shimmied.

"Moreen," O'Hara said in a low voice. "You are Moreen, are you not?"

The answer was a hissing sound. A yes, perhaps?

"Moreen," O'Hara continued, "you're dead. You don't belong here anymore."

More sharp twittering followed, and even though Daisy couldn't tell what Moreen said, she suspected it was not pleasant.

"You're not going to kill anyone," O'Hara said calmly. "You can't. You have no body with which to harm us. All you can do is scare a sweet lady who has done you no harm." He turned his head to look toward Daisy. She couldn't tell, in the dark, if he was smiling or not. "Don't let her scare you," he added in a lower voice. "Don't let anything that happens here scare you. It's what he wants."

Scrydan. He was trying to use the souls he'd trapped here to frighten them all, to produce a tangible fear he could feed on. And when he was stronger, he would take over Lucien completely.

"I understand," she said softly. "I really do. But how am I supposed to remain unafraid when I'm trapped in a room with a ghost?"

O'Hara walked slowly toward her. "Not worried about being trapped in here with me?"

Her heart skipped a beat. "Of course not. You're a perfect gentleman."

He laughed lightly. "Actually, I'm not a gentleman at all." He stopped when he stood just a few feet away. "And I'm definitely not perfect. But you're right. You don't have to worry about being trapped with me."

"I thought not." Oddly enough, that was the truth.

A tremble worked its way through Daisy's body when the ghost in the corner, Moreen, made another of those annoying hissing noises.

"If we're not afraid," O'Hara said calmly, "if we don't let her scare us, she'll go, sooner or later."

For the life of her, Daisy could not think of a way to wash away her fear. Logically she knew O'Hara was right, but her heart was pounding much too fast and she couldn't take a deep breath. "But if she leaves," Daisy whispered, "will another one take her place?"

"I don't know. Perhaps."

A muffled voice drifted into the room. At first O'Hara turned his head toward the door, but when the muted shout came again he rushed to the window and threw it open. A cold wind rushed in, pushing back the lightweight curtains and the tail end of O'Hara's jacket. Daisy ran to stand beside him and look down. Lionel and Buster stood there, looking up at all the windows as they continued to walk along the perimeter of the hotel.

O'Hara leaned partially out of the window. "Up here!"

Lionel put his hands on his hips. "What are you doing on the third floor?"

"We came up here looking for candles," O'Hara shouted down.

"We?" Lionel repeated.

Daisy leaned forward so the men below could see her. "Hello," she said timidly.

"Daisy!" Buster yelled. "Are you all right?"

Of course she wasn't all right! How could he ask such a thing? "I'm fine," she said, hoping to soothe Buster's fears on her behalf. There was no need to tell him that there was a ghost in this room.

"So far we can't get any of the doors or the ground floor windows to open," Lionel bellowed.

"We can't get the door to this room open, either," O'Hara explained loudly. "I suspect every door in the house is tightly closed."

"Why don't we just break a window?" Buster suggested sensibly. "We could get inside that way, and maybe once we're . . ."

"No," Lionel said sharply. "I believe breaking a window would be an incredibly unwise course of action."

O'Hara just nodded. "Do you think you could find your way to Elijah's house? You two can't stay out in this cold indefinitely."

"I saw the direction he took this morning," Lionel said. "Once I get close enough I'll be able to find him. Still, I hate to leave you all here."

"Go," O'Hara said. "There's no telling how long it will be before the doors open."

That matter-of-fact statement did nothing to calm Daisy's nerves.

Buster spoke up. "We can get the horses, go to town, and bring back some help."

Lionel nodded, not happy to be leaving but accepting that it was, perhaps, the best way.

As they walked around the corner of the hotel, O'Hara closed the window with a resounding thud.

Eve tugged at the doorknob, even though she knew full well that it wasn't going to open.

She finally turned to face the bed and her bound fiancé. Lucien sat with his back against the headboard. His head dipped down, and long strands of dark hair fell over his pale cheeks to conceal much of his face. It had been three days since he'd shaved, and the uncontrolled channeling of so many spirits—and the powerful possession by Scrydan—had drained him. His bare chest rose and fell with deep, even breaths, but to her eyes he looked barely alive.

Her heart broke a little. No matter what had happened, she hated to see him tied up this way, his hands and feet bound so that he was spread-eagle on the bed.

He slowly lifted his head and looked at her. "Let me go," he whispered.

She wanted to do just that. Lucien shouldn't be tied up this way. It wasn't right. But she couldn't. She shook her head.

"If you love me, Eve, you'll release me." His voice was low and smooth, and it cut her to the quick.

This wasn't Lucien. "I can't. You know that."

"After everything we've shared," he whispered. "How could you let them do this to me? I'm cold, Eve. I'm hungry. I want to wrap my arms around you and kiss that sweet mouth of yours until you beg me to take you. Come to me. Untie me and feed me and make me warm again."

She shook her head. "Open the doors."

He smiled. The thing on the bed had Lucien's face, Lucien's voice, Lucien's body. But that was not Lucien's smile. "Let's make a deal, lover. You let me go, and I'll unlock the doors."

"That's not much of a deal, is it?" she asked. "You'll kill us all if you get the chance."

"Not you," he said in a low, rough voice. "Lucien won't let me kill you." His brow furrowed, as if he could not comprehend the concept.

"What about the others?"

He shrugged, the motion subdued thanks to his position on the bed. "What do they matter? They're nothing. They're annoying insects who mean so very little. The two of us, we can walk out of here and start a new life somewhere else. Anywhere else." He smiled at her. "When I get out of here, you'll be amazed at the things I can do for you. I have magic inside me. Power. Nothing can stop me. I can give you everything you've ever wanted."

"I want Lucien," she whispered.

"Almost anything," he said with a wry smile. "Do you wish to be famous? Rich? Beautiful?"

Eve turned her back on him. She couldn't bear to see that evil spirit talking out of Lucien's mouth! "I won't let you go," she said.

"Yes, you will," Scrydan said to her back. "Eventually. I can wait. The others, they're going to make me stronger. By morning I'll be able to free myself. I'm not so sure the man in the hallway can wait until morning," he said casually. "I suspect he'll be dead long before then."

"Hugh," Eve whispered.

"Release me," Scrydan said again. "And I'll let them all live. You and I can walk out of here together, and I'll allow these simpletons you call friends to live. We're talking about a difference of a few hours, no more. I'm already getting stronger. Soon I won't need you at all. The girl above," he said, briefly turning his eyes to the ceiling, "she's going to be particularly tasty. She's been filled with fear for a very long time. She began to feed me the minute she walked through the door."

"Daisy?" Eve turned to look at the monster on the bed. "You leave Daisy alone, do you hear me?"

"If you insist, lover. She can be safe. She can remain untouched. It's up to you, of course. All you have to do is untie these ropes that bind me."

Eve shook her head.

Scrydan glared at her. "You've been possessed before," he whispered. "I see it in you."

"Twice," she said. "Very briefly."

"I can enter your body in more than one way. Not as easily as I can take this one, and I can't stay within you as long, but I can certainly control you long enough to make you untie these ropes." He tugged violently, and the headboard shook and creaked.

"If that's possible, why haven't you done it already?" Eve asked, taking a single step toward the bed, her mind spinning. "Spread a little bit too thin, perhaps? This is a quiet room. You're not as strong here as you are in other parts of the house. It must be a real struggle to keep all the doors closed and control the spirits and hold onto Lucien at the same time. You're afraid to completely let go of Lucien, because you know when you do he'll be in control and you won't find your way back. Once he regains complete control, he can block you."

Eve could tell by the expression on his face that he was perturbed by her observations. She must be at least partially right.

"You think I'm weak here in this room?" he whispered. The fire in the fireplace roared to life, and a cold wind came out of nowhere to whip around Eve, making her full white skirt billow and dance.

"Parlor tricks," she said.

Lionel said Scrydan had slipped into sleeping, unaware bodies, during his years in this hotel. He'd entered through dreams, taken control, and under his direction perfectly ordinary people had turned into murderers. Some had committed suicide. But his possession of these people had been draining for him, and short-lived. How long had he been able to stay inside? Minutes, perhaps? Not long, and not easily.

He'd slipped into Lucien more easily, since Lucien's gift was accepting the messages and spirits of those who had passed on. It was Lucien's gift that made this possession possible, not Scrydan's power.

As long as she stayed alert and awake, she didn't think he could use her body to untie Lucien, as he'd threatened. Besides, he really didn't want to let go of this receptive body he had found. If he did, what was left of Lucien might be able to block him from returning, and he didn't want to risk that possibility.

Unless he grew stronger and was somehow able to control them both. That wouldn't happen unless the others in the house were so filled with fear that they did, indeed, feed him well.

"You might as well let Lucien go, Scrydan," she said. "You can't win, not this time."

"Lover," he answered. "I always win."

Katherine tugged on the door between the kitchen and the dining room, while Garrick banged on the door that opened onto the back porch. By the light of one measly candle, they both struggled in vain.

There was one small window in the kitchen. It was certainly not large enough to fit Garrick, but she could probably squeeze through.

That wasn't an option. Not only was that window stuck, she didn't relish the idea of being alone outside the house. In the cold.

Frustrated, Katherine turned around—opening her mouth to tell Garrick that they were wasting their time—and there before her stood Jerome.

She couldn't make a sound. Her entire body was numb. The ghost before her was misty, a vaporous vision of her dead husband, and Jerome smiled the way he always had right before he'd beat her.

"Go away," she finally whispered. "You're dead."

Garrick spun around. For a moment she thought he'd think her crazy. But he saw Jerome, too.

"You still mourn me," Jerome said, reaching out a ghostly hand to almost touch her black gown.

"I still despise you." Her heart beat too fast, and her voice trembled.

Jerome's misty hand went through her, and she

felt his ghostly caress. His touch was like ice. "You didn't always despise me."

Garrick circled around the nasty shade to stand beside her. Instinctively she reached out and took his arm. She held tightly onto the warm, substantial man, so she wouldn't fall to the floor.

"He's here," she whispered. "I can't believe he's here."

"You've seen him before, right?" Garrick asked in a low voice.

"Not like this," Katherine admitted. "I've sensed him, several times. I've turned quickly on occasion and caught a glimpse of . . . something. But I've never actually seen his ghost."

Jerome grinned. Oh, she hated that grin! "You see me now, don't you, sugar? I'm home, and I'm not ever leaving you again. You're mine, forever. Now, lie down on the floor and spread your legs for me."

"You're not real," she whispered. "Go away!"

"Never," Jerome whispered. "I will always be with you. You will never be rid of me. I will haunt you till the day you die, and when you join me we'll be together for eternity."

Garrick jerked away from her, ran to the stove, and grabbed a cast iron skillet. He rushed up behind Jerome and swung the skillet at his head. The weapon swept right through Jerome's image.

"Go away, you son of a bitch," Garrick shouted. "Leave her alone."

Jerome turned, faced Garrick, and swung out an insubstantial arm. The unexpected force of the blow knocked Garrick to the floor.

"What do you want from me?" Katherine screamed. "Why can't you just go and leave me in peace?"

Jerome dismissed Garrick, who rose slowly to his feet, and turned to Katherine. "You don't want to be left in peace," he answered calmly. "I still live in here . . ." he reached out, and his hand went through her body. "In the heart."

"No," she protested. "I don't love you. You managed to kill any affection I might have once had for you. You might as well have killed me," she whispered. "Because you made my life a living hell."

"I can, you know." He moved so close she lost her breath. "I can kill you any time I want."

Garrick grabbed the skillet he had dropped. He didn't head for Jerome this time, but for the small window. He reared back as if to strike. Before he could smash the glass, Lionel's face appeared in the window.

"No!" Lionel shouted. "Don't break the window!"

Garrick paused in mid-swing. "Katherine needs to get out of here."

"You'll never fit through that window," Katherine argued.

He turned to her. "No, but you will."

"You can't break the window!" Lionel said again. "Stay here. Buster and I are going to try to find Elijah's house."

"Take Katherine with you," Garrick insisted.

Lionel tried to open the window from the outside, but had no more luck than Garrick had had. "Sorry," he finally said. "We haven't been able to open any of the first floor windows. Just wait here."

"But her . . . her damned husband is here."

"Ignore him, if you can," Lionel instructed. "Remember that he wants your fear."

Katherine covered her face with her hands.

"Ignore him," she said against the palms of her hands. "How can I do that?"

Garrick dropped the skillet and Lionel moved on. He and Buster were heading to Elijah's house. In the dark and the cold. And they didn't know the way, not really. Elijah would've left a trail in the snow, but would they be able to see it in the dark? What if they never came back?

"Look at me, Kat," Jerome said. "Look at me!"

"No," Garrick said, as he came to her again and took her arm. "You're going to look at me, not him, and we're going to talk about something else."

"What? What on earth could we talk about that would make me forget that the ghost of my dead husband is watching?"

A small table filled one corner of the kitchen. There was one chair. Garrick made her sit in it, facing the table and the wall. Then he sat on the edge of the table and looked down at her.

Jerome sat beside him.

Katherine kept her eyes on Garrick. He smiled wanly. "Did you know that my mother is not really my mother?" he asked. "Before Lucien announced it, did you know?"

"Oh, Garrick." She laid a hand on his knee. "Of course I didn't know." Suddenly the hand seemed much too personal, much too intimate. She withdrew that hand and placed it in her lap. "You don't seem too terribly surprised."

"Kat," Jerome whispered. "Look at me. We aren't finished. We will never be finished."

Garrick tilted his head to one side. "It explains a lot, actually. I have always suspected that Mother hated me, just as Lucien said. She never said anything to make me think that, but there were times when I just knew. She always blamed me for her poor health, said her pregnancy was terribly difficult."

Jerome whispered. "Your mother was a whore."

Neither of them acknowledged the ghost.

"What are you going to do?" Katherine asked. "Are you going to let her and your father know that you've discovered the truth?"

"I don't know." Garrick smiled down at her. He did have such a nice smile, even if it was understandably strained. "I might just decide to pack up and leave Plummerville altogether."

"Where would you go?" For many years she had not particularly liked Garrick. He was rich, for one thing. That wasn't his fault, but she had worked so hard for every little thing in her life, while he'd had everything he needed or wanted given to him. He took nothing seriously, it seemed. Life was a lark. Nothing about that life was difficult. It simply didn't seem fair.

But lately they had become friends, thanks to the Plummerville Ghost Society. It was amazing to her that she could have a male friend. Jerome had made her hate them all, at one time. Men were all the same. They were mean, abusive bastards who always had to show a woman that she was weak, and that he was the one who commanded her.

"West," he said. "I would like to find a town where I'm more than a rich man's son. Where I can do something on my own. In Plummerville, nothing I have is my own, not really. Father's mill, Father's house, Father's money." He paused and took a deep breath. "I think it would be nice to have something of my own. I guess that sounds selfish."

"Not at all."

"It's just that as long as I stay in Plummerville, no

matter what I do I will always be Douglas Hunt's son, and everyone I know thinks I've had every good thing in my life handed to me on a silver platter."

She felt a warm blush rise to her cheeks. She had thought just that. "It sounds like you've been thinking about this for some time."

"The thought of leaving comes and goes," he confessed. "Mostly, it goes. Leaving and starting over would be difficult."

"Kat," Jerome said angrily. "You're mine. You will always be mine. Isn't that why you still wear black, so everyone will know that you're mine and always will be?"

She wore black to remind her of the hell she'd lived through with Jerome. To remind herself, every day, that he was really and truly dead.

"Where out west?" she asked, ignoring Jerome.

Garrick shrugged his shoulders. "I don't know." He winked at her. "Why don't you pick a place and you can come with me."

Katherine shook her head. "No. I'll never leave Plummerville."

"Why not?"

"I hold her there," Jerome's ghost whispered. "I gave her a house that has become her prison. She's branded as mine, and she knows better than to think she can ever have a life somewhere else."

Her life was her prison. Jerome was the jailer. She couldn't ignore him any longer. "I hate you," she whispered. "I hate you so . . ." Garrick grabbed Katherine's hand, pulled her to her feet, and wrapped an arm around her waist before he kissed her.

He kissed her. Soft and tender even though he held her so tight she couldn't move away. Inside her, something hard and icy melted. She grew warm. Her body tingled. It had been so long since she had been kissed . . . and she had never been kissed like this. Her own mouth began to move against his. She felt this kiss down deep. It moved her. It made her want more.

She jerked her head away and raised her hand to slap Garrick soundly across the face. "How dare you?"

His answer was to kiss her again. She returned the kiss, for a moment, and then she jerked away. Garrick imprisoned her wrists in his hands so she couldn't slap him again.

"I've wanted to do that for years," he confessed.

Katherine was stunned. "You have? Why?"

He smiled at her. "Why? You're the most beautiful woman in the county, for starters. You're sassy and fierce, which did give me cause for alarm at one time, but I'm beginning to like that about you. And did I mention that you're beautiful?"

"I'm not beautiful," she whispered. "Not at all."

Garrick shook his head. "How can you say that? Everything about you is beautiful."

"Just a few months ago you said I scared you."

"You do," he whispered. "You definitely scare me. You make me want things I shouldn't want, dream dreams I shouldn't dream."

Chills ran up and down her arms. She did like Garrick, more every day. But she could never take another man into her life. "I'm sure when you head out west you will find many other beautiful women along the way. You'll meet someone else who makes you . . . dream."

"Maybe I won't go west. Not for a while, anyway."

Was Garrick saying that he'd stay in Plummerville?

For her? Katherine leaned forward to kiss him once again, but she stopped before her mouth met his. Who was she kidding? "I think you should go."

"I'm not going anywhere for a while," he teased. "It looks like we're stuck here."

"I mean you should go west," she snapped. "I think you should get out of Plummerville once and for all."

"You do?" he asked with raised eyebrows. "How can I court you if you're in Plummerville and I'm thousands of miles away?"

Courting? The very idea gave her cold chills. "You can't court me. We're not . . . well suited."

"How can you say that when we've just begun?"

Her heart skipped a beat. "We haven't begun anything!"

"Yes, we have."

He kissed her again, laying his slightly parted lips over hers. A part of her wanted to fight this feeling that washed over her, but another part, the part of her that had once hoped for a better life, accepted and cherished the sensations and the hope.

But it wasn't real and it wouldn't last. "I don't want a man in my life," she insisted.

"Since we might never set foot outside this damned hotel, I don't think we need to talk about forever just yet," Garrick said. He grabbed her tight and pulled her close. He sat on the table, she stood before him. "We'll take it slow. Maybe try another kiss."

"Garrick . . ." He cut off her argument with his mouth over hers. She didn't fight it. She did want the kiss. No one had ever kissed her this way, and no one ever would again. For now, she would just enjoy this closeness and store the memory of this kiss and the way he held her to draw on in darker times.

He was right; they might not survive the night. She didn't want to spend her last night afraid, the way she'd been afraid all her adult life. She wanted, for once in her life, to feel truly good. To hold onto a human being who wanted to hold onto her. To kiss, and touch, and talk about packing up everything and going west. So she gave herself wholly to the kiss, and she held onto Garrick with all her might.

Deep inside, a spark of hope came to life. How strange, to have found that hope again when matters were so dire. She made herself forget the dire situation and concentrated on Garrick's lips. On the arms that held her. On the luscious way he smelled and felt and tasted.

A few minutes later, she realized that Jerome was gone.

Eleven

Daisy stood in the center of the room, hands clasped tightly before her. Lionel and O'Hara both said Scrydan was in the hotel itself, in the walls and the furnishings and even the floor. She wiggled her toes nervously. She couldn't do much about her feet, but she didn't have to touch anything else!

O'Hara was apparently not worried about such things. At the moment he sat on the bed, on the edge of a bare mattress. Until just a few moments ago he had paced, quick, even steps, the heels of his shoes clipping against the floor. He had even stopped pacing to place the palms of his hands on the wall once . . . but he hadn't held them there for long. He'd pulled those talented hands away from the walls as if touching them had burned him.

"So," she said conversationally as O'Hara left the bed, shooting to his feet once again. The man was never still for long. "What is your given name?"

"What?"

"I need a way to pass the time," she explained.

In the corner, their ghost laughed. Moreen was not alone. The ghosts Daisy could not see clearly kept coming. They had begun their entrapment with only Moreen to haunt them, and now there were at least three other ghosts here. They laughed, moved about, sent cold drafts circulating through the room. As the minutes ticked silently past, their number grew.

O'Hara saw the apparitions, too. Given his experience, perhaps he saw them more clearly than she did. His eyes went from one to the other as he walked toward Daisy.

She could see the ghosts quite well, much better than she wanted to, even though they remained less than substantial. They walked through walls, appearing and disappearing in that remarkable way. The haunting spirits were primarily women, she noticed, but there were also soldiers and men dressed in fine suits. Thankfully, they did not venture toward the center of the room, where she and O'Hara stood. The ghosts lurked in the shadowy corners and against the walls, hiding so that when she tried very hard Daisy could almost convince herself that they were figments of her imagination.

O'Hara moved closer to her, in an almost protective manner.

Daisy pursed her lips. She couldn't think about what she saw around her. She couldn't stand here and wonder who these ghosts were, what they wanted, what they would do before the night was over. It was all too shocking, too unreal.

So she thought about the man before her. O'Hara was such a cretin! Her request concerning his name was small, her curiosity larger than the situation called for, perhaps. Since she might not live until morning, she didn't think it was too much to ask! Oh, why was she so curious about O'Hara's given name?

"Obviously you don't want to discuss your name," she said.

He continued to study the ghosts that remained in the corners and against the faded walls. "Not now, Daisy," he hissed.

"I'm supposed to stay calm!" she explained. "I'm supposed to look at these things around us and not be afraid! How can I do that? Can't we at least try to . . . to ignore what's happening here and carry on a normal conversation?"

"You're right," he said softly. "We should do just that."

"If you refuse to tell me your name, perhaps you can explain to me how putting your hand under Eve's skirt could possibly be an *accident*." Ha! Surely he would prefer to discuss his name than to try to justify something so crude and unforgivable.

O'Hara sighed. It was actually more of a groan. He took another step toward her. Oh, he was almost too close. "It had been more than a year since Lucien . . . forgot to show up for their wedding. More than a year, and she was still so sad."

"So you decided to cheer her up by . . ."

"May I finish before you rake me over the coals?" Daisy pursed her lips. "Of course."

"Thank you." O'Hara reached out a hand as if to touch her, but he let that hand drop before it came too close. "Eve was so unhappy. She did her job and she did it well, but the sparkle was gone. She was hiding inside herself, trying to pretend that it didn't matter that the man she loved had forgotten her."

"I still don't see how being crude and improper . . ."

"You will," he interrupted sharply. "Just be patient."

She could be patient. Daisy threaded her fingers

together and moved up onto her tiptoes. She kept her eyes on O'Hara's face, as she tried to ignore the spirits and the sparks of unnatural light in the room.

"So," he continued. "There she was, standing by the second story railing, looking over her notes, scribbling something in the margins. In my defense, it's true I had had a little bit too much wine with supper and was feeling a tad lightheaded."

"You were drunk," she clarified.

"I suppose," he admitted. "But that didn't make Eve any less melancholy. I wanted to bring that spark I remembered back into her eyes. I wanted to make her care about . . . something. Anything. So I walked up behind her, pretended to stumble, and slipped my hand up her leg."

"That's so incredibly ill-mannered," Daisy said.

"But it worked." She could hear the smile in O'Hara's voice. "Eve was furious. She hit me with her notes and kicked me in the shin."

"Good for her." Daisy looked O'Hara square in the face. Yes, Eve had gumption, something she herself did not possess. Every confrontation was a major event for Daisy Willard. She was mollified to know that Eve had given O'Hara what he deserved.

"It would kill her to lose Lucien again," he said in a more serious tone of voice, making Daisy immediately regret her momentary pleasure at the thought of his pain.

The ghosts, and there were more than a half dozen of them now, left the corners. Bits of shadow and soft light as well as almost substantial forms, they moved toward the center of the room where Daisy stood with O'Hara.

"They're coming," she said, taking a step closer to O'Hara.

"They can't hurt you," he said calmly. "Remember that."

"I'm afraid," she whispered.

The ghosts did not descend upon them. They stopped several feet away, in a circle surrounding the couple, and played out their horrid deaths in silent reenactment. A man in a nice suit drove a knife into a half-dressed woman's chest. One soldier turned on another and wrapped his hands around his comrade's throat. One female ghost sneaked up behind another and slit her throat, and a man drew a gun from his waistband and started to shoot. The entire spectacle was silent and bloody, and Daisy shivered as she watched each scene unfold.

O'Hara reached out, grabbed her, and pulled her against his chest. "Don't look," he said.

She gratefully buried her face against his shoulder. Had she once thought him too short? He was just right, for her. Her face fit into his shoulder perfectly, and here she didn't have to see the spirits that haunted this hotel. And it was nice, to be held. It was nice, not to be alone at this terrifying moment. She only hoped he was right and the ghosts couldn't hurt her. Or him.

Daisy grasped O'Hara's jacket with both hands, hanging on tight. Even though she tried to stay calm, it was impossible. She began to tremble. Even with her head buried against O'Hara's brown jacket, she saw the bits of light that twirled around them, a ghostly arm, a hand clutching a bloody knife. Heavens, she could hardly breathe!

"Shut your eyes," O'Hara said, gathering her even closer than before. "They're trying to scare you. They can't hurt you."

She closed her eyes tight, she clenched her fists

and pressed her face against O'Hara's shoulder. Somehow she could still see the ghosts, as if they danced behind her closed lids. It was a trick of the mind.

O'Hara ran his hand up and down her back. "Remember that they want you to be scared. Your fear makes Scrydan stronger. Think of something besides ghosts and haunted hotels. Think of something beautiful."

"I can't think of anything beautiful, at the moment," she confessed.

O'Hara held her tight. He was scared, too, she suspected. He just didn't want her, or the residents of the hotel, to know.

"Quigley," he said in a low voice.

"What?"

"My damned given name," he said without heat. "Quigley Tibbot O'Hara."

In spite of everything, she smiled against his shoulder. "Really? Quigley?"

"If you tell anyone I will deny it," he insisted. "I have gone to great lengths to keep those outside my immediate family from discovering the horror."

"Horror is a bit . . . strong." She laughed softly. "Well, maybe not."

He started to laugh with her, and Daisy opened her eyes. The ghosts that had encircled and tormented them were fading. She laughed a little harder. "Quigley Tibbot? That must've been a family name."

"My great-great grandfather," O'Hara said.

"I hope he was very rich and left you a fortune, since you were his namesake."

"Alas, he was a farmer who died up to his neck in debt."

The noise and bright lights of the ghosts faded. Daisy caught a glimpse of a woman's ghostly face. It was more sad than horrific. More hauntingly tragic than frightening. One by one the images and the lights faded until the ghosts were completely, magically gone. Daisy lifted her head to look up at O'Hara. Yes, he would always be simply O'Hara to her. Quigley certainly didn't suit him!

His face was so near. She wondered if he would kiss her. His hands raked up and down her back, slow and firm and comforting beyond belief. She could release her hold on his jacket, but she did not. She hung on tight.

Yes, he was going to kiss her. His face dipped toward hers, his head slanted to one side. He stopped while his mouth was still inches from hers. Then he retreated a little bit.

"Viking?"

How long would it take Lionel and Buster to get help? And what kind of help could they bring to this terrible place? At the very least, it would be morning before help arrived. Eve suspected hoping for help by morning was a true grasp at optimism.

Lucien's eyes followed her as she paced. Lionel and O'Hara said her love would save him. But how? The man she loved was in there, still hanging on and fighting Scrydan for his heart and his soul.

"You won't win," Eve said as she stopped by the side of the bed. The room was dimly illuminated with the light of the fire and moonlight through the uncovered window. Pale light danced over Lucien's face, his bare chest, his spread legs. The firelight made the glimmer in his eyes seem to burn.

"I'm already winning," Scrydan said smugly. His fingers swayed, as if they caressed the air.

"You don't look like you're winning anything," she snapped, annoyed and frightened by his lack of concern at his present situation. "You're tied to the bed, helpless as a kitten, and you're not going anywhere until I get Lucien back."

"He told the others to kill me, if it came to it."

Her heart hitched. "I know."

"Lucky for me, there's not a single person in this house who's capable of killing me while I'm in this body." He smiled. "Not one," he added softly. "They look at this face and they see Lucien Thorpe, not me. That's why I'll beat you all."

He glanced up at the ceiling and frowned.

"What's wrong, Scrydan? Things not going as planned?"

"Not yet," he said. "Soon enough." And still he stared at the ceiling.

"I want to talk to Lucien," Eve said.

Scrydan stared at her. "No. He's almost gone, you know. Fading, fading . . ."

Eve sat on the side of the bed and reached out to touch his face. She loved that face, so much. She loved Lucien more than she had ever imagined possible. It wasn't possible that she could lose him this way, when they were so close to happiness. True, their life would never be normal. But shouldn't they have more time? Maybe they didn't have forever. Maybe no one did. But they deserved better than this.

Lucien . . . Scrydan . . . tugged at the ropes that held him tightly bound. Eve stared down at that heavy, knotted twine. The knots looked sturdy enough, but if Scrydan was right he'd eventually be able to break them on his own.

But he wasn't strong enough yet.

She caressed the roughness of his beard, raked the back of her hand over his throat. "Lucien," she whispered. "I need to talk to you."

"Stop it," he whispered.

"Fight him, for me."

Scrydan was no longer calmly confident. "It's too late . . ."

"Fight him, Lucien. I love you, so much."

Scrydan tugged at the ropes again, leaning as far toward her as possible. "You think love will help him now? Don't be ridiculous."

"Then why do you suddenly look so scared?"

She rested her hand over his heart. It was cold in this room in spite of the fire, Lucien wore nothing but his trousers, and still his skin was hot. And his heart raced, his heartbeat was faint and much too fast.

"I'm not scared of you." He leered at her. "I know what you want. You want this body. Go ahead, lover, use it. I can't stop you. Have you always dreamed of taking Lucien this way? I think you have. I think you like the idea of having that power over your lover. Have you always wanted him bound and helpless? Perhaps you would prefer to be the one who's bound. Love me, as you desire."

"You have no idea what love is."

"Move your hand a little lower and I'll show you."

She ignored his crudeness, the way he leered, the way he rocked his hips. With a gentle, hard-won smile on her face she moved her mouth closer to his. "I love you, Lucien. I need you."

He moved his head forward and snapped his teeth at her.

Eve lowered her head and kissed the bare skin over his heart. He was too tightly bound to stop her. "Come back," she whispered as she kissed again.

"Why would you want him to come back?" Lucien asked. Lucien, and not Lucien. She had to remember that. "He's a weak man, an imperfect man, and he forgot you so many times. So many. You don't know how many times he forgot you. I do, though. I know everything. I'm stronger than he is. I'm more powerful. I can give you everything."

"Then give me Lucien." She lifted her head from his hot chest and looked him in the eye. "Give me Lucien." This time when he snapped at her she didn't back away. The man she loved was still in there, and he wouldn't allow Scrydan to harm her. She tilted forward and laid her mouth over his, kissed him soft and sweet. After a moment's stillness, he kissed her back. His mouth moved against hers, and she tasted tenderness, fear, and Lucien's passion.

Tears ran down her cheeks, slipped between their lips, and still they kissed. "I love you," she whispered between quick, tear-damp kisses. "I love you."

"Evie?" Lucien whispered.

She rested her hands on his neck and kissed him deep. "Yes," she said softly as she drew her lips away, filled with relief. For a moment she had thought she'd never speak to Lucien again. "I'm here, and I'm not going anywhere. I'm here, Lucien. Stay with me."

"I don't think I can."

She shook off her own doubts. "You will. You must. Scrydan is holding all the doors closed. Lionel and Buster were outside when it happened, and they've gone for help. Last I heard, Katherine and Garrick were going to the kitchen to make coffee. I guess they're still there." She licked her lips. "O'Hara and Daisy are on the third floor, and . . . and Lucien, I think Hugh is hurt pretty badly. He fell down the stairs and I haven't heard anything from him since."

"I don't care about them," he whispered. "There's no one in this room but the two of us. I've missed you, so much. I want to hold you. Untie me, Evie. Release me so I can wrap my arms around you."

Instinctively she reached for the ropes at his right wrist. Her fingers touched the knot there . . . and then she stopped to look Lucien in the eye.

And he leered at her.

"The *Evie* gets to you every time, doesn't it?" Scrydan asked. "So sweet. So adorable. And it almost worked. You were seconds away from untying me when you came to your senses. Kiss me again, woman, and I'll make you forget again."

Eve backed off the bed, holding her breath as she made her escape. He'd fooled her again, at a time when she should have known better. He'd whispered and kissed her and made her think he was her Lucien. She'd been so certain it was her Lucien she kissed and spoke to.

Like it or not, she had to face her greatest fear. What if Scrydan was right and Lucien was gone forever?

* * *

Scrydan watched the woman pace. So close. So damned close! He'd almost convinced her to untie him.

It was disturbing that Lucien had been able to work his way to the surface once again, even if his control had only lasted for a minute or two. He should be too weak for such an effort. He should be dead! But he had awakened and fought his way to the surface. All for a kiss.

What a fool.

"Your friend in the hallway is dead," he said. "His soul is now trapped here, like so many others." He smiled at the woman's obvious pain. "The others will follow, soon enough." He glanced up. Things were not going as he'd intended, but he didn't have to let the woman know that. "Upstairs, in a room where many have died, this O'Hara you dislike so much is going to eventually wrap his hands around the throat of that pretty little girl and choke the life out of her. Goodness only knows what he'll do to her first. Anything is possible. He's such an angry young man, and he does find your friend attractive. I doubt her death will be a quick one."

When Eve flinched and turned her face away so he could not see her pain, he smiled widely. If he did this right, he wouldn't need the others at all. This woman would feed him, and then she would either release him from these annoying bonds or he'd become strong enough to free himself. "When he realizes what he's done," he added in a whisper, "he'll toss himself out of the window and break his neck."

"Shut up," she whispered hoarsely.

No, he didn't need the fear of the others. Lucien's Evie would feed him well enough.

"Downstairs in the kitchen, the lovely widow is having a nice chat with her dead husband." He leaned forward, stretching the limits of the ropes that confined him. "In just a little while she's going to mistake your drunken friend Garrick for the ghost that torments her, and she's going to slit his throat. When that's done, she'll slit her own wrists with the same kitchen knife, and they'll die together in a puddle of mingled blood."

"Do I have to gag you?" Eve snapped.

"I don't think you will. You're foolish enough to think that Lucien might come back. You think he might fight his way back to tell you that he loves you, one last time, and you certainly don't want to miss that particular moment." He grinned at her stupidity and her hope. "Besides, don't you want to know what will happen to the two who wandered off?" He tsked loudly. "The morons went in the wrong direction. They're already lost. And it's so cold. So very cold. In just a little while they're going to fall asleep and never wake up."

"That's not true," she whispered.

"It's a fairly painless way to die," he said sensibly. "I do wish that farmer was closer," he pined. "The boy is filled with fear of things he cannot see or understand. His death would be invigorating, if only he were near."

The fear was growing in her. He could smell it, taste it. That fear sent a surge of energy through these veins, a tingle of pleasure through this entire body. "Don't you want to know what I have planned for you, lover?"

A light in the corner of the room distracted him. The spirit of that damned witch! She had all but ruined this room with her cursed spells. And she had been a most unreliable ghost! The others obeyed his every command because they were rightly afraid of him. She . . . she had always defied him.

Even now, she was trying to communicate with Eve. Fortunately, Eve did not have the gift her beloved possessed. She was oblivious to the assistance that was being offered her.

The humans in this house were as defiant as the witch. They fought the fear, they clung to one another. There was too much love in this house. Too much hope.

Even though the night was not progressing as quickly as he had planned, Scrydan was not concerned. The hope would die soon enough, and so would they.

"Is he really gone?" Katherine asked, glancing nervously around the room.

Garrick nodded. "He might come back, though. If he does, we must ignore him. No matter what he does, no matter what he says."

She nodded, but she knew ignoring the ghost of her late husband was all but impossible. But in truth, the man had hurt her more than the ghost ever could.

Garrick had distracted her with that kiss, and it had worked too well. No one had ever kissed her that way. In the beginning, Jerome had occasionally given her rough, coarse kisses. He had never kissed her sweetly. He had never made her feel soft and warm all over, simply by moving his mouth over hers. He had certainly never held her the way Garrick did.

Katherine shook off the memory. It was perfectly

all right to like Garrick as a friend, but to think of more was impossible. Judging by the light in his eyes, he was already thinking of more.

Jerome used to get something similar to that light in his eyes, and what followed was never pleasant.

Women were so sloppily sentimental! Love and affection were pretty dreams, dreams men never shared. Katherine had learned to think like a man, to be cold and practical. She wouldn't let herself be fooled by pretty words, not ever again.

She walked across the room, trying to get away from Garrick. She had a feeling he was very good at spouting pretty words a woman liked to hear. Lies. Pretty promises. The kitchen was too small for her to go far, but she certainly didn't want to be within touching distance. Not until she had a chance to reconstruct the wall with which she protected herself.

As if he knew she was now unprotected, Jerome appeared before her. Smiling. No, sneering. That twist of his mouth was not a smile.

Garrick came up behind her quickly, and she stepped protectively between the ghost of her husband and her friend.

"Stop this, Jerome," she ordered. "I'm not afraid of you. You can't hurt me anymore."

"Of course I can," he said, his misty eyes on her face, his unworldly fists reaching out for her.

Katherine didn't move away, and those fists never touched her. Garrick placed his hand at the small of her back, gentle and supportive. And so warm and real! She needed that now. Reality and the warmth of another human's hand.

"Tell him to go away," Garrick whispered.

Such simple advice, and she had never taken it. When her husband had been alive she hadn't dared. When she'd sensed his spirit in the house, after his death, she had cursed and railed at him, but she had never simply told him to go away.

"You're the only one who can send him on," Garrick whispered.

Katherine Cassidy had never possessed power of any kind. No matter how strong she tried to appear to be, she knew she was weak. Helpless.

"Tell him, once and for all, how you really feel," Garrick prodded when she remained silent.

Katherine straightened her spine and took a deep breath. "I despise you," she said to the misty Jerome. "You were a mean, abusive drunk and a bad husband, and it isn't fair that you never had to pay for those sins. You never had to suffer." In her heart and soul, something broke. A wall crumbled and gave way to her long-hidden fears.

She swung out at the ghost with a clenched hand, but her small fist went right through his image. "You died too quick!" she shouted. "It's not fair! You should have been tortured, you should have died a slow, painful death. It's not fair!"

The ghost of Jerome backed away from her.

"Katherine," Garrick said softly. "Tell him to go. Tell him to leave you forever."

Tears burned her eyes and she pushed them back. She did not cry. She certainly shed no tears for Jerome. "No, that's too easy. He can't just die and rest in peace. I want him to suffer."

"Honey," Garrick whispered. "I think he is suffering."

She spun on Garrick. "Don't call me honey! Just because I let you kiss me one time, that doesn't mean you can call me *honey.*" She hit him on the chest with the flat of her hand. Jerome had called her "honey." She had hated it when he called her that! She hit Garrick again.

Garrick didn't back away from her or even flinch. "Tell Jerome to go," he whispered. "I think if you tell him to go away and you mean it, if you feel it in your heart, he'll leave."

"It can't be that easy." She hit Garrick again, and in answer he wrapped his arms around her. She struggled, but not hard and not for long. His arms felt good. The way he held her—it was warm and close and made her feel safe. Exhausted, she rested her head on Garrick's chest and took a deep, unsteady breath.

"What if it is that easy?" he asked. "Tell Jerome to go away, tell him to stay out of your home and out of your life. Think of all the things you can do when he's completely gone." He kissed the top of her head. "You can dance. You can laugh. I'll buy you a yellow dress, and we'll burn all the black."

She shook her head.

"We'll walk down the street arm in arm."

Again, she shook her head vigorously.

"We'll start a new life," he said. "Together."

She pushed away from him, escaped from the false security of his warm embrace. "No. There will be no new life, and you and I are definitely not doing anything *together.*"

"I think I love you," Garrick said in a low voice.

She slapped him soundly across the cheek.

"You can hit me all you want," he said without rancor. "It won't change anything."

Suddenly Katherine realized what she'd done. Jerome had hit her, so many times she'd lost count the first year of their marriage. Was she just like him, now, lashing out at Garrick with her fists and the flat of her hand because he wouldn't tell her what she wanted to hear? No, she couldn't be like Jerome. She threaded her fingers and clasped her hands tightly.

"I'm sorry."

"I do . . ."

"No," she said, taking a quick step back. "Don't say it again. Please don't. I don't want love. Not from you, not from anyone."

Garrick reached out a hand, but when she backed away so she'd be out of reach, he let that hand drop. "You're too young to give up on love."

She lifted her chin. "Pretty words from a man whose idea of love is a trip to Savannah and a woman paid to warm his bed." Yes, Garrick was just like his father. They didn't dare to take their pleasures with any of the local willing women. As the richest family in Plummerville, that might cause some sort of scandal, and they could not afford lurid gossip or little Hunt bastards littering the streets. No, they both made trips to Savannah to buy their women. At least once a month, the Hunt men each managed to ride off on a purported business trip.

Her anger faded quickly. If Lucien was correct, Garrick was a Hunt bastard. He hadn't dealt with that news yet.

"If you've been paying attention," Garrick said tightly, "you will realize that I haven't been to Savannah in five months."

"That doesn't mean . . ."

"It means maybe I want something more than a woman who warms my bed because she's paid to do so. It means maybe I want something more in my

life than work, my angry family, and shallow friendships." He reached out to her again, and she didn't
back away this time. "Maybe I'm ready for love,
Katherine."

She shook her head. "Love is just a pretty disguise.
A trick of the heart. It can kill you, if you let it."

He shook his head.

"I once loved Jerome," she confessed in a shaking voice. "Before I knew what he was really like, I
loved him with a young girl's heart and unfailing
optimism. That love died piece by piece, and it
hurt. It still hurts."

"Is that why you won't let him go?"

Heaven above, it was true. She held Jerome with
her. Did she think she could punish him for all his
sins? Or did she believe that the love she'd once felt
for him still lived, buried in her cold heart? It was a
frightening thought.

"I don't know how," she whispered.

Twelve

"*A Viking?*" O'Hara dropped his hands and took a step back.

In all the excitement, Daisy had forgotten all about O'Hara's power to see inside a person when he touched them. Oh, she never should've let him lay his hands on her! "I don't know what you're talking about," she said primly, seeing denial as her only option.

"Of course you do." O'Hara sighed and shook his head, and when a ghostly form of a woman in white formed to circle around him, he waved his hand at her as if she were an annoying fly. "I shouldn't be surprised. Women like you always go silly over Lionel."

Daisy wrinkled her nose. She shouldn't have to explain away a brief whim, not to O'Hara. "I haven't gone silly over anyone. And if I did, perchance, in the back of my mind think Lionel resembled a Viking in some vague way, it was an unconscious thought surely brought on by the fact that he is fairly tall and has long blond hair."

O'Hara scoffed.

Turning the tables would be nice, right about now. "And what exactly does that mean? *Women like you.*"

He didn't answer her question. Instead he snorted, "Viking."

"I hardly think this is the time and place to get into an argument over some absurd, stray thought I *might* have had," Daisy said. "Besides, my thoughts should be my own, no matter what or who they concern."

O'Hara's face went strangely calm. Oh, she didn't think that was a good sign, not at all.

"I know why you like Lionel," he said in a low, soothing voice.

"I don't like or dislike . . ." she began.

O'Hara continued as if she hadn't spoken. "He's safe, isn't he? Lionel Brandon is aloof and cool. He lives most of his life off in another world, so he can't possibly be a threat to you."

"That's the most ridiculous . . ."

"He's not real. You see a pretty face and you dream of Vikings."

"I did not dream of Vikings," she insisted.

"Yes, you did," O'Hara whispered. "You just don't remember."

She felt a rush of warmth to her cheeks. "Even if I did . . ."

"You've been pushing me away since we got here," O'Hara insisted. "I'm not a pretty picture, and no matter what abilities I have, I make an effort to live very solidly in this world. I'm real, Daisy. Are you really so afraid that a real man might hurt you?"

Her heart thudded too hard in her chest, and it had nothing to do with ghosts and haunted houses. She wondered how much O'Hara had seen, when he'd touched her. "Now that you've laid your hands on me, does that mean you know . . . everything?" That last word came out as a high-pitched squeak.

"Of course not," he said testily. "No one sees everything. We're not meant to see everything. I have no control over what comes through when I touch someone or something."

"Is the power, uh, only in your hands?"

"Yes."

So if he ever actually kissed her he wouldn't see anything he wasn't supposed to see, as long as he kept those hands to himself.

"What else do you know about me, besides that silly notion that I thought Lionel might resemble a Viking?" She held her breath and awaited his answer.

O'Hara crossed his arms over his chest. Oh, he was still annoyed with her! "Nothing shocking," he said in a low voice. "You're much stronger than you allow others to believe, stronger than you know. You have a good heart. When you love someone, you love them completely," he added in a lower voice. "And you hate squash."

"Mother always kept a garden," she explained. "There were a couple of summers that we had an abundance of squash. She served it at every meal. She even tried to make me eat it for breakfast once!" She shuddered. "I do despise squash."

"Fascinating," O'Hara said dryly.

Since she and O'Hara were standing apart, the ghosts around them began to take shape again. Together, they were stronger, less afraid. Apart, as they were now, they were more vulnerable. The female ghost in white, another woman, two older men. They circled and floated around the room, and one of the women settled on the bed. Daisy tried to keep track of their movements, her head turning this way and that as the haunting spirits twisted and turned.

When one of the men drew a misty knife, she let out another high-pitched squeak. Real or not, the reenacted murders were painful to watch.

"They can't hurt you," O'Hara assured her. "Don't look at them, look at me."

She focused her eyes on his shadowy image in the dark room. There was just enough moonlight to keep them from being lost in complete darkness. She couldn't deny that she was glad O'Hara was here. No one else in this house could make her feel more protected. "How can I not be frightened?" she whispered.

"Think of Vikings," he said sharply.

Daisy sighed. "I'm not . . . you only saw a tiny portion of . . ." There was no good way to talk her way out of this one! "Oh, you are the most impossible man!"

"Me?"

"Yes, you, Quigley Tibbot O'Hara."

"That's not very sporting of you," he said sullenly, "to bring up my name at a time like this."

She was so afraid. She was afraid of everything and had been for a very long time. Not of the ghosts O'Hara assured her would not hurt them. She didn't think he would lie to her about that. She was more afraid of living than she was of dying. Maybe O'Hara was right, and she was drawn to Lionel Brandon because in her heart she knew he was no threat to her.

And deep inside, she wanted that kiss she'd almost gotten.

O'Hara would never kiss her, now. One all too brief touch, and he believed she was besotted over Lionel merely because he was beautiful.

She looked at the ghost on the bed, the sad-looking woman who lounged there . . . a foot or two off the mattress. "Leave," Daisy said succinctly. She looked at all the spirits in turn. "All of you, just go. I know you mean to be frightening, but in truth you're simply annoying. Each and every one of you looks more sad than threatening. So go." She waved her hand much as O'Hara had, shooing them away. "I can't carry on a private conversation with all of you watching."

One by one they did as she asked. She suspected the only evil spirit in this hotel was Scrydan himself. The others were as trapped as she and O'Hara.

"It worked," O'Hara said. He sounded more than a little surprised.

"Of course it worked."

"Most women would be hysterical, right about now."

"I'm not most women."

"No, you are not," O'Hara said softly.

Daisy closed the distance between them. She took a deep breath before reaching out and taking O'Hara's right hand with hers, as if for a handshake. But instead of shaking his hand she held it tight, palm to palm, fingers snugly closed. His hand was so large it engulfed hers. And it was warm. Wonderfully warm in this chilly room. His fingers tightened and loosened. His eyes drifted closed.

"For a very long time," she said, "I've been afraid to let anyone know me the way you now do. Maybe you can't see everything, but I believe you can see more of me than you did before. I believe you can see further than my dislike of a particular vegetable or a silly, passing notion about a man I didn't even know when I allowed my mind to . . . wander."

"Daisy," O'Hara whispered. He tried to pull his hand away, but she held on tight.

"Maybe you're right, about me living safely and setting my mind on men who won't ever be a threat to my heart. Maybe I do push away any man who might mean more to me than a passing pretty face."

"I never should've said those things," he said. "I was angry."

"It's all right to be angry," she whispered. "Losing your temper is a part of living, isn't it?" She shook her head. "O'Hara, I can't even remember the last time I cared enough about anything to get angry."

His hand gripped hers tightly. "Daisy, I'm trying not to pry, I'm trying not to see any more . . . but I don't have that kind of control. I can only block you for so long. Let go of my hand."

She shook her head. "If Scrydan wins and we die in this house . . . I don't want to go alone. I want to be holding hands with someone who knows the real me. All of me, good and bad. I don't want you to block anything."

O'Hara reached out his left hand and laid it on her cheek. She closed her eyes and let him caress her there, his fingers gentle and knowing. And she was afraid. Not of the ghosts, not even of Scrydan. She was afraid of what O'Hara would think of her when he let his hands fall.

Eve caught a glimpse of herself in the mirror over the dusty dresser. Good heavens, she looked as frightful as any ghost! Her hair was down, tangled and waving in all directions. Her face was too pale. And her dress . . . her wonderfully elegant wedding gown was ruined. It was stained in several places, and there were a few tears. Nothing major, just popped stitches and missing seed pearls. The bodice was oddly misshapen, the once pristine skirt so wrinkled it couldn't possibly be saved. Tears filled her eyes and dulled the image.

If Scrydan was right they were all going to die in this hotel, and she was crying over a ruined gown! A ruined wedding gown, a white symbol of purity and celebration and forever. A symbol of the life she wanted so badly and would never have.

"Oddly enough, he thinks you're beautiful," Scrydan said.

Eve turned to look at the man who was bound to the bed. Scrydan . . . using Lucien's face and body . . . sneered at her. "Just keep quiet," she insisted, wiping away the tears. "I don't want to hear another word from you."

"What are you going to do?" he asked. "Gag me?"

"I might," she whispered.

"And what will you do if Lucien comes back and wants to speak to you? What if he wants to tell you that he loved you to the very end? What if he wants one last kiss?" He flicked his tongue at her in an obscene way.

"Gagging you is sounding more and more like an excellent idea."

Scrydan's eyes turned to a corner of the room, and his wicked smile faded. "Silencing me is a chance you won't take."

Eve turned to look into the dim corner that had drawn Scrydan's attention. Did something move there? Yes. A shadow in a shadow. A shift of the low light.

She had channeled Viola Stamper, for short

periods of time, while she and Lucien had been trying to solve the mystery of her murder. Could this newly arrived ghost possess her the way Scrydan had possessed Lucien? She wasn't sure the weakened spirit was capable of taking over her body, but the last thing she needed was to be controlled by a force who was in Scrydan's command.

Lucien often spoke of building walls in the mind, to keep unwanted spirits out. Eve constructed those walls within her own mind, as the figure in the corner twisted and turned.

She forgot about the ghost when she heard a scraping noise in the hallway, as if someone or something were being dragged slowly down the hallway. For a long moment she held her breath. The scraping sound came closer and closer. Something breathed raggedly. Scrydan was holding the door closed. Could he open it if he wanted whatever was out there to enter this room?

"Eve," a soft voice whispered.

Relief rushed through her body, making her weak in the knees. "Hugh?" she said as she laid the flat of her hand against the door. "Are you all right?"

He hesitated. "I'm not sure. I hit my head and everything's rather . . . muddled. It's very dark. I only found the door because I felt my way down the hall. What happened?"

Eve explained, as simply as she could, what had happened and where the others were.

"Whatever you do," Hugh said, "don't release Lucien."

"It's not Lucien," she said in a low voice.

"That's right." His words were slightly slurred.

"He's not . . ." Hugh shifted against the door. "Eve, something's here."

"Hugh!" Eve banged her fist against the door. "Block it. You can keep it out."

There was no answer, not even when she banged on the door and shouted his name. She sank to her knees to move herself closer to the man on the other side of the door. "Hugh!"

"We could walk out of here right now," Scrydan said casually. "Just you and me. Once I'm a few miles away from the hotel, everything will return to normal and your friends will be safe."

She stood quickly and spun to face him. "You're a liar. You said Hugh was dead." He'd said other things, too, about the ways her friends would die before the night was over.

"Are you sure that was Hugh?" he asked with a smile. "It might've been a figment of your imagination, or a ghost masquerading as your friend. It might have been anything at all."

She shook her head.

"You can save them," Scrydan whispered. "Only you. And in reward I will give you anything you want. Beauty. Riches. Fame."

As Eve walked toward the bed, Scrydan smiled at her. She leaned down, moved in so close she could feel the heat radiating off his body. But she stopped before she got too close. "You're a liar."

He shrugged his shoulders.

"And all I want is Lucien."

Scrydan yanked against his bonds. He was getting no stronger, that she could tell. When he grew strong enough to free himself . . . how would she stop him?

* * *

Jerome had vanished, for the moment, but Katherine suspected he was still there. Watching. Waiting. The flame of their single candle flickered, and as it did Garrick reached out and took her hand. Neither of them wanted to be lost in darkness.

"Come over here," Garrick said gently. "You need to sit down." He sat on the only chair in the room and pulled her onto his lap.

"I don't . . ." she began, as she started to rise.

He wrapped his arms around her waist and tugged, and she fell back onto his lap. "I need to sit," he said. "And I don't want to sit alone." He shifted his arms so they were firmly around her, but not holding on too tight. "Please, Katherine."

She didn't think she had ever heard Garrick Hunt say *please!* So she stayed. It was nice, considering the circumstances, to be so close to another human being. To be warm. She stayed where she was, sitting on Garrick's lap, and told herself that she stayed for his sake, not her own. She stayed because he asked it of her, not because she liked the way he held her. Not because for the first time in years she was not alone.

Katherine watched the candlelight flickering and prayed that it would stay strong and bright. She didn't want to be lost in the black of night. She didn't want Jerome to come after her in the dark.

"When we get out of here . . ." Garrick said in a lowered voice.

"If we get out," Katherine said sharply. "If."

"*When* we get out of here," he began again, "and we return to Plummerville, would you give me permission to call on you?"

Her heart leapt. "Of course not."

"Why not?"

"For one thing, you're going out west. I see no reason to . . . to start something we're not going to be able to finish."

"I don't start things I can't finish," he said.

"The answer is still no."

He didn't seem alarmed or disappointed. "Why?"

Katherine sighed. At least she was facing away from Garrick and didn't have to look him in the eye. "I don't want a man in my life, not ever again. I won't remarry, I'm not interested in romance of any kind, and I will not pretend otherwise."

"We're not all like him," Garrick said defensively. "Many men are trustworthy and gentle. Many husbands love and care for their wives in a way Jerome never did. They're kind and solid and . . ."

"You're a drunk, just like he was." She wanted to rise, but Garrick held her tight.

She had hoped to make Garrick so angry he would release her, but her ploy didn't work. "I do drink too much, I can't argue with that. But I don't love the bottle, and more than that I don't need it. For the right reason, I could be persuaded to give up drinking altogether."

"It's not that easy," she whispered. "I can't tell you how many times Jerome promised he would never drink again. If the desire for liquor is in you, it's in you and there's nothing to be done."

"I could give it up for you," he said confidently. "I *would*. I suppose you think that's tripe."

"I do."

"Do you think I would say anything, tell any lie, to get what I want?"

"Yes."

"I want you," he whispered. "Here. Next week. Next year. Forever."

Her heart clenched, every muscle in her body went tense. "Don't . . ."

"But I won't lie to you about anything, Katherine. You're too important to be won with lies and deceit."

"Rubbish . . ." She choked on the word.

"But I will do anything else in order to get what I want. I'm horridly spoiled, you know," he teased.

How could he joke at a time like this?

"There's a problem with what I suspect you want from me." Best to be blunt. She couldn't allow Garrick to go on expecting things she could not give him. "If I never touch a man again, that will be fine with me. More than fine. I won't take another man into my bed, not ever. I don't want it." She swallowed hard. "I don't want you."

"How can you say that?" he asked, apparently not at all offended.

"Marriage offers women stability. A home they would not otherwise be able to have. Children, if they want such troublesome things about." She stiffened her spine. "I imagine the women you've paid to have sex with you pretended to enjoy it," she snapped. "But it's not at all . . . I can't imagine . . . I will never . . ."

"You have to give me a chance," he whispered. "Give me a chance to prove to you that things would be different for us, if you'd allow it."

She shook her head. "You've become a wonderful friend," she admitted, her heart all but flipping over at the confession. "You've been good to me, especially since we came here." And the kiss had been nice. Very nice. "But I'm not interested in anything else."

He sighed. "Too bad."

The candle flickered again, and then it went out

as if someone had extinguished it with a gentle breath. A trill of soft laughter filled the air, and Garrick gathered her closer against him.

It took a few moments for her eyes to adjust to the new darkness. Was it her imagination, or was the room alive with ghosts? Shadows danced and fell, cold wind out of nowhere, the same wind that had snuffed out the candle, brushed across her face.

"Do you have more matches with you?" she asked.

"No. The few matches we gathered are in the lobby. I was going to start the stove with the flame from the candle, but we never got that far."

It didn't matter, not really. There wasn't much left of that extinguished candle.

Something to her right moved, a darker shadow in a shadowy corner.

"Look at me," Garrick said sharply. Obviously he saw the ghosts, too.

Katherine twisted to the side and wrapped her arms around Garrick's neck. She kept her eyes on his face, even though she could not see his features well enough to suit her. The window in this room was small, and did not allow much moonlight to find its way in. "We have to try not to be scared," she whispered. "That's what they said."

"We'll talk of other things," Garrick said.

What other things? Oh, there was no safe subject, not that she could think of at the moment. "I'm beginning to like Daisy's idea of a pie society. If we get out of here, I don't want to so much as speak of ghosts again!"

"*When,*" Garrick said. "*When* we get out."

She wasn't so sure. "All right. When we get out of here, we'll disband the Plummerville Ghost Society

and form a pie society instead." She sighed. "That
is the most ridiculous idea I have ever heard."

"Forget Plummerville," Garrick whispered. "Come
west with me."

"What? I have a home, I'm quite comfortable . . ."

"Forget being comfortable. Life isn't comfortable,
Katherine. It's hard and unpredictable, and if you
don't grab what you want when you have the chance
it's gone." His voice was tense, not angry but disappointed, perhaps. "Leave the ghost of Jerome and
your house and your quiet life behind and come with
me."

It sounded like a fine plan. Too fine. Such a life
wasn't meant for her. "Why should I?"

In answer, he kissed her. Softly, but with a quiet
demand.

Katherine pulled her mouth from his. "I told
you, I don't want . . ."

"You don't know what you want."

She wanted to argue with him, but no words left
her mouth. Garrick was right. She knew what she
didn't want, but she had no idea what would make
her happy again. She had been happy once, hadn't
she? She hadn't always been scornful about people
and life.

So she kissed him. That, at least, was pleasant.
And distracting. She dismissed the ghosts, the
knowledge that they were never getting out of this
kitchen, and most of all she dismissed her fear.

She held onto Garrick, and he held her. Their
mouths were locked together, their hearts pounded
together, and in the midst of a horrible experience
they made something beautiful happen.

Yes, the kiss that went on and on was beautiful.
Having Garrick hold her was beautiful. Beauty in

the midst of horror. Maybe it was the horror that made this kiss so bright and wonderful.

She had never dreamed that kissing could be so powerful.

Garrick let one of his large hands slip up her side, slowly stroking the silk. He hesitated before cupping her breast in his hand. His fingers moved against the giving flesh, unexpectedly arousing. A chill shot through her body, and this chill had nothing to do with the cold of the winter night.

No one had ever touched her there, not with gentleness. Not with tender, stroking fingertips. Garrick continued to caress her. One finger brushed over her nipple, and unexpected sensations shot through her entire body. She almost whispered, "Again, please," but held her tongue. Garrick didn't need to be instructed. He touched her that way again, without being asked.

She knew she should tell Garrick to stop. She should primly order him to return his hand to her back and be satisfied with just a kiss. But she didn't. His caress stirred her in a way she had thought impossible.

"Garrick," she whispered, her lips lightly touching his. He mumbled an incoherent response. "We can kiss. I'll let you . . . touch me. But that's all. Nothing else."

"If that's what you want," he murmured.

"And if we get out of here . . ."

"When," he interrupted.

She didn't argue with him. Not this time. "When we get out of here, you're going west and I'm staying in Plummerville, where I belong."

He flicked his tongue against her lower lip. "We'll see about that."

Thirteen

Lucien opened his eyes as if from a long sleep. His mind was foggy, and for a moment he didn't know who or where he was. Eve paced beside the bed, restless and tense, her full white skirt rustling loudly, her hair tumbling down her back. He tried to reach for her, and when he discovered that he couldn't, he remembered everything.

"Evie," he said, finding his voice didn't come to him easily.

She spun around. "Didn't I tell you to shut up!"

"It's me," he said. He gave her a smile. "I think holding the doors closed and trying to direct the other spirits in the house while he's in this protected room has weakened Scrydan. He's still here, but he's gone quiet."

Eve stared down at him. "I've had enough of your tricks." Her eyes narrowed. "You lie, you confuse." She studied him closely. "If you're Lucien, then how do you know about him holding the doors closed?"

"I just know," he said. "He's with me, now. It's like when Alistair Stamper spoke through me and I remembered bits and pieces of his past as if they were my own."

"How do I know you're not just . . . just drawing

information from Lucien's mind in an attempt to deceive me?"

"I guess you don't."

"I guess not."

"Evie," he said as she turned and started to walk away. "I don't know how much time I have. He could come back at any moment, and I can't fight him much longer."

She spun around to face him defiantly, wild and angry. "I should untie you, I suppose, so you can . . ."

"No!" he snapped. "Don't you dare let me go."

Her face softened, and two tears ran down her cheeks. Her fingers trembled, and her legs were not as steady as she would have him think. She was barely holding herself together.

"I want to believe it's you, I really do, but . . ."

"Just listen." He hated her tears. He wanted to wipe them away. He wanted to hold her. But there was no time for either.

"There is one spirit in this house capable of defeating Scrydan, with Lionel's assistance."

"Lionel's gone."

Lucien shook his head. "It was not coincidence that Lionel was outside the hotel when the doors closed and locked."

Eve sat on the side of the bed and reached out to touch his face. "Lucien, I want to believe it's you . . ."

"Believe."

He could see by the expression on Eve's tired face that she still had reservations. She was rightfully suspicious.

"Listen carefully," he said softly. "There was a witch. Her name was Melissa."

"A witch named Melissa," Eve said skeptically.

"Melissa's younger sister died here, committed suicide, so she came to investigate."

"And found Scrydan."

"Yes. She got a job as a housekeeper, when the place was a fancy hotel, and with her powers it didn't take her long to discover what was happening."

"Why didn't Scrydan just kill her?"

"He did, eventually." Lucien shook off the memory of the horrible way Melissa had died. He saw it as if he had been there, tasted her fear and felt Scrydan's joy. He pushed deep the memories that were not his own. He tried to hide them away. "But Melissa had a protective spell that kept Scrydan from her for a while. She tried to cast these spells on the rooms, which is why some are more active than others. This room was where she cast her most successful spell, which is why it's so quiet."

"What's the spell?"

He shook his head. "I don't know. I'm hoping that with the witch's name and the little bit of knowledge I was able to glean from Scrydan, Lionel will be able to reproduce the spell on a grander scale that will actually trap the evil spirit so he won't be able to do any more harm."

"Can Lionel accomplish this?"

He nodded his head. "I believe so. He has the power, and he's had experience with casting spells."

"I didn't know that."

There was a lot Eve didn't know, about him, about the others. He had always tried his best to protect her, when she was his colleague, his friend, his fiancée.

"Scrydan's been blocking her from Lionel, but he's spread himself too thin." Lucien wrinkled his nose. It itched. Of course it itched! He couldn't scratch his nose or anything else. He did his best to dismiss the discomfort. "Keeping a hold on me and trying to control the house and the spirits in it as well . . . he doesn't have the strength to do it all, and he won't, as long as the others remain calm." From the little bit he could see, through Scrydan, the others were doing fine. Hugh was not in good shape, but he'd be all right. If they got him out of here in time.

"What if Lionel doesn't make it back?"

"He will."

Eve turned away, as if she couldn't bear to look at him any longer.

"Evie?" he said, when she took a step away from the bed. "I'm so sorry. I'm sorry that you're stuck here, sorry that I ruined everything. I wanted our wedding to be perfect. I wanted . . ."

"No, you didn't," she said softly. "I don't think you cared if we were married or not. You would have been just as happy to have the justice of the peace marry us in the middle of the street. I was the one who wanted the perfect wedding. You didn't care."

"I did."

"Then why did you come here?" She turned to him, and he saw the tears on her face. That's why she had turned away. She didn't want him to see her cry. More tears fell as he watched. "You should've stayed in Plummerville instead of running away."

"I didn't run," he insisted.

"Well, what do you call it?"

Maybe she was right and he had been running, the way he'd been running from one thing or another all his life. He'd run from his power to see into the world of the dead, when it had been hard to understand and more of a curse than a gift. He'd been running ever since, or had been until he'd met Evie. "I love you."

"It's not enough this time," she whispered. "You can't just tell me you love me and expect everything to be all right! You came here on a whim, and now we're all going to die. Both of us and most of our friends are going to die because you came here alone when you should've been getting married."

She was right. He had unknowingly led them all into this trap. "Give the information to Lionel, when he arrives."

"If he makes it at all, it'll be morning at the earliest. We could all be dead by then."

"Have faith, Evie."

She shook her head. "It's too late for that. Much too late."

O'Hara dropped his hand, and Daisy let her fingers trail over his palm. He had been right all along. She did have a good heart, and when she loved she did it well. Too well.

"There's no need to be afraid."

"Of course there is," she said sensibly.

"I'm not talking about the hotel and the ghosts."

"Neither am I." Daisy licked her lips, stared up at him wide-eyed. "Do you hate me?" she asked softly.

"Of course not." He reached out to touch her cheek, and she didn't flinch. There was no need. He had seen what she'd tried to hide for so long. It was as if she'd pushed the knowledge at him, as if she needed him to know. As if she needed someone to know.

"No man will ever love me enough to forgive what I've done."

Daisy was so fragile, and still so strong. Like most people, she was much more complicated than he'd initially suspected. "You made a mistake a very long time ago. Any man worthy of you will understand that." He stroked her cheek. "You only need to forgive yourself."

"I loved him," she whispered. "At least, I thought I did."

"You were very young."

"Seventeen."

"And he tricked you." If ever he'd wanted to kill someone, it was the man who had seduced an innocent girl and broken her heart.

"He said he was taking me to a preacher in another town so we could get married before my father could stop us." She didn't cry, her voice didn't tremble. "Then we lost our way and came upon this little deserted cabin, and it seemed like a good enough place to spend the night." Her hands began to tremble, and he caught them in his. "And he said we were as good as man and wife," she whispered, "so . . ." her voice trailed off.

"That's no good reason for you to give up on love and marriage." He hated to think of her being alone, when she should be surrounded by her own family. A husband. Children. She wanted and deserved it all. "You've been hiding long enough, Daisy. Let it go. Release all that old pain."

"How can I ever marry a man without telling him what happened?" her voice was small, uncertain. "A husband would expect . . . certain things."

A husband would expect a virgin in his marriage bed, that's what she would not say aloud. That's the fear he'd caught when he held her hand. "Any man worthy will dismiss all your worries. He will love you, and cherish you, and thank his lucky stars every day that you love him." He lifted her soft, tender hands and kissed them, one and then the other.

He didn't want to release her hands, not ever. They were such feminine hands, gentle and quiet, unlike his own. They were just hands, made for touching, for holding and caressing. He adored her hands, so he kissed them again.

"When I got up the next morning, he was gone," she whispered.

"I know."

"A couple of months later I found out I was going to have a baby," her voice faded to almost nothing.

His heart broke for her. "I saw that, too."

"I cried so hard when I found out," she said, her voice barely a whisper. "I cried for days and days. That's why I miscarried. It was all my fault." She sniffled softly. "I killed my own baby, and no one ever knew. Not the baby's father. Not my parents."

"You did not kill your baby," O'Hara insisted. "Put that thought out of your head forever."

"How can I know for sure?"

"You know because I tell you so." He pulled her close and placed his hand on the back of her head as he held her tight. "What happened to him? The bastard who did this to you. I didn't see that."

"He moved away. I saw him in town a couple of times before he left Plummerville, and he laughed at me." She shuddered down the length of her body. "I wouldn't let him see that I hurt inside. It was just a game to him. I was just a game."

Daisy was so tiny! He hadn't truly realized that before, but as she burrowed against him it hit him.

She was fragile and petite, with gentle curves and delicate bones. She had no business fighting ghosts or hiding her battered heart. Daisy should have a loving husband, a nice home, a couple of beautiful children to take care of. This was the kind of woman a man cherished.

Most women who knew of his abilities stayed well clear of him. They didn't want to be involved with a man who could touch them and know their darkest secrets, their most profound desires. And those who didn't know of his gift . . . there were so many he had touched and been repelled by. So many who cared only for themselves, or for what a man could give them. There were too many hearts touched with selfishness and hate. That's why it had hurt him so to see Eve hurting, after Lucien had left her at the altar. There were too few truly exceptional women in the world. Eve Abernathy was one of them.

So was Daisy Willard.

"You're exhausted," he said softly.

Daisy nodded her head.

"We might very well be here all night."

She trembled gently.

"Why don't you lie down and rest."

She tilted her head back and looked up at him, studying him closely. She wondered if he would try to seduce her, now that he knew she was not a virgin.

"No, I will not," he said without waiting for her to say a single word aloud. "I'm not nearly as wicked as my reputation would have you believe."

"Good." She glanced at the bed. "But I don't think I could lie on that mattress. If Scrydan is in the hotel and the furnishings, is he in the mattress on that bed? Besides, we don't know what happened in that bed. People died there. And . . . other things."

Yes, people had died there. They'd seen that fact too clearly tonight, as the ghosts had replayed their deaths. "I have an idea." Holding her hand, he led her to the window. A chair had been placed there, long ago, and it caught the moonlight now. He pulled it away from the wall, sat down, and waited for Daisy to follow. "Sit," he finally said.

"On your lap?"

"Why not?"

"It's . . . unseemly."

"Are you going to stand on your tiptoes all night?"

She sighed and sat, perching stiffly on his knee. "Maybe just for a little while. I need to rest my feet."

"Yes, you do."

It was nice, to have her there so close. To have her touch him without fear. It took only a few moments for her to relax, in a subtle way. She did not lean back against him, and most likely would not. Not tonight. But she was comfortable here. That alone was amazing.

She stared out the window, moonlight on her beautiful face. "It's not fair, you know," she said softly.

"What's not fair?"

"You can see into me, and yet I see nothing of you."

"There's not much to see."

"I doubt that." She relaxed a little. "I believe you are a very interesting man."

"I'm very simple, actually." He ran his hand up her spine. Ah, she was still a little bit afraid that he'd try to seduce her, and she wasn't sure if she liked the idea or not. "I'm a simple man with simple needs."

She squirmed on his lap. "You don't seem at all simple."

"I need the same things any man needs. A good meal, a warm fire, and a beautiful woman sitting on my lap. What else can a man ask for?"

"How about a ghost-free place to spend the night," she suggested.

"Can't have everything."

Daisy didn't seem to mind that he touched her with his hands, even though she knew what he could do.

She didn't have to worry about his trying to seduce her. After everything she'd been through, she deserved better. He knew that not because he'd touched her, but because she'd touched him, deep inside. Daisy Willard deserved a man who would court her, adore her, and seduce her well and good on their wedding night.

It crossed his mind, briefly, that he might be that very man.

Katherine didn't know how long she and Garrick had been kissing in the dark. A long time, but not long enough.

There was no fire in this dark kitchen, and yet she wasn't chilled. Not at all. She was hot, as if her blood was heated and rushing too fast through her body.

While they kissed, he touched her constantly. He caressed her face and her neck, he fondled her breasts through black silk until she leaned into him, silently asking for more. And while he caressed her, she touched him. She trailed her fingers over his stubbly jaw, and touched his neck, and laid her hand over his heart.

She was almost thirty years old, and she'd never been kissed like this. Was it being trapped in this hotel that made her feel hungry for this kind of touch? Was it the fear that she might not live until morning? At the moment she didn't care why she felt this way. She liked it.

Garrick groaned, his mouth against hers, one hand at her back, the other over one breast. His fingers trailed over the peaked nipple, once and then again, and a shudder of pleasure worked its way through Katherine's body.

"I want to touch you," he whispered.

"You are touching me," she answered, her lips barely leaving his.

"I want more. I want to touch *you*, Katherine. I want my hand on your bare flesh." He kissed her hard, flicked his tongue into her mouth, and then drew away slightly. "If you don't want me to touch you just say so and I won't mention it again."

This was exactly the kind of touch she had been determined to live without. And yet . . . she wanted it. She craved it. The very thought made her heart beat fast. "All right."

She began to unbutton her bodice, but Garrick placed his hand over hers and stopped her. "Let me."

He kissed her while he very slowly unfastened the tiny buttons that ran from her neck to her waist. There was fever in his movements, and yet he didn't rush. When his fingers brushed against her skin as he accomplished the chore, she felt that caress to her very bones.

Every button that came loose set her free, in a new and miraculous way. Cool air on hot skin was as sensual as the way his mouth moved over hers.

When her bodice was unbuttoned to the waist, Garrick slipped his hand inside and cupped her breast. That hand was so warm and gentle, so . . . so right. She had never been this close to another human being, not in her entire life. It was as if she breathed Garrick in with every breath. He stroked his thumb over her rigid nipple, and she felt that touch so intensely she shuddered and almost came apart.

They continued to kiss, while Garrick caressed her breasts. Sensations she had never known assaulted her. There was so much pleasure here, in a touch, in a kiss. Gradually and surely, something unknown grew inside Katherine. It started at the center of her being and grew outward, like a smoldering fire. This new something grew quickly, spiraling out of control.

She wanted him. Her clothes and his were in the way. She couldn't get near enough to him, no matter how she twisted and turned. Never had she craved a man's touch, and yet she craved Garrick. She needed him.

Her lips parted wider than before, and his tongue danced with hers while his fingers aroused and surprised her. An involuntary moan came up from her throat, a hoarse and urgent cry.

"Katherine," Garrick whispered. "If we're going to stop, we need to stop now."

She knew what he was saying. The growing need, the gnawing hunger, it was not what she'd expected from this encounter. The kissing had been pleasant, but they were far past pleasant at this moment.

She wanted more, and so did Garrick. Unbelievably, she didn't want this moment, this coming together, to end.

"Don't stop," she whispered.

"Do you know what you're . . ."

"Don't stop," she said again.

The hand that had been caressing her breasts dropped lower, to brush against her belly, against her thigh. Garrick lifted her skirt and his hand began to climb. His hand was on her leg, accompanied by the rustle of her rising skirt and the way they both breathed fast and hard.

Her thighs fell apart, and for the first time since they'd begun she felt a rush of alarm. Right now everything was beautiful, but as they continued it would become less beautiful. It would be rough and hurtful, and in the end she would only feel pain.

But something hopeful inside her whispered that this would be different. Garrick was a different man, and tonight she had become a different woman.

When he touched her intimately, slipping his hand through the part in her drawers, she forgot all about her fear. She was wet, hot and empty, and Garrick stroked and aroused her as the fever grew.

Shimmers of pleasure shot through her body, and she quivered. She ached and she yearned, and both were new sensations for her, just as the kissing and the caressing were new.

"What are you doing to me?" she whispered as she rocked against his hand.

"I'm loving you," he answered, his mouth over hers, his hands doing unexpected and wonderful things to her until she thought she would shatter. She couldn't help but move her hips in time with the stroke of his hand.

Soon there was nothing else in the world but the two of them and the need to have Garrick inside her. Katherine unbuttoned his trousers and freed his erection. Without a moment's uncertainty, she wrapped her fingers around his arousal. He was long and hard and hot, and he moaned when she stroked his length once.

With his help she twisted on his lap until she straddled him. For a moment she hesitated. How had this happened to her? What was she doing here? She dismissed the momentary doubts and lifted herself up, and Garrick guided his erection into her.

There was no pain and no regret, as he slowly entered her. As her body accepted his, there was only pleasure and love. She had given up on both long ago, and yet here they were, discovered in the most unlikely place and time.

Garrick was inside her, deep and thick, stretching her and filling her and bringing her closer to something new and wondrous. She moved against him, riding him at a slow and easy pace. Every move was gentle and yet breathtaking. She rode him gracefully, finding a rhythm that satisfied them both. To have him inside her, her body and his on the edge of something wondrous, was a true miracle. While she undulated gently, he caressed her breasts and kissed her neck. She wanted this to last all night, but her need for more grew with every stroke. Soon she was moving faster and faster, taking him deeper, craving more. He brought his mouth to hers and kissed her with a passion she tasted and answered.

It was so dark, even with Garrick's face close to hers, she saw nothing of his features. She could not see, but every other sense was in working order. The scent of their bodies coming together, the taste of his lips, the sound of his sighs and hers mingling. And most of all, there was the sensation of touch.

Katherine cried out when the intense pleasure of completion hit her, taking her by surprise. She was overcome in so many ways. Physically and emotionally, Garrick captured her. Her body thrummed and throbbed, her hands shook, and with one last thrust Garrick found his own release.

He moaned, clutched her body close and tight while he shuddered around and inside her. What had been frantic became slow. Easy. Katherine felt a boneless sensation sweep through her body.

Breathless and sated, she rested her head on Garrick's shoulder and closed her eyes. He remained inside her, a part of her, and she didn't want to let him go. Not yet.

He stroked her hair and kissed her temple. "Not the most romantic circumstance for our first time," he teased, "but you won't catch me complaining."

"Me, either." She smiled. "I never . . . when I was married we didn't . . ."

He grabbed her chin and made her look at him. "No more talk about the past, not for either of us. If we get out of here, we're going to start over. We're going to burn your damned black dresses, dress you in yellow and blue and emerald green, and head out for some place where there are no memories except the ones we make."

"When," she whispered.

"What?"

She kissed his lips with a gentleness she had just discovered. "*When* we get out of here."

Fourteen

The scratching at the door startled Eve so that she almost jumped out of her skin. Lucien slept once again. It was as if he didn't have the strength to stay awake for long. But when Lucien slept, was Scrydan stronger elsewhere in the hotel?

The scratching noise came again, only this time it was accompanied by a hoarsely whispered, "Eve. Eve, are you all right?"

Eve dropped to her knees beside the door. "Hugh?" Tears came to her eyes. It might be a cruel trick, one of Scrydan's tortures. When Hugh had gone silent before, she'd allowed herself to believe the worst. "It's so good to hear your voice again. I thought you were . . ." Her heart leapt into her throat. "I thought you were unconscious." She didn't want to tell him that she'd believed him to be dead.

"I fell down the stairs," he said. She heard his body shift, as if he leaned against the door. "It's dark out here. Let me in."

"I can't. Scrydan's holding all the doors closed, remember?"

He sighed and shifted again. "Is anyone alone?"

"I don't think so. Daisy and O'Hara are upstairs, and Garrick and Katherine are in the kitchen."

"That's good. It'll make it harder for the spirits to frighten them. They must stay together, they must stay strong."

Hugh himself was alone, but he was familiar with the workings of such a place. He could fight what he might see in that dark hallway better than anyone but Lionel.

"How badly are you hurt?"

"I'm not sure. My head hurts, and I think it's bleeding. I feel . . . sticky. And my shoulder hurts. I twisted something when I fell."

"Scrydan can't hold these doors closed forever," she said, not very convincingly. "We'll all be free soon."

Hugh said nothing for a long while, and then he whispered a few low words she could not decipher. A moment later he said, more loudly, "Jane? Is that you?" He called out to his long-dead wife, the woman he had adored and lost. Scrydan had known Hugh blamed himself for Jane's death, so long ago. She knew he didn't mind using that guilt and sorrow against a perfectly helpless and lovable man. It was so unfair!

Eve stood and grabbed the doorknob, and once again she fought. She tugged and kicked at the immovable door. "Let me out of here, you bastard!" Scrydan was torturing Hugh. Was he also torturing the others? He knew their fears, their weaknesses. It wasn't right that he could control them all this way.

She stopped struggling with the door and turned to face a sleeping Lucien. Arms and legs spread, tied to the bed so that he could barely move, he looked helpless. But he wasn't. Whatever was inside Lucien was holding the doors closed. That thing was torturing Hugh. If she wanted the doors to open, she needed to be fighting Scrydan, not an immovable door.

It didn't matter that she was angry with Lucien, that she wasn't sure they'd ever get married, that in her heart she knew she would never come first in his life. She did love him. And at the moment, Scrydan wore his face. This was not going to be easy.

She leaned over the bed and tapped Lucien lightly across the cheek. "Wake up," she commanded. He slept on. Her fingers clenched and unclenched, and she slapped him again, harder. Again, he seemed unaffected.

In the hallway, Hugh began to sob.

Eve climbed onto the bed and straddled Lucien so that she was directly above him. The skirt of her ruined wedding gown spread around them, her loosened hair fell across her face. Firelight flickered across Lucien's cheeks and his mussed hair as she gathered her strength, drew her arm back, and hit him with her fist. Hard.

His eyes fluttered and opened slowly, and he lifted his head to meet her glare. It wasn't Lucien, she knew immediately. It was Scrydan, and he smiled.

"Ah, lover, I know what you want when I wake to find you atop me this way."

She hit him again, so hard his head snapped to the side. "Open the doors," she commanded.

He laughed at her. "Do you really think it's that easy?"

She hauled off and hit him again, tears building in her eyes. *It's not Lucien,* she told herself as his head snapped back again. *It's not really Lucien.* "I

don't think you're as strong as you'd like me to believe, Scrydan. I think it's all an act. You're weak.
This room makes you weak. My love for Lucien
makes you weak. Our love for our friends confuses
you and makes you *weak.*" She hit him again, and
his smile finally faded.

"If I'm so weak, then why are you trapped here?
Why are your friends trapped?"

"It's all you can do," she whispered. "You're not
all-powerful. You control this hotel, you catch
lonely spirits, but you're not so strong that I can't
beat you."

"You're a child," he whispered, giving her a
crooked smile.

"The only reason you can remain in Lucien is because he has the power to accept you. Without him,
you're nothing." She hit him again.

"If that's true, then all you have to do in order to
save your friends is kill Lucien." He leaned toward
her, as far as possible given his bound state. "But
you won't do that, will you?"

"You're not Lucien," she whispered. "You look
like Lucien, but . . ."

"I smell like him, too, don't I?" he interrupted.
"And the voice is the same, Evie, isn't it? Do you want
me to tell you that I love you? Would those words
whispered in this voice make you feel better?"

"You're not . . ."

"I am. If you laid those luscious lips on my skin I
would taste like him." He flicked his tongue at her.
"If you'll untie me, I'll plow you again and you'll
see that I take my women exactly like he did." He
rocked his hips up against her. "You don't have to
untie me for such a test, but I promise you, you
won't regret . . ."

He stopped speaking when she hit him again. "Shut up! You're nothing. You don't scare me, you don't scare anyone. You're a pathetic, sad shell of a spirit. My insipid cousins are more frightening than you are." It took a great effort, but she smiled at him. "Look at you, helpless as a kitten. If you're so strong, then why don't you fight me? Come on, Scrydan, at least pretend to put up a fight." She hit him again, with her left hand this time.

"Stop it," he commanded.

She hit him again. "You're so pathetic. Melissa got the best of you, and now I'm winning, too. You just can't seem to defeat a woman, Scrydan."

"She was a witch," he said tersely, "not a woman. And you are nothing. You can't hurt me. You can't change what's going to happen here tonight."

"Can't I?" she whispered, and then she hit him again.

O'Hara glanced around the suddenly quiet room. It was too quiet here, as if everything had stopped. The ghosts were gone, or at least hiding.

"Can you stand for a moment?" he asked, assisting Daisy to her feet.

"Of course," she said, stepping away from him.

He walked to the door, reached out and touched the doorknob. It turned, but when he pulled it didn't open. Still, it seemed less sturdy than it had been a few hours ago when they'd first been imprisoned here.

He turned to smile at Daisy. "Come give me a hand."

She ran to join him, placed her hands over his, and together they pulled. The door didn't open, but it did move. A little. They tried a few more times, but were still unable to get the door open.

"I think we'll be out of here soon," he said.

"Really?"

He nodded, and then moved back to the door to lay his hands against it. There was no shock, this time, no heat of the fire. Just a restlessness. Restlessness and a lot of pain. Old pain. New pain. Struggle.

"O'Hara?" Daisy said shyly.

He dropped his hands and turned to her. Daisy Willard was likely the most beautiful woman he had ever seen. More than that, she had allowed him to lay his hands on her. Women who knew what he could do didn't do that. Not ever. There had been no lasting relationships for him, no one to talk to at the end of the day. Truth be told, he had once envied Eve and Lucien so much it tasted bitter.

"Everything's going to be fine, I think," he assured her.

"I think so, too." She squirmed where she stood, looking very much like a lost little girl. "Everything feels . . . different, doesn't it?"

She had no powers, to speak of, but her instincts were in fine working order.

"Yes, it does," he answered.

Daisy Willard, more beautiful than any woman had a right to be, rocked up on her tiptoes and lifted her chin slightly. What a magnificent woman she was! When they got out of here, he was going to stay in Plummerville for an extended visit. He was going to call on Daisy like a proper gentleman would. He was going to take her flowers and candy. He was going to court her, well and proper.

"You won't . . . tell anyone what you saw when you touched me, will you?" she asked nervously.

"Of course not."

He could see well enough to notice that she bit her bottom lip in consternation. "Given the circumstances, it would probably be best if you didn't even tell anyone that you touched me at all."

His heart fell. "Certainly," he said dryly.

"I . . . I thought we were going to die," she explained. "I never would have . . . you know what I'm trying to say, I suspect."

It hurt, more than he'd expected it would, to hear Daisy admit that she'd only allowed him to touch her because she'd believed it was her last night on this earth.

"You don't tell anyone my name, and I'll keep your little secret, as well." Hers was not a *little secret,* of course, but a deep-seated pain. One he would never share with another living soul no matter what she said or did when they left this room.

She nodded. Had he actually thought for a while that when they got out of here Daisy Willard would give him the time of day? She had clung to him tonight because she was afraid. She would have clung to any man who had been here to protect her.

"The power in the walls is weakening," he told her. "Since we're not feeding Scrydan the fear he needs, he's losing his strength. Right now he's . . . fighting." Fighting and losing, perhaps.

"And besides," he added in a biting voice. "I'm sure your *Viking* will be here to rescue us all as soon as the sun comes up."

* * *

Katherine rested her head on Garrick's shoulder. Jerome was gone, and the kitchen was quiet. Very quiet. She suspected that Jerome was gone not just for tonight, but forever. Garrick had taught her to let him go. She wished she could be certain that he was truly gone.

No one had ever held her the way Garrick held her now, warm and tender. It was very nice, in an unexpected way. She couldn't get close enough to the man who held her.

"I don't want to die," she whispered.

"I know." Garrick raked his hand up and down her back in an attempt to comfort her.

Katherine lifted her head to look at him. She had never suspected that he had feelings for her. Not Garrick. She had never suspected that she might have feelings for him. Feelings that slept so deep she hadn't know they were there. "You don't know. For a very long time, I didn't care. There wasn't much to live for."

He smiled. His neat little world had been turned upside down, the dire situation they were in was far from over, they both knew that there couldn't ever be anything between them if they made it out of this hotel alive, and still he smiled.

"You're so beautiful," he whispered.

"You say that in the dark," she teased.

"I can see you, Katherine. In my mind, I carry this precise picture of you." His fingers barely brushed her cheek. "Your skin, so pale and soft. Your nose," he brushed the tip of his finger there, "regal and perfect. Your lips"—his finger brushed against her mouth. "Which I now know feel and taste as wonderful as they look. And when morning comes and I see you by the light of day, I know you'll be even more beautiful."

"I'm not . . ."

"You are," he interrupted. "Don't argue with me about this, Katherine."

She touched his hair, those soft, fair strands, and he leaned forward to lay his mouth on her throat. The unexpected sensations he had brought to life began to slowly and insistently grow once again. All it took was that sensual touch of his lips to her skin. She closed her eyes and sighed. She felt so alive.

Katherine Cassidy was no untried maid. She was a widowed woman who had shared a bed with her husband for years. But until tonight, no man had ever truly made love to her. She hadn't known what love was, until now.

No one had ever taught her to be bold, and she had certainly never wanted to be. Garrick made her want to be bold. She wanted to surprise him, the way he had surprised her.

While he kissed her, she untucked his shirt and slipped her hands beneath to touch his skin. He was warm, hot even, and when she stroked his skin he brought his mouth to hers and kissed her deeply. Her lips parted as she tasted him. Her body shuddered.

"Why couldn't we have been trapped in a bed-room?" Garrick asked hoarsely. "With a nice, soft bed and a quilt or a blanket and . . ."

Katherine decided to be truly bold, and reached down to touch his erection. "Are you complaining?"

"No."

* * *

This is not Lucien, Eve reminded herself as she hit him again. She wasn't an extraordinarily strong woman, but still the effects of the blows she'd delivered were beginning to show on his face. A trickle of blood marred the corner of his mouth. His jaw was red, the flesh by the corner of his eye beginning to swell.

"Fight me, you son of a bitch," she whispered.

"Evie, I couldn't possibly hurt you."

This was not Lucien, no matter what he said. Not entirely, at least. Lucien was in there, but Scrydan was in control. It was Scrydan she fought.

The sky outside her window was no longer black. It was gray. Morning gray. With any luck, Lionel and Buster would be here soon, and she could set Lionel to discovering the spell that would weaken Scrydan. That wouldn't happen if Lionel couldn't open the front door and come inside.

Fighting Lucien was harder than she'd expected. Every strike hurt her, more than it seemed to hurt him.

Eve drew back her hand again, but stopped with her fist in midair. She couldn't bear to hit the man beneath her again. There had to be another way to fight him, another way to weaken Scrydan. She relaxed her fingers and laid her trembling hand on his face. Her knuckles were raw and red, she had hit him so hard, so many times.

"Lucien, can you hear me?" she whispered. "I know you're still in there." She let her fingers stroke his stubbled cheek. "I love you. No matter what happened to bring us here. No matter that I don't know in my heart that we'll ever make things right. I love you."

Scrydan scowled from behind long strands of

dark hair that had fallen across his face. "Do you really think that matters?"

"I do," she answered calmly as she lovingly brushed those strands away from his face. "I believe love is stronger than hate, stronger than fear. It's certainly stronger than you. I don't imagine you understand that concept. Love."

"Lust," he countered. "What you two felt for each other, before I arrived, was lust. Nothing more."

"Not lust, not mere affection . . . love. It's what brought me here. It's what keeps Lucien alive, even now."

"Not for long," Scrydan whispered. "He's almost completely gone, you know. He's weak."

"I don't believe you." She wondered if he could tell how much of a lie that was. Probably so.

"Would you care to make a trade?" he offered casually.

Her heart clenched, and every nerve in her body went tense. "What kind of trade?"

"I let your friends go. All of them."

"They're still alive?" she asked.

"At the moment, yes."

She couldn't believe him, couldn't trust him at all. But what choice did she have but to listen? "And what do you want in return?"

"You release me, and then we walk out of here together."

"Why? Why would you let us all live?"

"I see no reason not to be honest with you, Evie. I won't keep *you* alive very long. These hands will choke the life out of you, once and for all." He flexed his bound fists. "When the time is right, of course. When it's just the two of us. I might allow Lucien to hang on just long enough to watch. Between the two of you that should provide a feast of fear that will keep me strong for a very long time."

"If you have Lucien's body and you're away from the hotel, why do you need the fear?"

He leaned close to her again. "I like the way it tastes."

If Lucien didn't walk out of the hotel, she didn't care if she survived or not. She didn't want to die . . . but to sacrifice herself for five other people didn't seem like such a bad idea.

"You would have to let them go, first," she whispered.

"You don't trust me, Evie?"

"No. I don't trust you and I never will." She took a ragged breath. "And stop calling me Evie," she commanded hoarsely.

That request made him smile again. "Do we have a deal, lover?"

Her life for five. It wasn't much of a choice. "Deal."

O'Hara was pacing again, hands behind his back and steps long and quick, while Daisy stood very still, hands clasped and mind spinning. They were no longer lost in complete darkness. Morning was coming, and with it a gray light that broke through the window and illuminated the room. It was a shabby, dusty room, she now saw, and there were spiderwebs in every corner.

It was best not to look at the spiderwebs or the old bed or the chair where they had passed much of the night. Watching O'Hara was more comforting than allowing her mind to wander.

He was angry, still. He would never forgive her

that one foolish lapse, in thinking Lionel a Viking-like manly creation! Not that it mattered if he forgave her or not. If they got out of here, Quigley O'Hara would leave Plummerville rather quickly, she assumed. Why would he stay? Certainly not for her. He led an exciting life. He'd surely find Plummerville, and her, incredibly boring. It was just as well that he get out of town before he could inadvertently let her secret slip.

Everyone made mistakes. Most were not as colossal as hers, but still . . .

Who was she kidding? Even if O'Hara had once liked her a little, he didn't now. He knew she was weak, and flighty, and stupid. And she'd been right all along. He didn't care enough about her to forgive her one mistake from so long ago that she no longer felt like the same girl who had fallen in love and let her heart and her body rule her head.

It might be different if that night hadn't been so memorable, in a wonderful way. She might be able to dismiss the horrid mistake if that night had been dark and painful and frightening.

That night had been none of those things. She'd loved lying with Tucker just as she'd loved him. She'd adored being a wife, before she was actually a wife. She'd enjoyed the sensations, the closeness, the way it felt to have the man she loved inside her. That wanton streak she'd discovered that night, the passion she tried to hide, only made her guilt sharper, harder to bury.

She tried to soothe her worries about O'Hara and the jaded past by thinking of other things. Poor Katherine and Garrick. Until recently, they hadn't been able to get along at all. They had done much better, of late, but she wondered how they were faring, wherever they might be trapped. The kitchen, she supposed.

Eve was with Lucien . . . or Scrydan. What if he managed to get free? She'd seen him there as they'd walked down the second floor hallway, tied to the bed and looking terribly wicked. Would Eve be persuaded to let him go, in these circumstances?

Hugh had fallen, O'Hara said. Which meant that if he had survived he was all alone. That would be the worst, she imagined, to be alone in this hotel all night with no one to talk to. With no one to hold.

"Thank you," she whispered.

O'Hara stopped pacing and glared at her. "For what?"

Daisy shrugged her shoulders. "Just for . . . everything. I would not have survived the night sane and sensible if not for you."

"I suppose you're welcome," he said ungraciously.

"There's no need to be snippy."

"I think there's every . . ."

Before he could finish the sentence, the door popped open. All the doors popped open. She heard them, up and down the hall, on the floor below. The doors creaked and banged and whooshed, as they opened one after another. O'Hara wasted no time. He grabbed her wrist and pulled her from the room. As they ran down the hallway he gave her one brief, biting instruction. "Don't look back."

She didn't. O'Hara practically dragged her through the hallway and down the stairs to the second floor. It was a quick, breathless trip.

Even the front door had been thrown open, and morning light spilled into the lobby and up the stairs. Hugh was lying on the floor in front of Lucien's room, conscious but barely so.

One door in the hotel remained closed, and that was the door to the room where Lucien was bound and Eve waited.

"O'Hara?" Eve called through the closed door.

"I'm here," he called. "What happened?"

"Take Hugh and Daisy and get out of here. Katherine and Garrick are in the kitchen. Make sure they get out, too."

"What about you?" O'Hara asked angrily.

A deep voice mumbled something indecipherable. Lucien, but not Lucien.

"You don't have much time," Eve said desperately. "Take everyone and get out!"

O'Hara looked at a dazed Hugh and then at Daisy, and cursed beneath his breath. "Let's go," he mumbled as he lifted Hugh to his feet. The older man could walk, but not without assistance.

"You're not leaving her here!" Daisy said as she followed O'Hara to the stairs. "You're not leaving Eve here to . . . to battle that thing alone."

"I'll come back when the rest of you are safe," he said in a low voice.

"That might be too late!" Daisy said as she followed him down the stairs. As they reached the lobby, Garrick and Katherine emerged from the dining room. It looked as if they had passed a dreadful night. They were both rumpled and flushed, and their clothes were askew as if they'd been fighting something horrid all night long. Poor dears.

"Out," O'Hara said with a nod of his head toward the front door. "Now."

It was all the instruction Garrick and Katherine needed. They ran for the open door, hand in hand.

Daisy stopped a few feet back from the door, while O'Hara assisted a weak and groggy Hugh onto the front porch. "I can't go," she said softly. "I can't leave Eve here!"

O'Hara said nothing. He handed the care of Hugh over to Garrick and stalked back into the hotel lobby. He was going to help her save Eve. Together they would . . .

He grabbed her, tossed her over his shoulder, and carried her onto the front porch. And the moment he unceremoniously dropped her onto her feet, the front door to the Honeycutt Hotel slammed shut.

Fifteen

Eve perched nervously on the edge of the mattress. Scrydan smiled at her. She didn't even try to fool herself into thinking that Lucien was with her. The man before her was all Scrydan.

"Well?" he snapped, tugging at his bound wrists.

"When I'm sure everyone is safe I'll let you go," she said softly. Calmly. She needed calm, at a time like this. Eve rose from the bed and walked to the window. Dawn was here . . . so beautiful. The snow would probably all melt today. There were no clouds to keep the sun from the frozen ground.

She lifted the window and let the cool January air wash over her. In the distance, she saw Lionel and Buster riding toward the hotel, leading several horses as they hurried in this direction. Good. The others would be safely away from here soon.

From this vantage point, she saw that Elijah followed at a distance. Her breath hitched. The boy who had done his best to save Lucien could not come near this hotel. Not with the battle that was still being waged.

How close would Lionel have to be to sense that Elijah was following? How close to the hotel before the psychic might receive a message from her? This place was not safe for a child, she knew that with all her broken heart.

O'Hara walked around the corner of the hotel, staring up at her window the entire way. "What do you think you're doing?" he snapped.

"It was the only way," she explained. "You're all out and safe. That's all that matters."

"It is not!" he shouted. "How can I get back in?"

"Tell him not to try," Scrydan whispered. "Tell him if he comes back into this hotel, I will have his entrails for supper."

She didn't even look toward the bed. "You can't," she said, her insides twisting. "It's too late for that."

Daisy came running around the corner, and O'Hara snapped his head around to look at her. "I told you to stay with the others!"

"I don't have to do what you say." Daisy tilted her head back and looked up at Eve. "I didn't want to leave you in there," she explained. "This cretin carried me out of the hotel."

"Cretin?" O'Hara repeated.

"Good for him," Eve said. "Now I want you to make him do something he doesn't want to do."

"Gladly," Daisy said.

"Make him take you and the others back to Plummerville." She nodded toward the approaching Lionel, Buster, and tethered horses. "There's your escort home. Go out to meet them, and tell Lionel that Elijah is following. Send the boy home. Tell him not to come here again."

"Why not?" Scrydan asked softly. "I won't be here much longer. The boy never seemed very tasty, in any case. He doesn't have the proper imagination."

"Can't you climb out the window?" Daisy asked in a loud whisper everyone could hear.

"Tell her if you try the very walls will shake you loose and you will break your sweet neck," Scrydan whispered.

"I can't," Eve answered simply, staring down at Daisy and O'Hara. "Tell Lionel there was a Melissa here . . ."

"It's time for you to untie me," Scrydan interrupted angrily. "I held up my end of the bargain, now it's your turn."

Eve closed the window, turning her back on O'Hara and Daisy's shouts.

"As soon as they're gone," she said confidently.

"That wasn't part of the deal," Scrydan said, yanking at his right hand and making the headboard crack and jump.

With only her in the house, his energies would be more focused. He would get stronger. Eventually he wouldn't need her to untie him. He'd break free on his own.

"It's a part of the deal now," she whispered. "What's your hurry?"

"I've been trapped here for a very long time," Scrydan said. "Too long. Until Lucien came along, I had forgotten what it felt like to breathe and taste. I had forgotten what it felt like to glide inside a willing woman."

She had begun making love to Scrydan, last night. God in heaven, just last night! But it had been Lucien who made love to her. Lucien who came to the surface to protect her. He wouldn't let Scrydan hurt her, not if he had any strength left.

Lucien was still there, weak but not yet gone.

"If you've waited this long, you can wait a while longer," she said.

"I've waited long enough."

Eve paced restlessly, while Scrydan muttered and yanked at the ropes that bound him. After a few long minutes had passed, she returned to the window. Sure enough, O'Hara and Lionel were leading the others away from the hotel. Elijah was heading toward home. She closed her eyes. They were safe. It was the only way.

She turned around to find Scrydan smiling at her. "Now you will let me go?"

"Not yet." Her wedding gown had what seemed like a hundred tiny buttons down the front. Yes, they were elegant, but what had Laverne been thinking! She began to unfasten those buttons.

"What are you doing?" Scrydan asked.

"You're going to kill me. You have at least been honest with me about that." She did not so much as slow down as she continued her chore, eyes on Scrydan. "Maybe I want to hold Lucien one last time before I untie you. Maybe I want to touch him, flesh to flesh, once more."

"Lucien isn't here."

"Yes, he is." She took her time removing her wedding dress. It was a chore Lucien himself should have taken on days ago, in their own bedroom, standing beside their own bed. She didn't hurry, but it wasn't a pleasant task. She only got through it remembering that Lucien was in there, somewhere, and this might be the only way she could reach him.

They were at least a mile away from the hotel, and still Daisy chattered in O'Hara's ear. "I can't believe you'd leave them there!" She sniffled and wiped at the tears running down her face. "How could you? What kind of a man are you?"

She didn't take her anger out on everyone. She didn't harangue any of the others. Only him.

"If I were a man," she continued, "I'd still be there fighting for my friends. If you hadn't physically dragged me out of the house . . ."

"Daisy, be quiet," he insisted.

"I will not . . ."

O'Hara glanced at Lionel, who rode blissfully alone. "Have we gone far enough, do you think?"

Lionel closed his eyes and took a deep breath while his horse continued unerringly forward. "Yes," he finally said.

"Far enough for what?" Daisy asked.

One by one they all brought their horses to a halt beneath the shelter of a cluster of trees that grew beside and over the road.

O'Hara ignored Daisy—no easy task since she was riding behind him and hanging on for dear life—and addressed the men. "Garrick, Buster, we'll leave it to you to see the ladies safely home and get Hugh to a doctor."

"I'm fine," Hugh said, in a voice that told everyone present that he was not at all fine. "My place is with you two."

"You're going back?" Daisy asked breathlessly. She leaned as far to the side as possible without falling off, so that all O'Hara had to do was twist his head slightly to see her.

"Yes," he said, offering a hand to assist her to the ground. "Of course."

She took his hand comfortably, no doubt forgetting for the moment about his ability. He tried to block out the feelings that came through, but the sensation of worry was too intense to ignore. Worry for her friends. Worry for him. She hung tightly onto his hand for a moment before she made an effort to swing down. Buster was there to assist her.

"Be careful," she said, looking up at him.

"We will."

"I didn't really mean what I said," she chattered. "I know you're not a coward. I knew you wouldn't just ride off and leave Eve and Lucien there to . . . to . . ." Maybe even Daisy knew that death wasn't the worst of the outcomes that awaited her friends. "Be careful," she said again.

Lionel started riding slowly back toward the hotel, and O'Hara followed. Leaving Daisy behind was much more difficult than he'd expected it might be.

"Will he know we're coming?" he asked, setting his mind on the task ahead.

"Maybe," Lionel said, his mind already working. "It depends. If Eve is putting up a fight, maybe Scrydan will be too occupied with her to sense us."

"Maybe," O'Hara muttered.

"I think I know what to do to get them out," the *Viking* said thoughtfully. "It will be dangerous, but it might be the only way."

"Just tell me what to do. I think we're well beyond worrying about danger, at this point."

"True enough," Lionel said absently.

Much of the snow was gone, but patches of white remained in the shadows of the tall evergreens. Icy snow crackled beneath the horse's hooves, as they retraced their steps. At least Daisy and the others were safe, and Hugh would soon see a doctor. No matter what happened, he could take comfort in that.

"O'Hara," Lionel said in a lowered voice, as they passed beneath the limbs of a tall evergreen tree. "Daisy Willard doesn't like me. She likes *you.*"

"We agreed a long time ago not to read one another," O'Hara snapped.

Lionel grinned. "Oh, I didn't read you, *Quigley.* I read Daisy."

"What's the knife for?" Lucien asked as Eve climbed onto the bed, her wedding gown and underclothes discarded. She had to think of him as Lucien, not Scrydan, to do what had to be done.

"For cutting the ropes," she explained as she clutched Buster's knife a little tighter in her right hand, "when the time is right."

"Now is the time," he insisted.

"Not yet."

She unfastened the buttons that kept his trousers closed, her fingers trembling. They'd made love many times, but this was different. Scrydan ruled Lucien's head and his body. But not his heart. Somehow she was sure of that. The demon hadn't taken over completely. Not yet.

Beneath the confines of his trousers, he was already hard. She freed him, caressed him.

"You could untie me so I can properly participate," Scrydan said, a leer in his voice. "Or are you perverted? Ah, I'll bet you and Lucien used to play this little game. Did he ever tie you up and take you rough? Did he ever hurt you?"

"You know he didn't," she whispered. "Lucien loves me. He would never hurt me."

"So you think I'll let Lucien come out to play just because you want to be his trollop one last time?" Scrydan grinned and winked at her. "You may continue. I don't find you at all unpleasant. But understand that there's no one here but me, Eve. Maybe you know that. Maybe you like me more than you've been letting on."

Surely he knew suggesting that she might find him attractive would be repulsive to her. Scrydan was a demon, a monster. She loved the man he had captured.

"Lucien is here," she whispered. "I can smell him. I can feel him." She ran her hand up his chest and rested her palm over his heart. It beat too fast, and had since the battle inside Lucien had begun. She leaned in close, dangerously close, and raked the tip of her nose against his throat. Her tongue flicked out and tasted his sweat.

"I'm still going to kill you when we get out of here," Scrydan promised.

She straddled him as she had earlier, only this time his manhood was freed and she was naked. He was so close to being inside her, so very close.

"It won't work," he whispered hoarsely. "All you're doing is making me stronger." He leered at her, stared at her bare breasts and flicked his tongue in that direction.

"Then why are you so worried?"

"I'm not worried," he assured her. "You're nothing, lover. You can't hurt me. You can't push me aside to bring back a man who no longer exists. Continue, if you insist, but it's me you're ravishing, not your beloved Lucien."

She couldn't believe that he was right. Lucien had fought his way to the surface once before, when Scrydan had been inside her. He would do it again. He loved her that much, she knew it.

"I think you know it's only me," Scrydan whispered. "Maybe you don't care whose spirit is inside this body. You only care about the body itself."

He was trying to repulse her, trying to make her surrender before she'd even begun.

So many nights she'd touched this body, this man. She knew him so well. Every curve, every hollow. More than that, she knew the heart that beat in this chest, the spirit that was Lucien Thorpe.

Eve held her breath as she guided him to her, as she moved against him so that he entered her slowly. He lay there, motionless, that damnable smile on his face. Scrydan was here, he was in control, but Lucien was here, too. She felt it with all her heart.

"I love you, Lucien," she whispered as she moved gently atop him, her hips swaying. "I love you more than I've ever loved anything in my entire life. Even when I'm angry, even when I don't think there's any hope for us, I love you."

The knife was in her right hand, grasped tight. Her left hand reached out to touch Lucien's cheek. A cold wind from nowhere circled around her, chilling her bare body. She paid it no mind. There was only Lucien, and the way they came together. Nothing else mattered.

He didn't make a move to bite her, as he had earlier. She rose and fell slowly, taking him in deep, closing her eyes and remembering all the times they'd been together this way. It was more than sex, more than physical.

Lucien was the better half of her, just as she was the better half of him. Separate they were less than they were together. Together they could do anything. Together they could fight this thing that had taken up residence in Lucien's body.

The cold wind died, the man beneath her moved his hips and moaned low in his throat. Eve opened her eyes and knew without a doubt that she was looking at Lucien. Those were his eyes, staring at her. "Fight him," she whispered as she lowered herself to take him deep again. "You're mine, Lucien. I won't let you go so easily."

She reached out to sever one rope.

"No," he said as the blade touched twine. "Not yet. It's not time. He's still here."

"Fight him, Lucien. Fight him for me. For us. For the life we will never have if he wins."

"Evie," he whispered.

"Fight him for the children we haven't had time to make. For all we know the first of those babies is growing inside me right now. If we let Scrydan win that baby will never be born. We'll die here in this awful place, you and me and our babies."

"I won't let that happen," Lucien whispered hoarsely.

"I know you won't. Resist him, Lucien, push him out. You have the strength, you have the will, and you have me." She swayed into him, rose up slowly. "Don't let him sleep, don't let him hide. Push him out and once he's gone close the doors in your mind so that he can't find his way back in. He's been working too hard to hold on to you and control the hotel and the spirits in it. He's weak. Now's the time." She reached out and cut the rope that tethered one hand to one headboard post.

Lucien's arm snapped up and around to grasp her tight. He swayed against and into her, and she shifted the knife to the other hand and cut the other rope. As before, that arm encircled and held her.

It was Lucien who held her, she knew it as the angry hotel began to shake. The walls, the floor, the furniture. It all quivered with anger.

"Lucien?" she whispered.

"Yes, Evie, it's me."

She kept her arms around him, smiling as one last time she sank down to take him as deep as possible. The pleasure exploded inside her, and as she clenched around him Lucien quivered and found his own fulfillment. While the angry house shuddered, while the doors banged open and shut, they dismissed everything but each other.

Eve was warm again. Lucien's heart had returned to a normal rhythm. They were one, still, physically and spiritually. Together they had pushed Scrydan out. At least, it seemed that way to her.

"He's gone?" she asked as she disentangled their bodies and cut the ropes, one and then another, that bound Lucien's legs.

He nodded. "Completely. Can we get out of this cursed place?"

"Please." She grabbed her wedding gown and stepped into it, quickly slipping her arms through the sleeves. There wasn't time for anything else, not for shoes or her chemise or that expensive corset. She tugged on the gown and buttoned a few of the tiny buttons down the front.

"You can finish that outside," Lucien said, taking her hand and all but dragging her from the room. They ran down the stairs, toward the front entrance to the hotel. Lucien tried to open the door, but it wouldn't budge.

"No matter what you do," Eve said, "keep those doors in your mind tightly closed. Don't let him back in."

Lucien nodded as he glanced around the large room. "So many spirits."

"You can't let any of them in," she insisted. "You know what happened last time."

"I wish you had brought the specter-o-meter."

Now she knew she had Lucien back! "How do we get out of here?" She held his hand tightly. Separate, they were both vulnerable. Together they were unbeatable.

They heard quick hoofbeats, and ran to a window to look outside. It was O'Hara and Lionel, their horses approaching the hotel at breakneck speed. They both dismounted and ran toward the hotel. It was Lionel who saw them first.

"Is the door refusing to open again?" he asked loudly, so they could hear him through the shuddering walls.

"Yes," Lucien shouted back. With one hand he tried to lift the window. It didn't budge. "I'm going to break this window."

"No!" Lionel shouted. "Wait." He closed his eyes and went still there on the porch, but only for a moment. "When he opened his eyes he laid them on Lucien and stared a moment longer. Was he weighing Lucien? Making sure it was truly Lucien he was rescuing? Finally he smiled. "Stand close to the door and be ready to run, but stay well away from the windows. I have an idea."

* * *

"Are you finally going to tell me about this idea?" O'Hara snapped as Lionel walked away from the hotel.

"The message from Eve, the mention of Melissa, opened a new door. I had a vision that a window was broken, and it started a reaction of some kind."

"A reaction," O'Hara repeated.

"Windows exploding. Walls crumbling." Lionel looked at O'Hara. "The end of the Honeycutt Hotel and everything in it. Scrydan is weak, perhaps weaker than he has ever been. Now is the time to strike. If the hotel dies, he dies."

"And the trapped spirits?"

"Finally free to move on."

O'Hara nodded.

"But it's dangerous," Lionel added. "I can't be sure exactly what will happen. Nothing here is as it seems. My visions are altered in this place. Everything here is warped."

"Do you have any other ideas?" O'Hara asked.

Lionel shook his head.

Moving quickly, they led the horses away from the hotel and into the woods, where the animals would be protected by space and the wide trunks of old trees. As they returned to the weathered structure, they gathered a number of good throwing rocks.

"What if it doesn't work?" O'Hara asked glumly. "Basically we're throwing stones at a haunted hotel and expecting it will actually lead to something greater."

"It's more than that," Lionel said. "Melissa was a witch who cursed the place, years ago. For some reason I can't hear her clearly, but I do know one thing. Before she died she placed a curse on the hotel. The beginning of destruction will bring the end. I suspect she planned to begin the destruction herself, but was killed before she could complete the task."

"It's worth a try," O'Hara said.

They stood as far back as possible, and they each hefted a rock. O'Hara tossed one rock straight up and then caught it deftly in his hand.

"Stand away from the windows," Lionel shouted, for Lucien and Eve's benefit. Then he drew back his arm and threw a large rock toward a second-story window. And missed.

O'Hara snorted. "Some *Viking* you are," he muttered as he tossed his own rock to a second-story window.

The rock he threw found its mark, and a window shattered. There was a moment of complete silence. Nothing happened. Nothing! O'Hara groaned and tossed his rocks to the ground. So much for Lionel's vision.

And then, a heartbeat later, it began. Every window in the place exploded, glass flying out of and into the hotel. The sound was loud and shrill, explosive and angry.

They shielded their eyes from the few shards of glass that came that far, and Lionel said, "Nice throw."

"Baseball," O'Hara explained simply.

The destruction didn't stop with the explosion of the windows. The walls shook, the porch covering began to shake perilously.

"I'm going in to get them," O'Hara said, taking one step forward before Lionel stopped him.

"That won't be necessary."

The front door flew open, and Lucien and Eve

ran out. Lucien was protecting Eve as best he could, shielding her from flying glass and debris that seemed to come out of nowhere. Beyond the open door, it looked as if a small tornado was tearing through the lobby.

Lucien wore nothing but a pair of dark, half-buttoned trousers. Eve was barefoot, and her stained and ripped wedding gown was more off her than on. They were both wild-haired, and Lucien looked as if someone had recently pummeled him about the face.

But they were alive, and they were relatively well.

As the couple reached O'Hara and Lionel, all four began to run for the forest.

"Am I the only one who wants to stay and watch?" Lucien asked.

"Yes," three voices answered at once.

"But it is fascinating," he argued. "We might never witness such a phenomenon again."

"It's a dangerous place for you still, Lucien," Lionel said as he helped the battered man into the saddle of one of their horses. "I suggest we all move on, as quickly as possible." He then assisted Eve into the space before Lucien. "It's for the best," he added solemnly.

Lucien nodded, and Lionel jumped up to ride behind O'Hara. As they took their leave at a steady pace, O'Hara looked back, leaning to the side to see past the man who was perched behind him.

Shingles flew off the roof, walls shuddered and then fell to the ground in pieces. Four white columns dropped, one by one, and in a matter of moments the hotel collapsed in on itself.

At the sound of the crash, Lucien stopped his horse and turned it around. O'Hara did the same, and the four of them watched the ensuing destruction wide-eyed and silent.

O'Hara, who rarely saw anything supernatural without actually touching a person or a thing, saw a collection of lights rise as the building fell. Fully formed ghosts and bits of brightness amongst the dark ascended toward the blue sky in a colorful, bright swirl. Red, yellow, blue, all the colors of the rainbow escaped into the waiting sky.

Something darker tried to follow. A swirl of gray and black, a mass larger than the other spirits, chased them into the clouds. Scrydan. But while the other spirits escaped, the darker cloud was trapped. Scrydan was still tied to the house that was quickly destroying itself. He was still trapped in the land.

O'Hara expected to see the dark cloud drift down into the land, and it seemed the spirit tried.

But the witch's spell worked too well. The dark cloud swirled above the collapsed hotel for a moment, and then there was a howl—like the wind through the trees. But there was no wind, there was only Scrydan's scream.

And as they watched, the dark cloud literally fell apart. It broke into smaller pieces, dissolved, and screamed one last time.

Eve turned her face into Lucien's chest, and the two of them held each other tight as Lucien turned the horse around. Lionel sighed, in relief and exhaustion, as he and O'Hara watched the last of the dark cloud fade away.

"Is it really gone?" O'Hara asked.

"Yes," Lionel said.

"Should we go back and . . ."

"No," Lionel answered quickly. "There's no reason to go back."

Which meant there was no place to go but forward, and that was a very scary thought.

Sixteen

What do you say to a woman who saves not only your life, but your very soul? *I love you* seemed trite and inadequate. He'd said those words a hundred times, and he meant every word, every time, but it wasn't enough in this instance. Thank you? Not even close to enough.

Fortunately Lucien didn't have to say anything, at the moment. Eve was sound asleep in his arms, as they rode slowly toward home.

"Are you sure you don't want my coat?" O'Hara offered for the third time, as he pulled his horse up alongside Lucien's.

"No, thank you." He should be cold, he knew that, but he wasn't. Scrydan was gone, dead, no more, and yet Lucien still carried a small piece of him inside, as he always carried a remnant of any soul he channeled. It never lasted. An unfamiliar accent, the memories of another person, a slice of a personality unlike his own . . . they never stayed with him long. Minutes, hours perhaps. But then, he'd never been possessed by anything as evil as Scrydan, before, and he'd never kept another spirit inside him for such an extended period of time. Who knew how he might react? That little bit of evil that lived inside Lucien scared him.

Lucien remembered everything Scrydan had done, before his death and after. He remembered as if he had been there, as if he had done those things. Logically, he knew he had not. He knew the memories would fade.

But what if they didn't fade this time? What if Scrydan was always with him?

"I'm not cold," he said again. Barefoot and naked from the waist up, he should be. "But if you don't mind I will take that coat, for Eve." She wore her wedding gown, with those long satin sleeves, but it wasn't enough. The gown was low cut, and she shivered even as she slept.

"Of course," O'Hara said eagerly.

They brought their horses to a halt, and both O'Hara and Lionel quickly removed their jackets. Lucien took them both, and arranged the garments around the sleeping Eve. She stirred, but did not wake. She was truly exhausted.

"I still despise you," Lucien said to O'Hara as he tucked a bit of one of the jackets around Eve's arm. "And one day you and I are going to have a long discussion about the proper way to treat a lady."

O'Hara sighed. "Why don't you just pummel me and get it over with," he said passionlessly.

"I might." It was a tempting idea, but at the moment there was nothing he could do. He had no strength, and he certainly didn't have the heart to lash out at the man who had helped to save his life and Eve's.

"Looks like someone pummeled you pretty good," O'Hara added. "What happened?"

Lucien lifted one hand and touched a sensitive place on his jaw. It was bruised, surely. One eye did seem to be a little bit swollen. He had to think for a moment, and then it came to him, in a flash. He'd been tied to the bed, and Eve had been atop him, hitting him, crying, begging him to come back.

"It was Eve," Lionel said absently. "She fought Scrydan the only way she knew how."

Lucien prodded his horse to move forward, and O'Hara and Lionel followed.

"She was a warrior," Lionel continued in a softer voice. "She truly saved you, Lucien. She saved us all."

"I know."

They had hours ahead of them before they'd reach Plummerville, especially with two riders to each horse. Hours where he didn't feel the cold, where he wondered if the demon still lived inside him. Hours where he'd pass the time wondering if he should marry Eve or let her go. He loved her too much to let her go; but at the same time he loved her too much to take the chance that something like this might happen again.

"You're a very lucky man," O'Hara said.

"I know."

"Do you really?" O'Hara asked sharply. "Do you know how few men ever know the kind of love Eve has for you? She knows what you can do, how you live your life, what you see every day, and still she wants you. She knows who you are in the pit of your soul, and still she loves you. It's more than lucky. You're blessed."

"I don't need you to tell me that," Lucien answered in a low voice.

"Someone obviously needs to. After all this . . . after what she did for you. If you leave it will destroy her."

Lucien glanced sharply at O'Hara. "Have you

taken up mind reading? You certainly haven't touched me."

"I don't need to," O'Hara said. "The truth is written all over your face. Any member of that blasted idiotic Plummerville Ghost Society could decipher it."

"Eve is none of your business." Lucien held her a little bit tighter.

"Eve is my *friend,* and that means anyone who mistreats her makes their behavior and her safety my business."

"Touching," Lucien muttered.

"Stop it," Lionel commanded. "You two are giving me a headache, squabbling like a couple of old women."

"O'Hara obviously thinks he has the right . . ."

"Stop it!" Lionel said again. "This is not the time or the place for you two to argue. We're cold, we're hungry, and we've been through hell."

Lucien took a deep breath of cold air and glanced down at Eve. As if she knew he was watching her, her eyes fluttered and opened. She smiled up at him, briefly and wanly, and then closed her eyes again and instantly fell back to sleep.

Plummerville. Home at last. Katherine didn't know whether to be elated or disappointed. Coming home meant an end to what she'd found with Garrick.

For the first part of their journey, Garrick had ridden with Hugh, since his strength was needed to support the injured man. Daisy, who did not ride well, had hung onto Buster. Katherine had a saddle and a horse to herself. Too bad. She would have liked an excuse to hold onto Garrick for a while longer.

Once they'd collected their abandoned wagon and made Hugh comfortable, she'd sat next to Garrick for a while, on the driver's seat.

But coming home meant an end to fanciful dreams. There would be no yellow dresses. No going west. No anything, not for her and Garrick. In the end she was a widow who eked out a meager existence, and he was the son of the richest man in town. They didn't belong together, no matter how good it felt when he touched her.

They didn't have a future together, and she refused to be his mistress. It would be tempting, if he came to her one night and looked at her with those beautiful eyes of his. But that would make her no better than one of his Savannah whores. Katherine Cassidy might not have much, but she would be no man's harlot.

People ran out to greet them, emerging from shops along the main way, and Garrick asked one man to fetch the doctor. He guided the wagon close to the doctor's office, and when the physician who served all of Plummerville came rushing out, the two men assisted Hugh from the wagon's bed.

Garrick and Buster supported Hugh, and the three men and Daisy followed the doctor toward his office.

Katherine left the wagon, but she stood apart from the others, watching them all band together to aid the injured man. When they reached the door, Garrick stumbled and glanced back.

"Aren't you coming in?" he asked.

Katherine shook her head. "I can't. I need to get home."

He nodded and returned his attention to Hugh Felder, who was having a difficult time remaining on his feet.

And just like that, it was over.

Once they reached the main road, Lucien seemed to be confident of the way. O'Hara hung back and allowed him to lead.

Lucien, the sonofabitch, was going to leave Eve again. O'Hara saw the truth on Lucien's face. Eve had almost died to save him, she had been willing to sacrifice herself to save them all, and he was going to leave her! It would crush her, to lose the man she loved. It would kill her as surely as Scrydan would have, if he'd been given the chance.

O'Hara wished he could knock some sense into the man. Didn't Lucien know how rare Eve was?

He'd believed Daisy to be rare, for a while. Once she'd discovered that they weren't going to die after all, her tune had changed. She'd expressed her regret over allowing him to touch her, and even though she had seemed sincere in her wishes that he take care in his rescue efforts, he suspected her real concern was for her friends. Not for him.

Was he doomed to live a life alone? Hugh had done so, since his wife's death, and he seemed content enough. Lionel apparently liked being alone most of the time. He didn't seem to mind at all that there was no room in his life for a woman of consequence.

O'Hara did mind, very much.

Eve moved. Her hand raked up Lucien's bare

back, the movement slow and easy. Was she shifting about in her sleep? Or had she awakened just long enough to tell her sweetheart that she loved him?

"It's not our business," Lionel said softly, the voice intrusive in O'Hara's ear.

"You're not supposed to do that!" O'Hara insisted.

"I can't help it," Lionel protested. "I feel like you're shouting in my head. What happened at the hotel, it drained me. I don't have the strength to block everything, at the moment. For God's sake, let it go."

"What if I can't?"

"I don't think you have any choice."

Like the rest of his life, from the beginning to this moment, he had no choice. Lucien was going to break the heart of a good woman, Eve was going to wither without the man she loved, Daisy was going to hide from him and every other man, and he would continue on as he had, solving other people's problems and ignoring his own.

What he wouldn't give for a somewhat normal life. Surely he wasn't alone in his desire for the little things other men took for granted. A woman. Children. A home. Did the others ever long for something more than this? Did they ever crave what they could not have?

"Yes," Lionel whispered.

For once, O'Hara didn't chastise his friend for peeking into his mind.

Plummerville waited before them, quiet and peaceful. Eve belonged here. It was the home she had made for herself, the sanctuary she had come to after he'd broken her heart. No matter what happened in the days and months and years to come, she would be safe here.

It was late afternoon, and already the sky was turning gray. The days were short now, but winter would soon turn to spring and the days would grow longer. Eve could plant that garden she'd been talking about. She and Daisy would plan cozy dinner parties. With or without him, life would go on here.

Buster saw them and came running out of the doctor's office. Lucien slowed the pace of his horse, but did not stop. "Hugh?" he asked simply.

Buster nodded. "He'll be okay, the doc says." His eyes flitted to Eve. "How is she?"

"Sleeping," Lucien said in a low voice, so as not to disturb her. As if he could! She had barely stirred on the long trip from the Honeycutt Hotel.

"She's not . . ." Buster began, swallowing the last word he could not say.

"She's fine," Lucien assured the farmer. "Just fine."

Lionel and O'Hara halted their horse and dismounted, anxious to check on Hugh and see for themselves that their colleague was doing well. Lucien didn't stop, but continued on toward Eve's cottage.

He was beginning to feel the cold. Was that a good sign? He couldn't be certain, but he thought . . . perhaps. People stared as they passed, and he was not surprised. He was half dressed, Eve was asleep in his arms, in her wedding gown. Stories of the weekend's disaster had surely begun to circulate, since the others had arrived earlier in the afternoon. How many of those stories were based on truth? They were so fantastic, no one who hadn't been there would ever believe what had happened.

As he reached Eve's little house, the red door welcoming them, the door swung open and four people poured out. Eve's aunt and uncle, two wide-eyed cousins.

"Wake up, darling," he whispered into Eve's ear. "You're home."

Her eyes fluttered open and she smiled up at him. "I don't think I have ever been so happy to be home in my entire life."

With effort, he gave her a smile. It seemed to comfort her, for the time being. He assisted her down and into her uncle's steady arms, and then he dismounted and lifted her into his arms once again. She sighed and laid her head on his shoulder, and closed her eyes.

"Good heavens!" Eve's Aunt Constance shouted as Lucien carried Eve through the open doorway and into the house. "What happened? Look at the two of you, dirty and bedraggled, and Mr. Thorpe, you are barely dressed! Girls!" she snapped. "Turn around. This is not a proper sight for innocent eyes."

Eve's meek cousins obeyed without a single protest.

Lucien did his best to ignore them all, as he stepped onto the staircase to the sound of the front door being slammed shut.

"Stop right there!" Constance commanded.

Lucien stopped, then turned with a sleeping Eve in his arms to look down into the entryway. The two girls faced the closed door. Constance and Harold Phillips glared angrily up at him.

"What have you done to my niece?" Constance screeched. "And how dare you presume to walk into this house as if you live here!"

Eve had been trying for months to quell his need for telling the truth at all times. She said while honesty could be an admirable trait, when it was overdone it could be annoying.

At the moment, he didn't have the time or the energy to sort through the consequences of his words. "I do live here," he said in a calm voice. "And if you raise your voice again and wake Eve, I will toss you out on your ear, family or not."

Aunt Constance turned red in the face, and one of the girls, the older one he thought, took a quick peek over her shoulder.

"How dare you," Constance's husband said irately.

"Go home," Lucien answered in a calm voice. "Eve is exhausted, and she needs me to take care of her. I can't do that and argue with you at the same time. Go home," he said again, and then he turned and resumed his trek up the stairs.

"Stop right there," Constance ordered. "Something is very strange here. Something is not quite right. What kind of a scientist are you? What is going on?"

Lucien stopped at the top of the stairs and turned to face the intruders again. "I'm not a scientist," he said. "I'm a medium."

"A what?" Eve's uncle asked sharply.

"I talk to dead people. I see ghosts in every corner, I speak to spirits that no one else sees or hears."

Aunt Constance placed a hand on her forehead and swayed as if she might swoon. When she saw that her husband was paying no attention and would not be handy to catch her, she quickly regained her composure.

"Really," Lucien said with a shake of his head. "If you'd pay attention to what's going on around you, you would have heard about me by now. I'm fairly well known in Savannah, and everyone in Plummerville knows what I do. But you . . . you two are so wrapped up in yourselves that you can't see anything beyond your own rather large noses."

"That's rude and uncalled for," Constance snapped.

"It's the truth," Lucien said as he turned away. This time when they called, he refused to listen.

He stepped into Eve's bedroom—their bedroom—and very gently laid her on the bed. She sighed, but didn't move. "I love you," he whispered. "More than I thought I could ever love anything on this earth."

She slept on, oblivious, as he covered her with the quilt. They both needed a long hot bath, food and drink. But for now, what they needed most was sleep. He placed his head beside hers on the pillow, draped his arm around her waist, and closed his eyes. Images he didn't want to see danced behind his closed lids. They had been Scrydan's memories, and now they were his.

He pushed the memories away and forcibly replaced them with his own. In all his good memories, Eve was there. He held onto her and fell into a deep, dreamless sleep.

Katherine nearly jumped out of her skin when the rap on her front door startled her. Who could be calling so late? It was nearly ten o'clock.

Her heart climbed into her throat. She knew very well who it was. She knew very well that only Garrick would come to her house so late. For a moment she considered not answering the door, but then the knock came again, more insistent this time.

She steeled her spine and her heart as she opened the door on the cold night and the man who waited on her doorstep. As soon as she'd arrived home she'd taken a long hot bath, donned clean clothes, and brushed out her freshly shampooed hair. She had almost washed the scent of the Honeycutt Hotel off of her, but she didn't think she'd ever be rid of the scent of Garrick.

Garrick looked just as he had when they'd ridden away from the house, in the suit he'd chosen for Eve and Lucien's wedding, with his hair mussed and his eyes so very tired. The heartless order to go died on her lips, when he looked her in the eye.

"I spoke to my father," he said. "It's all true. Everything Lucien said is true."

She took his hand and drew him inside. "It's too cold for you to stand outside," she said sensibly. "Come in, and I'll make you some tea."

"I don't want tea," he said as he came into her house. "I just want to be with you." He reached for her, and when she didn't respond he let his hand drop. "Is he still here? Jerome?"

She shook her head. "No. I haven't felt his presence at all, since I got home. He's gone."

"Good."

Compared to his own home, Garrick must find her little house depressing and small, cramped and ordinary. But then, he didn't look around him. His eyes remained on her. "In the back of my mind, I'd convinced myself that what Lucien said about my mother wasn't true, that he'd made it up because I didn't have any dark secrets for him to reveal. Pretty stupid, don't you think?"

"No. That's not at all stupid."

"When I confronted my father, I expected him to deny everything." He ran a hand over his tired, stubbled face. "He didn't deny anything. My real mother was his mistress. She was murdered, right here in Plummerville, when I was a child."

"I'm so sorry."

"All I could think about, while he was confessing every ugly detail, was coming here to see you." He sounded as if that fact surprised him as much as it did her.

"You can't stay," she whispered.

"Why not?"

"You don't belong here."

He wrapped his arms around her and pulled her close. "I think I do."

He was tired and upset, so she allowed him to hold her. She even wrapped her own arms around his waist and held on tight. Just for tonight.

"Everything will be all right," she said, speaking into his shoulder. "Your father is still your father, and your place with him is secure. I'm sure he . . . loves you." If she had a child, she would love it no matter what. Surely it was the same for people all over the world. Even Douglas Hunt.

"He was furious to hear that I'd found out about my real mother, but once he started telling me what had happened, it was like he couldn't stop."

"The excitement will blow over soon enough."

"I wanted him to stop. I wanted to come here

and see you. I needed to see your face, to touch you." He shifted his body back and, with a finger beneath her chin, made her look up at him. "I feel better already."

She allowed him to kiss her, because she sensed he needed the closeness, that he needed a friend. But she didn't fool herself. They were home, and everything had changed. His father would forgive him for discovering the secret, he would forgive his father for keeping that secret for so long. Garrick would settle back in at the mill, and there would be no room in his life for a poor widow who had been there when his world had fallen apart, for a while. He would have felt some warmth for any woman who had been with him at that time. He would have turned to anyone who had the ability to comfort him, when they thought they might not live through the night.

So she kissed Garrick, and held him tight, and made herself forget that she loved him.

In the middle of the night, Eve woke with a start. It took her a moment to realize that she slept in her own room, in her own house, with Lucien beside her.

He slept soundly, and oh, he looked terrible! His face was battered and he needed a shave. His hair was tangled and, in spite of the fact that he'd slept long hours while they'd been in the haunted hotel, there were bags under his eyes. She knew she must look just as bad, after everything they'd been through.

She snuggled a bit closer. There had been a time when she had been so sure they would not survive.

Not both of them, perhaps not either of them! And yet here they were, together, safe, happy. They were home.

Lucien didn't look particularly happy, but then he had been through a lot. He had almost died . . . he had almost lost the essence of his being. His spirit, his soul. Scrydan would have gladly trapped it there in that awful hotel with all the others.

Eve rolled gently against Lucien, crinkling loudly in the process. Lifting the quilt, she peeked beneath. She still wore the wedding dress, which was now beyond ruined. The gown had cost her a small fortune, and it had been so beautiful! At least for a while. Now it was simply a mass of wrinkled satin. It could not possibly be saved.

At the next wedding she'd be practical, as she had been the first time around. No more white satin. Nothing fancy for her. Lucien had been right all along. They should have let the justice of the peace marry them months ago!

As if he knew she was thinking about him, Lucien opened his eyes sleepily. He looked at her hard, as if he could see right through her. He reached out and laid his hand on her neck, letting the fingers drift slowly downward. "I love you, Evie," he whispered, still half asleep.

"I love you, too."

He wrapped an arm around her and pulled her close. "I wish I could make everything right again, with a snap of my fingers and a wave of my hand."

"Everything is right," she assured him. "We're here. We're together. Everyone is safe."

"Hold me," he whispered. "I'm cold."

She complied, wrapping her arms around Lucien and snuggling against him. He was indeed cold, his skin chilled. After days of being unnaturally warm, the coolness seemed more pronounced than usual.

"Is that better?" she asked.

"Yes," he whispered, and then he drifted off to sleep.

Seventeen

The hot bath had been an amazingly effective therapy, Eve thought as she made a nice hot cup of tea. It was one of the small things a person might take for granted, until they ended up spending a weekend in a haunted hotel where there were no such comforts as warm baths and steaming sweet tea.

Lucien still slept. She looked in on him frequently, just to assure herself that he was breathing correctly and that his skin was not turning warm again. Every time she opened the door to peek in, her heart stopped and she half expected to find him tied to the bed, a Scrydan grin on his face and the heat radiating off his skin.

But he slept peacefully and unrestrained, and when she crept to the bedside to touch him, his skin was cool—as befitted a January morning.

The knock on the kitchen door was familiar, and Eve rushed to answer with more than a touch of relief. As soon as she opened the door Daisy rushed in, arms opened wide.

"You're truly all right," Daisy said breathlessly as she hugged Eve with all her might.

"Yes," Eve answered, still not quite believing her luck, herself.

"And Lucien?" Daisy asked as she released her hold on Eve and stepped back, closing the door on the blast of a winter breeze that made her black cloak dance. "Lionel and O'Hara said he was going to be fine, but . . . I wanted to be sure."

"He'll be back to normal in no time," Eve said, a false lilt of assurance in her voice. She couldn't be sure that anything would ever be truly right again.

Instead of professing her own relief at the simple fact that they'd survived, Daisy broke into tears. "I'm sorry," she said as she fanned her face and tried unsuccessfully to stop crying. "It's just . . . it was all so . . . I can't believe . . ."

Eve wrapped her arms around her friend and hugged her tight, understanding very well why Daisy was so upset. Until this weekend, Daisy had never been subjected to the realities of the supernatural world. Ghosts. Doors that wouldn't open. The possession of an evil spirit. All these things were new to Daisy. She'd held up quite well, considering.

When the sobbing stopped, Daisy backed away and held her chin high. Red-eyed, shaking slightly, she still managed to look strangely brave. "I'm sorry," Daisy said again. "I'm just not going to think of it again," she said firmly. "That's the only way to handle the situation. I will simply tell myself that the past three days did not happen." She seemed pleased with the convoluted idea. "If I do that often enough, eventually I'll be able to dismiss everything I saw and did as nothing more than a bad dream."

Denial. That was Daisy's way.

"I guess we all do what we have to in order to survive," Eve said. "Tea?"

"Please."

They passed the next half hour talking about everything but the Honeycutt Hotel. Talk about recipes, fashions, and good old-fashioned gossip kept them occupied. Eve began to think that maybe Daisy's idea wasn't so convoluted after all. She felt so much better after a little normal conversation.

Daisy had become her friend so quickly, even though in truth they had little in common. It was hard to explain how you could be drawn to one person and not another, in love and in friendships. Right now it didn't matter that she and Daisy had little in common. They were survivors. This weekend had bonded them to each other like soldiers who went into battle together. Daisy was no longer simply a friend; she was family.

The flow of their conversation finally ended, and Daisy sighed. It was one of those long, drawn-out sighs that signaled something was coming.

"You are so lucky, to have Lucien," Daisy said on the tail end of the sigh.

"Yes, I am." Was Daisy still smitten with Lionel? It didn't matter. Lionel wouldn't be in Plummerville much longer. Neither would Hugh or O'Hara. There was always another job right around the corner. Still, Eve didn't want to see her friend's heart broken. Daisy was so fragile. A broken heart would surely lay her low.

"Even though Lucien has his strange abilities, you two have managed to find love." Daisy lifted a hand, palm up. "Is it difficult, to know that he will always see things others do not?"

Oh, dear. Daisy was definitely still smitten. "Sometimes it is difficult," Eve said calmly. "But you have to remember that I've lived a very large part of my life among such curiosities."

"While your father tried to communicate with your late mother," Daisy said.

"Yes. So you see, I'm accustomed to the strange things Lucien sees and hears."

Daisy wrinkled her nose. "It doesn't bother you?"

Eve smiled and shook her head. "Not at all."

"But Lucien can't read your mind." Daisy said with a lift of her eyebrows. "He might talk to ghosts now and then, but it's not like he can see inside you. That would be just too difficult, wouldn't it? Why, think of the problems that would cause!"

Eve didn't know what to say. She certainly didn't want to encourage Daisy to chase Lionel, but at the same time she couldn't very well tell her friend that such a relationship was impossible. "I imagine it would take someone special to endure the hardships that would come with such an association."

Daisy seemed deflated. "Life just isn't fair," she said, practically pouting.

"No," Eve answered. "It's not."

Daisy walked home, dragging her feet. Eve had said that she had no idea when she and Lucien might reschedule the wedding. That meant as soon as Hugh was able to travel, the three visitors from out of town—O'Hara included—would be on the next train out of Plummerville.

It shouldn't matter. It *didn't* matter. No matter how unexpectedly adorable Quigley Tibbot O'Hara had turned out to be, the two of them weren't at all well suited. Daisy Willard pushed her secrets deep, but there was no place inside her deep enough to hide those secrets from O'Hara.

Not that he hadn't already seen them all.

It was mortifying that a complete stranger was privy to secrets her best friends didn't know about. Even if he were to stay, which he wouldn't, and even if she were to allow him to court her, which she wouldn't, and even if he did kiss her . . . and that would never happen . . . what kind of a future could she possibly have with a man who hunted ghosts for a living? Yes, it was best that he leave town as soon as possible.

Eve and Lucien would manage just fine. Eve was a part of that world. She could travel with Lucien, when she wanted to; she could even help him with his work. After this weekend, Daisy knew she would be of no assistance in such a situation. Not that she would ever put herself in that position again! No, she had battled her last ghost, thank you very much.

Still, it was rather disappointing that she hadn't gotten that one kiss.

The warmth of her own house waited straight ahead. She reminded herself that this was where she belonged. Plummerville was her home.

Less than a year after she'd lost her child, never telling anyone what had happened, her mother had died suddenly. Four years later, her father had gotten pneumonia and never recovered. She missed her parents terribly; she felt guilty for not trusting her father's judgment where Tucker was concerned and not trusting her mother in that terrible time when her heart was breaking and her world came crashing down around her ears. At the time she'd been so terribly embarrassed . . . but she shouldn't have been. She should have trusted her family, when they were with her. Daisy wished with all her heart that her mother were here now, so she could tell her all about O'Hara.

Daisy suspected Eve would never understand.

Sulking over O'Hara was a waste of time. Soon he'd be gone, and she had no intention of crying over a man she could never have. He had accused her of living cautiously, of turning her attentions to men who didn't pose a threat to her heart. But was there really anything wrong with that? Daisy tried to put more spring in her step. Maybe Garrick would ask her to marry him again. Maybe this time she'd surprise everyone and say yes. Marriage to a friend would be easy and comfortable, and she liked comfort. She most especially liked easy.

So why did her heart almost stop when she saw O'Hara standing on her front porch, banging furiously against the door? She knew it was him, long before she caught a glimpse of his face. His suit was the most awful green, with a pin-stripe . . .

"Is something wrong?" she asked as she hurried up the walk.

O'Hara spun around, apparently surprised by the sound of her voice. "I guess not. When you didn't answer the door, I got . . ." He stopped, swallowed, and then continued. "Curious."

"Oh." She stopped on the walk, several feet away from O'Hara and the front door. He had almost said *worried*, hadn't he? He'd been worried about her. A cold wind whipped her skirts and her second-best cloak. Her best cloak had been destroyed, along with the Honeycutt Hotel.

"I see you're just fine," he said, sounding almost disappointed.

"I've been to see Eve."

"How is she? And Lucien?" he asked, as if he really cared.

"Fine. Lucien was sleeping, but Eve said he's doing much better." She twiddled her thumbs. When O'Hara took a step toward her, she unconsciously took a step back.

That reaction made him go still in his tracks. Was he hurt by her response? Surely not. Surely he was accustomed to people who knew what he could do not wanting to be touched.

"I would invite you in for tea," she said anxiously. "But since you're alone I can't. It wouldn't be proper."

"Of course not."

Daisy could ignore the fact that she and O'Hara had spent the night trapped in a hotel room, along with several ghosts, that she'd sat on his lap, that she'd taken his hand. She was home now, and everything had changed.

"You seem to be . . . fine yourself," she said, hoping to change the subject.

"As do you," he said softly.

"I feel quite well, considering. How is Hugh?" she asked quickly.

"Much better today."

"So he'll be able to travel soon," she said, her heart sinking slightly.

"Yes." O'Hara continued forward, and Daisy held her breath. Surely he wouldn't reach out and touch her, not here, not now. He passed her without reaching out, and she spun about to watch him go.

He kept walking, down the walkway to the street. When he turned toward town Daisy shouted. "Wait!"

O'Hara stopped and turned to face her. "Yes?"

"You didn't say why you stopped by the house."

He paused a moment before answering. "I just wanted to say goodbye. I expect Lionel and Hugh and I will be on a train tomorrow morning."

"Oh."

"It's good to see that you survived the ordeal so well." He shook his head and gave her a half smile. "You look great."

"Thank you," she whispered.

Again he started walking toward town, and this time she had no excuse to stop him.

Katherine swiped angrily at the tears on her face, as she finished fastening the tiny buttons of her high-necked black dress. She'd said she would not be Garrick Hunt's whore, and what had she done? Fallen into bed with him much too easily when he'd come to her. Given in without a second thought.

And when she'd awakened, early in the afternoon after a very long night, he'd been gone. Without a word, he'd simply slipped away. What had she expected? She'd known all along that once they returned home she and Garrick didn't have a chance together.

Her eyes dried. She didn't cry, not anymore. She didn't crumble just because things didn't go her way. Garrick Hunt was just a man like every other, and all she had to do to weather this disaster without further pain was lay low until he left town. The way he'd been talking last night, it wouldn't be long before he did just that.

She had loved Jerome once, but she'd been a

child who was smitten with his face and his charm and the future he promised. She hadn't known the real Jerome Cassidy until after the wedding. The love had died quickly. Painfully, but fast.

This . . . this was so much more. She had fallen for Garrick like a wide-eyed girl, but with her hardened woman's heart. She had a feeling this love would take a long time to die.

The knock on the door made her literally jump. She wiped at her face again, straightened her spine, and left the bedroom with her stride long and purposeful. No one could know what a fool she was.

The knock came again, and this time it was accompanied by the call of her name. Garrick.

Katherine went still while several feet from the door. She didn't want to face him. Had he come to say goodbye? To seduce her again before he left town? No, she couldn't let that happen.

But she couldn't just stand here, either. She had to face Garrick and send him on his way. One last time.

By the time she opened the door, her face was impassive and her tears were dried. Garrick stood there with a grin on his face, hands behind his back. He'd bathed and shaved and changed into clean clothes, and his hair was neatly combed. And he was Garrick Hunt, charming rich man's son, once again.

"I did it," he said with a widening grin. "I told my father I was leaving town."

"When are you leaving?" she asked coolly.

His smile died slowly. "Tomorrow morning."

"Good luck to you," Katherine said as she began to close the door.

"Wait." Garrick's foot shot out and he stopped the swinging of the door. "What's wrong?"

"Nothing." She took a deep breath, for strength. "I'm home and everything's back to normal. It was very sweet of you to entertain me while we were trapped in that awful hotel, but it's really not necessary for you to continue . . ."

"*Entertain* you?" he interrupted.

It was best to make the break now, clean and harsh. Maybe if it ended now, before she was in so deep there was no way out, the termination of this senseless affair wouldn't hurt too badly. She knew that was a lie. It already hurt!

"Surely you didn't think this affair of ours was serious," she said coolly. "We have nothing in common."

"I think we have a lot in common," he argued.

"We're not well-suited and we never were."

Garrick stared at her as if he didn't know her at all. He didn't. "I'm not leaving with nothing, Katherine," he said softly. "I do have money of my own."

Oh, he thought she would send him away because he didn't have enough money? If he believed that, he surely couldn't love her the way he said he did. "How fortunate for you," she said distantly.

Katherine convinced herself, without a doubt, that what Garrick had proposed simply would not work. What they had found was beautiful but fleeting. It was lust, not love. It was physical, not of the heart. And he had never asked her to marry him, had he? He had only suggested that they leave town together. One day he would look at her and be sorry. Or else one day he'd pick up his flask, get drunk, and hit her when she said or did the wrong thing. And the nightmare would begin all over again.

Best to end it here and now, while she still had a few good memories to hang on to.

"I thought you were coming with me," Garrick said as he leaned toward the door. "When I told my father I was leaving town, I knew in my heart that you would be with me every step of the way."

"I can't," Katherine said sensibly. "I have my home here and I have a little money set aside. I don't need a man to take care of me."

"I never suggested that you did."

"Goodbye Garrick," Katherine whispered as she tried to close the door again. "Please don't make this more difficult than it has to be."

"Heaven forbid that I make it *difficult* for you." He whipped one hand out from behind his back. Yellow silk was bright on a wintry afternoon, the color startling and out of place on her dreary front porch. "Here," he snapped. "You might as well take this. It's not my size or my color." When she did not reach out for the garment, he tossed it over the porch railing.

"I don't want that," Katherine called as Garrick turned.

"Neither do I," he answered as he walked away.

With the door opened no more than an inch, she watched him leave. He reached into an inside pocket of his jacket, withdrew his ever present flask, and uncapped it.

But he didn't take a drink. He stared at the flask for a moment, emptied the contents onto the ground, and tossed the silver flask away with all his might. It flew across the street and landed in a mass of tangled weeds.

* * *

It had not been dark long, but Eve was exhausted. So was Lucien. They climbed the stairs together, the single candle Eve carried lighting the way.

"I'm sorry things didn't go well with your aunt and uncle," he said.

Eve seemed unconcerned. "They do tend to be irritable. When they've had time to cool off, I'll write them a nice long letter. I can smooth things over, when they're feeling more agreeable. Maybe . . . next Christmas. Or the next."

Constance and Harold Phillips had collected their things that afternoon and stormed away from Eve's cottage and Plummerville, red-faced and angry. "I didn't help matters any," Lucien said. "I'm sorry. I should have found a way to make things better before they left. They're your family, after all."

Eve smiled as they walked into the bedroom. "You're the only family that matters to me, Lucien Thorpe."

God, she was making this so difficult! He knew he could not marry her. He could never marry anyone. Scrydan still slept inside him, in a way no one would ever understand. Some of the memories had faded, but not many. There was now an evil inside him that would never be completely washed away. And if this could happen once, it could happen again. There were other spirits like Scrydan's out there, just waiting to discover a willing host like Lucien. He couldn't subject Eve to that danger again.

Hugh and the others were leaving in the morning. Lucien would ride out of town tonight. Alone.

Eve placed the candle on a bedside table, then

leaned over as if to blow it out. The remnants of a fire glowed in the fireplace, so they didn't need the candle.

But Lucien wrapped his arms around Eve and gently pulled her spine to his chest. "Leave it," he whispered. "I want to see you tonight."

She relaxed against him, as he reached up and began to unfasten the buttons that ran from her neck to her waist. "If you wish."

Lucien wished for their last time together to be here, not in that damned hotel. He wished to be the one to push inside her. Him and only him.

He undressed her slowly, kissing her neck and her shoulder when the urge to do so moved him. The taste of her skin was unique, her scent was all Eve, and he smelled her even when she wasn't with him. He would smell her forever, he suspected.

He marveled in the fact that she was so soft, so gently rounded and pale and beautiful. She was everything he was not, and he would love her until the day he died.

Eve was almost completely undressed when she turned to kiss him on the mouth. She gave him soft, sweet, brief kisses, as if she couldn't ever get enough. "I'm so glad you shaved," she said between kisses. Her fingers traced his smooth jaw. "It makes the kissing much nicer."

"I want everything to be nice tonight."

He finished undressing her, and then he let her hair down. Since the moment he had met her, he had loved her hair. Most especially, he loved it down. When they made love it wound around their bodies like dark spun honey, waving and silky. Sometimes she tried to be so sensible, so practical, so staid . . . but when he let her hair down she put those attributes aside and became his woman. Nothing more, nothing less.

While he kissed her neck and threaded his fingers through her hair, she reached out to unfasten the buttons of his shirt. He felt the tremble in her lips and her fingers, the quiver in her delicate throat. Tonight it wasn't fear that made her quiver.

Lucien wished with all his heart that Eve would never have to be afraid again, that the Scrydans of the world were oblivious to her existence, that she lived safe, always. He was going to do his part to make that wish come true.

He laid her on the bed, finishing the job of undressing himself quickly. The entire time his eyes were on her candlelit body, as if he could drink her in that way. Eve wasn't shy, not with him. She smiled up at him, lying bare and beautiful atop the quilt.

"I love you," she said as he lowered himself to lie beside her. "I thought you were gone, Lucien." She rolled onto her side to face him. "I can't lose you."

"We're not going to talk about that," he whispered. He couldn't bear it. "We're not going to talk about anything tonight."

Lucien knew where to touch Eve, where and how to stroke and kiss to make her forget everything else. Her neck, just below the ear. Her wrist. That spot on her inner thigh. He stroked and kissed them all, moving slowly even though something in him wanted to rush, occasionally stopping to watch the fascinating sight of his rough hands on her soft, pale body. He wanted tonight to be special. He wanted everything to be perfect for Eve, and for him. The memory of this night would have to last a lifetime.

Lucien tried to forget, as he touched Eve, that every caress of this place or that one was the last, that every sigh and undulation and catch of her breath was one of the last. He tried to forget, but he couldn't. So he savored each sound, each breath, each reaction to his touch. He tried to make time move slowly. He tried his very best to make time stop.

He circled the tip of his tongue around one hard nipple, then sucked it deep into his mouth. Eve arched up and into him, moaning deep and soft. His hand traveled slowly along her inner thigh from knee to apex, where he brushed his thumb against the nub at her entrance. He stroked her there, while he turned his attention to her other breast.

Her body moved gently against and into his, silently asking for more, gently urging him on. She sighed and he moved his mouth to hers to taste her passion. He pressed his hand over her heart to feel and remember the quick, steady beat.

Eve was on the edge of completion when he rolled atop her and entered fast and hard, burying himself inside her completely. Her arms went around him, her legs wrapped around his hips, and she rose to meet his thrusts. The way they came together was as much magic as any supernatural ability. They moved as one, they were coupled in every way. He could feel her heartbeat, taste her soul.

Lucien did forget, as he loved her, that this was their last time. He got lost in sensation and the energy their bodies created, in the impulse that drew him to her, until there was nothing but Eve. She took him into her body, she comforted and demanded and loved, and nothing mattered but the way they came together.

She came with a throaty cry while he was deep inside her, and as she throbbed around him, he joined her. The candle on the bedside table flickered, the low flame in the fireplace flared up and then eased.

Lucien laid his head beside Eve's, as they found their breath. "I love you, Evie," he whispered in her ear. "So much. Never forget that. No matter what . . ."

"Shhh." She stroked his hair. "No more talk about what happened. It's over, Lucien. We're fine and we're together and nothing else matters. Nothing."

He had never been good with people. Talking to ghosts was easier. He loved Evie. He needed her. And he could not come up with a proper way to tell her that he was leaving.

Eighteen

Lucien rode his horse down the main street of Plummerville, moving slow since he wasn't ready to leave. The blacksmith hadn't objected to Lucien's purchase of the horse he often rented, and he hadn't questioned it, either.

He really should have collected his specter-o-meter and ectoplasm harvester from the spare room in Eve's house where they were stored. But he'd been afraid he'd awaken her, moving those heavy pieces of equipment about. Besides, they were likely too heavy for the horse to carry for a long period of time, and since he had no idea where he was going . . . it was best this way. He could have Eve ship them to him later.

Even better, he could simply build new contraptions. Both could be improved upon. Yes, it would be better if he started over.

It was late, dark and cold, and all was quiet in Plummerville. So he was surprised to see a light in the church where he and Eve had planned to have their disastrous wedding. The *second* disastrous wedding. The light was soft, small. A candle, perhaps two.

He'd planned to ride past, but Lucien found

himself stopping in front of the church. All his life, he'd hated churches and the people inside them. How many preachers had tried to beat his curse out of him? How many times had his mother begged a frightened preacher to repair her damaged son? More times than he cared to remember.

Logically he knew it wasn't the churches he feared. It was the people inside them that still gave him chills, on occasion.

It was surely the Reverend Watts who worked so late. Lucien dismounted and threw the reins of his newly purchased horse over the hitching post. The Reverend Watts was not the worst of the preachers Lucien had dealt with. In fact, he'd seemed quite practical and friendly, on the few occasions Lucien had met with him. He'd gladly left the majority of the wedding planning to Eve, so his interaction with the preacher had been limited.

Perhaps this was one more thing he could do for Eve, before he left. He would explain that the wedding was off, and that Eve would need a shoulder to lean on until she recovered. And she would recover. She was strong, his Evie.

The Reverend Watts was vigorously wiping down the back of a pew, when Lucien opened the door. He stepped through the entryway and into the church, and the preacher stopped his chore to smile.

"It's a little late to be cleaning, isn't it?" Lucien asked.

The Reverend Watts smiled. "I'm not just cleaning. I'm pondering Sunday's sermon."

Lucien nodded. The words he had come here to say were on his tongue. I'm leaving town. There will be no wedding. Watch over Eve, for me. Instead he asked, "Reverend, do you believe in evil?"

The preacher was taken aback for a moment, but he answered firmly. "Yes, I do."

"Real, pure evil," Lucien clarified.

"I've never seen it." The Reverend Watts draped his cleaning cloth over the back of a pew. "But I believe it exists."

"I've seen it," Lucien said as he walked down the aisle, just as Eve should have done days ago in her fine wedding dress with her family and friends looking on. "I've touched it. It's touched me."

The preacher was not afraid, at least not visibly. "I'm sorry to hear that."

"What if it never goes away?" Lucien asked angrily. "What if that evil is always a part of me?"

Amazingly, the preacher smiled. "Don't concern yourself, son. The fact of the matter is, corrupt men don't worry about the state of their souls. Only a good man would be concerned that an evil might invade his spirit."

"I understand what you're saying, but what if that's not enough? I'm talking about an evil so dark . . ." he shook his head. How best to explain Scrydan and the memories Lucien carried?

"Sit down." The preacher indicated the front pew, and after a moment Lucien sat. So did the preacher.

The church was oddly peaceful, in the dim light and the quiet of night.

"If there is pure evil in the world," the Reverend Watts finally said, "then by all logic there must be pure good, as well."

Lucien shook his head. "It's not that simple."

"Of course it is. There's a balance to the universe, just as there is a balance inside you. Inside me. Every person on the face of the earth struggles between good and evil at one time or another. Perhaps it's a fleeting decision that might affect the rest of their lives. Perhaps it's an ongoing battle. No matter how or when the battle is fought . . . it's something we all go through."

"Not like this."

Pure good. Lucien didn't believe in the concept any more than he had believed in pure evil, before he'd met Scrydan in the most intimate way.

"Balance, Mr. Thorpe," the Reverend Watts said softly. "Where there is one, there must be the other."

Lucien turned his head to look at the aging preacher. "You don't know what I can do, what I have seen."

The preacher smiled. "I have heard stories."

Stories he likely dismissed as hogwash. "I talk to the dead," Lucien said sharply, making sure the preacher understood exactly who and what he was talking to. When he knew, he'd be frightened and angry like all the rest. "I see ghosts in every corner, around every person I meet."

"Then God has blessed you with a precious gift," Watts said serenely.

Lucien was taken aback. Most . . . no, *all* preachers were terrified of what he could do. He was an abomination. A freak. By his very existence, he threw what they knew of their faith back in their faces.

There was one spirit—not an earthbound ghost

but a being of bright light—over the preacher's right shoulder. A woman. She smiled. Lucien knew without asking that this was the Reverend Watts' late wife. Even now, years after her death, she gave him the gift of peace.

"What if the evil is stronger than the good?" Lucien asked hoarsely.

"It's not. Trust me. I've spent my lifetime believing that fact." He laid a comforting hand on Lucien's arm.

"What if it wins the battle?"

The old man shook his head. "Evil only wins if you allow it."

Lucien wasn't buying the simplicity that was offered here. Maybe life had once been simple, but no more.

"You're a very lucky man," the Reverend Watts said. "Love is the greatest good of all, and you have that in abundance."

"Love comes and goes . . ."

"It does not," the preacher interrupted, sounding insulted for the first time since they'd begun this conversation. "Love is the greatest power on the face of the earth. I believe that with everything I have, Mr. Thorpe. It's that belief that gets me out of bed in the morning, that sends me here to polish this fine wood and talk to God when I can't sleep."

It was a simple answer for a simple world. Lucien's world was anything but simple. He looked around at the modest elegance of the small church. No, he wasn't afraid of churches. He never had been. He was fearful of the people in them. He was afraid of people who were frightened, and angry, and dimwitted.

"All my life, people have run from me because they don't understand what I can do."

"People are not perfect," the preacher offered. "We're not meant to be."

"I don't expect perfection."

"From anyone but yourself?" the preacher asked.

"I've made so many mistakes."

"We all make mistakes. That's how we learn."

"You have an answer for everything, don't you?" Lucien snapped.

The Reverend Watts smiled. "That's my job."

Lucien slumped lower in the pew. This was not the conversation he had come here to have! He should've ridden past without stopping . . . but he couldn't do that. "Evie wanted to be married here," he said absently. "She likes you. She said you were a good man."

"I appreciate that. She seems to be an inordinately good woman."

"She is."

She was too good for him. Too good to spend her life chasing ghosts and pulling him back from the edge of death. And that would happen, wouldn't it? Time and time again until it killed them both.

"We all have difficult choices to make, now and then," the preacher said. "Sit here for a while and think yours over, if you'd like."

"I need to get going," Lucien said, but he did not stand.

"If you must." The Reverend Watts began dusting

again, and Lucien stayed put. He didn't move. He didn't argue with the preacher.

He only wanted what was best for Evie. It was all he'd ever wanted. He loved her enough to give her what she needed. What was best for her and what she wanted were not the same . . . not this time.

Eve was awakened from a deep sleep by two things. First, someone was banging on her front door. Two, Lucien did not sleep beside her.

Something was wrong. She leapt from the bed, lit a candle, grabbed her wrapper, and pulled it closed with one hand as she ran down the stairs. She threw the door open half expecting to see Lucien standing there, but it was Daisy who waited on the porch, wringing her hands. Lionel sat in the driver's seat of a small buggy.

Oh, no. What had Daisy done?

"It's Lucien," Daisy said as she rushed into the house.

"What's wrong?"

"He's lost his mind!"

Eve's heart dropped. Scrydan was back. The events of the weekend had made him mad. He was hurt and alone . . .

"Oh, not literally," Daisy said when she saw the expression on Eve's face. "I just . . . get dressed and come with us."

Daisy signaled for Lionel to come inside and wait in the warmth of the house, and then she followed Eve up the stairs. Eve had thrown open her wardrobe and blindly grabbed a dress. It was her old faithful brown.

"No!" Daisy said as she ran into the room.

Eve held the brown dress in one hand. "What difference does it make what I wear?"

Daisy reached past her and grabbed one of the new dresses Laverne had recently made. "This blue looks a little warmer, and it is quite chilly out tonight."

Not caring what she wore, Eve took the blue. When she began to remove her wrapper, Daisy turned her back. But she didn't leave the room to wait with Lionel.

"Is Lucien all right?" Eve asked as she quickly dressed.

"I suppose," Daisy said absently. "He is rather odd, Eve. The things he does don't always make sense, do they?"

"No."

"If I ever marry," Daisy said stoically, "it will be to a solid, dependable, ordinary, quiet, stable and logical man."

"Then I suggest you steer well clear of Lionel," Eve said.

"Lionel?" Daisy asked, sounding almost confused. "Oh, yes. I did think he was handsome when I first saw him, and I suppose he is. But he's not really my type."

Eve breathed a sigh of relief. "Then why are you two together tonight?"

"Oh, we're not *together*," Daisy said. "It's just that Lucien asked me to come here to fetch you, and O'Hara said he'd drive, in order to speed things along, but Lucien said no and asked Lionel to drive instead."

"Daisy, are you going to tell me what's going on here?"

"I can't," she said. "He made me *promise.*"

Eve glanced at the clock on her desk, as she finished dressing. It was almost midnight. What could have everyone up and about at this hour? Whatever it was, she suspected it was not good. Lucien simply wanted to tell her the bad news himself.

Eve twisted her hair up and used a handful of pins to hold the waving strands in place, and then she grabbed the candle and Daisy's hand and pulled her friend out of the room. Lionel waited at the foot of the stairs, distracted and impatient.

"Let's go," Eve said as she grabbed her dark blue cloak from a peg in the entryway, blew out the candle, and ushered her friends through the front door.

Lucien was nervous. He was never nervous! Not like this. He fidgeted, he stared at the front door of the church. Any minute now. Any minute, Eve would come through that door. What would she say? It would serve him right if she thought him presumptuous and arrogant and left him standing here.

Yes, that would be fitting.

The doors flew open, and Eve ran into the church. Daisy and Lionel were right behind her.

Eve stopped as she stepped into the aisle, her eyes on the candelabras that were filled with white candles that flickered in the dim church, then on the friends who were spread throughout the pews; on one side Katherine and Garrick sat far apart and in different rows; Hugh and O'Hara were seated side by side on the other. Lionel and Daisy parted ways as they came through the door. Lionel joined his colleagues. Daisy sat beside Katherine.

Finally, Eve turned her curious eyes to him and the Reverend Watts. "What are we doing here?" she asked as she walked down the aisle.

"Getting married," Lucien said. "I hope. If you'll still have me. I know there's no fancy wedding dress and no reception and no flowers. But we're here, and the people we care about are here, and . . . I thought maybe that would be enough."

His fear eased a little when she smiled. "You planned this all yourself."

"I did," he confessed as she reached him. His need to tell the truth compelled him to add, "I was leaving town, Evie." He made his confession in a lowered voice, so no one else would hear. "I was running away because I am so afraid that someday I might hurt you."

"But you didn't leave," she whispered.

"No. I couldn't. Even though I think you will be safer and happier without me, I could not make myself leave." His heart climbed into his throat.

"It's a good thing. I would have tracked you down like a criminal if you'd left me."

He smiled. She was a fine woman, and she was his. "I will spend my life trying to make everything right for you."

"And I will do the same for you," she whispered.

For the first time, he knew he was doing the right thing, in staying. Eve did need him, in a different way than he needed her. "Will you truly take me, for better or for worse?"

"You know I will."

He took her hand in his and bent to kiss the knuckles. "You are the good in my life. I need you. I will not survive without you. It's so incredibly selfish of me to take you as my wife."

"Do you love me?"

"You know I do, more than anything."

She smiled at him, and at that moment there was only good in his world. "Then let's get married."

O'Hara walked toward the train station, bag in hand. Lucien and Eve were finally married. It had taken them long enough! How appropriate, that they had been married at midnight. They were so perfectly suited, he wavered between being happy for his friends, and insanely jealous.

Lionel and Hugh walked ahead of him, and Lionel carried Hugh's bag, ignoring the older man's protest that he was fine and needed no assistance. Ha. Hugh was still not himself, and probably wouldn't be for weeks. He refused to talk about what had happened that night. Still, he was healthy enough to make his escape from Plummerville.

"Where are you headed?"

O'Hara, surprised by the intrusive voice at his side, slowed his step as Garrick Hunt joined him. Garrick carried his own satchel. "Savannah, first, and then north."

Garrick nodded. "I'm going to Savannah, too, and from there I'm going west." He didn't seem too pleased with the plan.

"Are you sure that's what you want?"

"It's what I'm going to get," Garrick muttered. "Are you married, by any chance?"

"No," O'Hara said too sternly.

"Any special woman in your life?"

O'Hara immediately thought of and dismissed Daisy Willard. "No."

"Then I don't suppose you can help me by explaining exactly what they want from a man."

"I have seen inside the mind of many a woman," O'Hara said wisely. "And no, I have no idea what they want. I don't think they know. Well, except to torture us, simply because we are men. They need no more excuse."

"Torture," Garrick muttered. "That's it."

"I know it's early in the day," O'Hara said as they continued down the street, "but I would be extremely grateful if you'd pass over that flask of yours."

Garrick muttered something O'Hara couldn't decipher.

"What?"

"I threw it away," he said more succinctly.

O'Hara was horrified. "Why?"

"I don't drink, anymore," Garrick said.

"Why not?"

"I prefer my pain undulled, at the present time," Garrick said bitterly.

O'Hara had a feeling Garrick would not make a pleasant companion on the ride to Savannah.

The station was ahead, the train waiting for the quickly arriving departure time. The two men reached the boardwalk when a breathless feminine voice called, "Wait!"

Daisy? O'Hara turned, and so did Garrick. Katherine Cassidy stood there, wearing a bright yellow dress and carrying a small bag of her own.

"Do you still want me to go with you?" she asked, her eyes on Garrick. She held her breath as she awaited his answer.

Garrick dropped his bag on the street and walked to her, a smile on his previously sour face. "Of course I do."

"I was going to let you leave. I'm so afraid . . ." she dropped her bag as Garrick put his arms around her and lifted her off her feet.

"But I couldn't do it," she said as he swung her around, "I couldn't just sit there and do nothing while you left." She took a deep breath when he placed her back on her feet. "So I wrote a note leaving the house to Elijah and his mother, since Buster said they don't have much at their little place. I put on my new dress and packed a comb and my mother's brooch and a couple of other personal things, and I walked away. I walked away from everything and I'm not going back. I love you, Garrick. I love you."

Garrick whispered some sweet nothings into Katherine's ear as he drew her close, and her answering smile told O'Hara too well exactly what he'd said. Love. What a load of . . .

"Care to come to another wedding?" Garrick

asked as he turned, one arm around Katherine while he grabbed up her bag.

"No," O'Hara said succinctly. He'd seen enough weddings for now. "I have a train to catch."

"So do we. We'll get married in Savannah." He looked down at a beaming Katherine. "Oh God, I never asked. You will marry me, won't you?"

"Of course I will."

Garrick's answer was a disgusting bright smile.

O'Hara picked up his pace and left the lovers behind. Listening to them was just too depressing.

Would he be forced to come face to face with happy couples for the rest of his life? Was God rubbing his face in the fact that no woman would ever have him? He'd thought perhaps Daisy was truly different, that she would be the one to set aside her fears about what he could do and see the man behind the freakish power.

But no.

At least he knew Lionel and Hugh were equally miserable, where women were concerned.

Inside the train Lionel and Hugh sat together, and O'Hara took the seat facing them. He could not wait to get out of Plummerville, once and for all.

"I thought perhaps Eve and Lucien would be here to see us off," Hugh said, glancing through the windows to the platform below.

O'Hara snorted. The way those two had looked when they left the church last night, he didn't expect they'd leave their cottage for at least a month, unless they ran out of food.

"I expect they're . . . busy this morning," Lionel said tactfully.

"Oh," Hugh said. "We'll have to pay a visit again and see how they're doing, perhaps in a few months' time."

"Good idea," Lionel said.

"Not me," O'Hara said tersely. "This little hick town with its little narrow-minded bumpkins is not for me. You two visit. I'll pass my spare time elsewhere, thank you very much."

New York, Boston, Savannah. Anywhere Daisy Willard wasn't.

Garrick and Katherine stepped onto the train, laughing and holding hands, the extra ticket for Katherine purchased just in time. They sat at the opposite end of the car, where they could continue to whisper those annoying sweet nothings to each other.

O'Hara tapped his fingers against his thigh. How long would he have to wait to escape from Plummerville? He was as much a prisoner here as he'd been in the Honeycutt Hotel. The train began to move at last. Thank God! The sooner he got away from this place, the better off he'd be. He willed the conveyance to move faster, as it crept along an inch at a time.

And then Lionel said, "Isn't that Daisy Willard?"

O'Hara's head snapped around. Sure enough, there was Daisy, squinting her eyes as she searched the smoky windows of the train. For him? Perhaps?

He jumped from his seat and ran to the door, holding onto a handrail while he stepped down onto the rail car's steps. Daisy saw him and she began to run. "I wanted to say goodbye," she shouted as she ran, keeping pace with the slow-moving train.

"You're late!"

"I couldn't decide what to wear!" She ran faster, came a little closer.

O'Hara shook his head. Women. He did not understand them. He especially did not understand this one.

"Goodbye!" she shouted. "Have a safe trip!" She continued to run, moving closer and closer. Then, to O'Hara's amazement, she offered her hand. Running, eyes bright, she offered him her hand.

He swung down and reached out, just as the train picked up speed. Daisy's fingers barely trailed over his palm, before the speed of the train pulled him away from her.

"Goodbye!" she shouted again.

O'Hara watched, his hand still out, palm up. She had barely touched him, and yet the message had been clear. *Cretin. You never did kiss me.*

He stood on the steps, the breeze the movement of the train made whipping his short hair and the tail end of his jacket about. When he could no longer see Daisy, he returned to his seat and plopped down with a strange sort of satisfaction singing through his bones.

"What did she say?" Lionel asked.

"Goodbye."

"And that has you grinning like the cat who ate the canary?"

"She also wished us a safe trip."

Hugh grunted. Lionel sighed.

"You know," O'Hara said as he watched the Georgia landscape fly past. "Perhaps I was hasty in dismissing Plummerville as an unpleasant place. It does have its charm. I think I might be persuaded to visit again."

"What made you change your mind?" Lionel asked.

"Nothing in particular."

"Cretin," Lionel added softly.

O'Hara shook a censuring finger at his friend. "You aren't supposed to do that!"

Lionel smiled and leaned back in his seat, closing his eyes, and O'Hara stared out the window.

Yes, he'd definitely be back.

Stella Cameron

"A premier author of romantic suspense."

Celebrate Romance with one of Today's Hottest Authors

Meagan McKinney

Discover the Magic of Romance With

Kat Martin

__The Secret
0-8217-6798-4   **$6.99**US/**$8.99**CAN

Kat Rollins moved to Montana looking to change her life, not find
another man like Chance McLain, with a sexy smile and empty
heart. Chance can't ignore the desire he feels for her—or the suspi-
cion that somebody wants her to leave Lost Peak . . .

__Dream
0-8217-6568-X   **$6.99**US/**$8.99**CAN

Genny Austin is convinced that her nightmares are visions of another
life she lived long ago. Jack Brennan is having nightmares, too, but
his are real. In the shadows of dreams lurks a terrible truth, and only
by unlocking the past will Genny be free to love at last . . .

__Silent Rose
0-8217-6281-8   **$6.99**US/**$8.50**CAN

When best-selling author Devon James checks into a bed-and-breakfast
in Connecticut, she only hopes to put the spark back into her relationship with her fiancé. But what she experiences at the Stafford Inn
changes her life forever . . .

Call toll free **1-888-345-BOOK** to order by phone or use this
coupon to order by mail.

Name_____

Address_____

City _____ State_____ Zip_____

Please send me the books I have checked above.

I am enclosing $_____

Plus postage and handling* $_____

Sales tax (in New York and Tennessee only) $_____

Total amount enclosed $_____

*Add $2.50 for the first book and $.50 for each additional book.
Send check or money order (no cash or CODs) to: **Kensington Publishing
Corp., Dept. C.O., 850 Third Avenue, New York, NY 10022**
Prices and numbers subject to change without notice. All orders subject
to availability. Visit our website at **www.kensingtonbooks.com**.

Thrilling Romance from
Lisa Jackson

Discover The Magic of Romance With
Jo Goodman